I0684907

Her Grand Plan

Meade Fischer

ISBN 0-9672523-8-5

First Printing Feb. 2013

1.

On a cloudy, central California December day, armed with a crisp, new teaching credential and barely twenty-two years old, Robert Spagnolo walked proudly through the door of the human resources department, dripping with idealism, and down a path he'd never even imagined.

Tired and frustrated, Barbara James, the human resources director, faced with a teacher who was taking a maternity leave, was struggling to fill a half year vacancy. After interviewing several district substitutes, she finally realized why they were perennial subs, never to work their way up the educational food chain. When Robert walked in, freshly filled out application in his hand, Barbara whispered to her secretary, "Looks like we finally got a live one."

Robert had that fresh teacher look, smiling and enthusiastic, bubbling over with the urge to make a difference in the lives of children. He was quite handsome, Barbara noted, in a boyish, not a rugged way, far better suited to this fifth grade position than, say high school, where the girls, not much younger than him, would be actively trying to seduce him. He also had all the right answers, the proper buzz words, the right attitude. Besides, winter break was only a week away, and Barbara wanted to get this done and enjoy the holidays with her family.

So, a deal was struck, and Robert was hired as a temporary teacher, with the vague promise that if he worked out, there might be a permanent job for him in the fall.

For Robert's part, while teaching elementary school wasn't his final life goal, it was what he wanted for this part of his life, a chance to get real world experience and to make some money for graduate school some time in the vague, but not too distant future.

He was taken to see the teacher he was replacing, an attractive, but very pregnant, young woman. She would fill him in on what had been going on the first semester and the general plan for the rest of the year.

The principal showed him in and introduced him to the teacher, who turned to the class and said, "This is the teacher who will replace me for the rest of the year, Mr Spagnolo. Say hello," which they all did in unison.

Then a freckle-faced little red head with a broad smile spoke up. "I'm so glad you're going to be our teacher. That is so cool. I'm Kelly. Don't forget."

Robert smiled and assured Kelly that he wouldn't forget, and he made a mental note to call her by name on his first day, some three weeks hence.

After the teacher dismissed the class for the day, she started to outline everything Robert would need to know to start out. She even noticed how he was taken aback by the girl, warning him that Kelly was quite precocious and would have things her way if he wasn't careful. "She's a good kid, really smart, but she's ten, trying very hard to be twenty."

Robert was understandably anxious when his first day of work arrived. He had worked part time during high school and college, but this was his first real, first professional job, and failure was unthinkable. He was as prepared as a teacher could be. He had the basic day lined up, alternative lessons in case things went wrong and enrichment activities in case the kids progressed faster than expected.

In spite of all the things he had on his mind, he didn't forget the kid's name, and when he walked in on the first day of the new year, he said, "Good morning class, and good morning Kelly."

She smiled in return, and that somehow made him feel accepted.

Robert decided to spend the first part of the first day on introductions, first asking the children their names and what they liked best about school. Then he introduced himself.

"I'm Mr. Spagnolo, and this is my first teaching job. I just got my teaching credential from our local university, and I've lived around here all my life and still live here in town. In fact, the junior high you'll be attending in a couple of years is the same one I graduated from nine years ago. I enjoy teaching everything, but my specialty is writing, so hopefully, you'll all become much better writers by June. Any questions?"

Kevin asked him what kind of a name was Spagnolo, and

Robert explained that his father's family was Italian. Then Bonnie asked if he got good grades in school, and Len asked if he was a Raiders or 49ers fan, to which Robert replied that he didn't really follow football.

Lynn asked his favorite color, and he had to admit that he liked them all just the same. Then Kelly asked him if he had any kids. "No kids. I'm not even married."

She persisted. "Why aren't you married? Don't you have a girl friend?"

Feeling uncomfortable, he responded. "You're getting a bit too personal, but I'll tell you that I've been too busy in college and getting this job to have time for marriage or even a girlfriend. Going to school is hard work, as most of you already know."

Kelly again. "Do you have a nice house or an apartment?"

Feeling really pressed and sorry he started answering questions in the first place, he decided to take this last step. "I'm living at my mother's house until I earn some money for my own place. Now, last question before we read?"

And again, Kelly. "Do you dye your hair?"

That came as a shock. "What?"

"I mean, you have this shiny dark hair and real pale skin. It's like they don't go together."

"I get the hair from my father's side of the family, and my skin color from my mother's Irish heritage. OK?" He realized how abrupt he sounded.

Kelly brightened. "I'm Irish too."

"Judging from how you look and from the name O' Mara, I already figured that out. Now, hands down, books out, and we're going to read."

It was a relief to have them sitting with open books. He realized that Kelly had pretty much taken control of things for a few uncomfortable minutes, and she'd had him on the defensive. He was feeling just a bit intimidated by her boldness.

By the end of the day, Robert figured that Kelly asked and tried to answer more questions than almost the whole class put together. He enjoyed that she was bright and inquisitive, but he understood that she would be a challenge, a kid who would test him daily.

4

Before he launched into writing again the next day, he stopped and thought that just making assumptions about their writing skills and attitudes wasn't very scientific, so he did a bit of a survey. "How many of you enjoy writing? Three or four hands came up, Kelly's being among them, which didn't surprise him. Then he probed deeper. "Who keeps a diary or journal?"

This time it was only Kelly, so he asked, "How often do you write in it?

"Almost every night, just before I go to sleep. I put down any-thing interesting that happens during the day, and feelings stuff too. You know."

"That's excellent. Perhaps after we've made writing less scary, more of you will feel like keeping a journal." With that he started talk-ing about how to build a sentence, taking short sentences from the kids and helping them enrich them and make them flow. By the time the lesson was over, the kids actually seemed to be enjoying it. Yes! I can teach this to kids, he thought.

After a week there were still questions from the class each time the schedule forced him to transition to another subject, and then the obvious hit him. "If anyone needs any extra help on this or anything, I'm always here after school, for at least an hour, so I'll be glad to help you."

In retrospect, he figured that about half the students stayed after school perhaps three times during the semester, with the notable exception of Kelly, who took him up on his offer that day and almost every day thereafter.

"I'm here to learn to be a writer." She had left after the bell, only to burst in five minutes later. "Am I the only one?" Saying this, she looked around the classroom and smiled broadly.

They sat down, and he started going over the idea of a sen-tence. "Give me a simple sentence."

"The girl ran home."

"Good," he said. "Now we're going to make that sentence do a lot more work. What about the girl? Little girl, big girl, happy girl, frightened girl."

Within a few minutes the sentence had been fleshed out to "The happy, little red-headed girl, anxious to tell her mother the news, ran home to announce she had just learned to write great sentences."

Kelly seemed genuinely happy doing these exercises, and Robert was happy having a willing and excited student. This kid wanted to learn what he wanted to teach, and that was a powerful feeling. It stroked his personal and professional ego, and he was in no hurry to end the session until he looked up and realized it was almost five and the school was closing up for the day.

"Can I stay tomorrow too," she asked over her shoulder as she breezed through the door.

"Of course. Any day you want."

When Robert got home and told his mother about this student who was showing great promise and was so eager to learn, his mother, Pat, frowned as he blurted out the story.

"What's wrong, mom? You don't seem pleased about my success."

"That part is great, but it's the girl I'm concerned about."

That stopped him. He had no idea what she was getting at, so she explained. "It sounds like there is more than the desire to learn going on here. It sounds like she has a crush on you."

"Good God! She's only ten years old."

"You don't think ten year old girls get crushes on their teachers. Trust me, they do. I did, and several of my girlfriends did."

"What, you don't think I should help her, teach her to write?"

"Oh, no. Do that, but be aware, be alert. Oh, and keep your classroom door wide open. These days even the hint of impropriety can cost you your career. A little girl's fantasies can make you look like some kind of predator."

That made him stop and think, and it also reminded him that his mother was more than just a mother. She was a woman who had probably once been just as precocious as Kelly.

At forty-three, Pat was not a matron. While slowly moving toward pleasingly plump, she still had a girlish look, with long blond hair and the smooth skin of a younger woman. She had pulled back from the world of men for a couple of years after divorcing Robert's father, but recently, she'd been going on dates, something that made Robert uncomfortable for reasons he couldn't or wouldn't articulate.

Putting these vague feelings aside, Robert thought it would be good for his mother to marry again one day, as she was too young to spend the rest of her life alone. His father, he'd decided was never worthy of her. He rarely contacted his father, still angry at him for his behavior. The divorce came after his mother found out that he'd been cheating on her with his secretary for a long time. Robert thought, even if the old man had fallen for someone else, he should have been man enough to come forward and end his marriage, rather than sneak around like some smarmy prick.

For his part, Robert felt that he wouldn't marry until he was sure it was something that would last, and once married, he would be faithful. Like his mother, he was very big on honesty.

The next day in class, Kelly made a big deal out of letting the class know how much help she'd gotten after school and how great a teacher they had. It embarrassed Robert, but there was something in the back of his mind that got a small thrill out of this obvious hero worship. It was, he realized, the first time in his life anyone had put him on a pedestal, and it was good for his ego. He was actually disappointed when Kelly didn't stay after class that day, and he thought that kids' interests and enthusiasm are short-lived. In his mind he suddenly went from teacher of the year to Mr. Ordinary.

Even though he knew it was childish and petty, he made a point out of being cool to Kelly the next day, not allowing her to be the star, the only one asking and answering questions.

After school, Kelly didn't leave at the bell. Apparently not noticing his less attentive attitude, she jumped right in. "I so want to learn some more stuff. I have questions about the book we're reading, and I've been writing some sentences that I want you to see. I wish I could have stayed yesterday, but I had stuff to do."

That made Robert brighten, but he told himself not to feel that way. He can't let some kid, some student affect his moods. He resisted the urge to tell her he missed working with her and was happy she'd stayed today. Rather, he adopted a more formal tone, telling her he was happy to give her all the help she wanted, while making a mental note that his door was indeed wide open.

As he explained the reading, she kept nodding in agreement, totally focused on what he was saying, and when he read her sentences and admitted that they were very good, she positively beamed, looking him straight in the eyes as if he were the source of all knowledge. It was hard, he decided, to not be affected by such enthusiasm. She was, after all, a teacher's dream student, anxious to learn and bright enough to absorb all he fed to her.

A pattern was developing. Kelly stayed after school four nights a week. On Tuesday she couldn't stay, but she never said why. Near the end of the second week, he suggested that, since she was interested in writing, that she should try writing something, a story perhaps, and he could critique it for her and give her pointers.

Robert was amazed at what he was talking to her about. He was explaining cumulative, periodic and balanced sentences as well as serial construction to a ten year old kid, esoteric topics he learned in college.

"But what should I write about?" She seemed genuinely puzzled.

"Write about anything you like, something you know about, perhaps yourself, your feelings, things like that."

She fairly bounced in her chair. "Yes, yes, that's it. I'll do that." With that, she picked up her stuff and dashed out.

After school on Monday, she dropped a three ring binder on the table, flipped it open to pages of long handwriting and said. "I wrote something. Read it, please."

He expected something trivial, but almost immediately, he was caught up in what she wrote. She talked about how hard it is starting a new school, with strange kids. He'd had no idea that this was her first year here. She also made some allusions to her father, for some unexplained reasons, no longer on the scene. Although his curiosity made him want to ask questions, he felt he shouldn't pry, but rather take what she said as she said it and reserve his comments for that.

"I'm impressed," He finally said. "You share your feelings, and your writing lets me see who you are. Is this how you write in your diary?"

"Sort of," she said, smiling rubbing her hands together. "But I kind of tried to make it better, you know, like in the diary I just put stuff down, not caring much about sentences and all that."

"Look, I've got an idea." He turned her binder back around to her. "We're reading a book in class. Write the next chapter, without

8

reading what happened. Write about what you think will happen or what you'd like to happen. Write it like you were the author, like you were writing the book. You understand?"

She nodded so hard her hair flopped into her face.

During the school day on Wednesday, she did nothing to indicate she'd done an extra assignment. However, she pulled out her binder as soon as the other students left and pushed into his hands. After a quick read, he saw that it was almost a fairytale projection of the story, very much the work of a child, but the writing was excellent. In fact, she had made an effort to copy the style of the author, and she'd done an amazingly good job of it.

As promised, she started to give an extensive critique of the writing, but after a few minutes another student came in, asking for help with the math assignment. Kelly sat there, looking impatient for a few minutes and then said. "I have stuff to do at home. I'll see you tomorrow." And without waiting for a reply, she grabbed her stuff and headed out the door.

Robert was disappointed to see her go, but soon he was caught up in explaining the math work to the other girl, Bonnie. He quickly realized that she was quite good at math, but she wanted to do more than just plug in numbers, she wanted to know what it all meant.

I'm blessed with bright students my first year, he thought.

He was in a good mood when he got home, and Pat asked him if it was his teacher's pet again. "That, and another kid who came in for help. I was beginning to think none of the others would take me up on it. This is going to be a good year."

"Has little Kelly asked for an autographed eight by ten of you yet?" She started to laugh.

2

Winter was turning to spring, and a pleasant routine had fallen over Robert's class. Bonnie and a few others came by occasionally, but Kelly was there, like clockwork, four days each week, leaving early when other students impinged on "her time."

Now that the days were longer, Robert started riding his bike to school. Biking was his exercise of choice, and he often rode with the local bike club on weekends, considering a fifty mile ride a refreshing jaunt.

Shortly after he started bring the bike and parking it in a corner of his room, Kelly looked at it and said in a matter fact way, "I usually ride my bike to school too."

Rather absently, Robert answered, "Good for you. It's great exercise."

"I'll ride with you after school."

"What? To where?"

"Home, I guess. I'll ride with you to your house and then I'll head home."

"Better idea, Kelly. I'll ride with you to your house before continuing home."

And so Robert climbed on his expensive road bike, while Kelly climbed on her discount store kid's bike. As they started down the street, she said, "We should take a ride together on a Saturday or Sunday."

Not wanting to decline outright, he sidestepped. "I don't think you could keep up on that bike. Doesn't look like it's meant for long rides."

"That's the best my mom would do. Says I'm growing too fast to spend much money on a bike I won't be able to use in a year or two. When I stop growing, I'm gonna get a really nice bike. I might have to get an after school job or something, cause I don't think my mom can afford a bike like yours, which looks like it cost a bunch."

"It did. You get your grown up bike, and we'll take a long ride, over the hills and down to the beach."

When they pulled up in front of her place, she asked him to come in, but he said he had things to do and took off before she could protest.

From then on, she would tag along on the ride home unless he made up some excuse about having an appointment and peddling quickly in a different direction. He was feeling a bit trapped from all her attention. She was with him all day, an hour or two after school and often on the ride home. If she had her way, he'd stay for dinner at her house.

Keeping her at arm's length was an effort. She was very outgoing and assertive, not afraid to say exactly what she wanted, and she wanted to monopolize all his time. However, when working with her on her writing, these concerns evaporated as he got caught up in how quickly she was learning from him. He was falling into the trap that snags many teachers, a student becoming a reflection of them.

With each bit of writing she shared, Robert learned more about her. Apparently, her father had simply left her mom, and not that long ago. And, while Kelly wrote about it in a matter of fact way, it was clear that it still hurt. Robert was torn between wanting to know about her life and wanting to pull away from it, feeling too much like a voyeur and disliking the feeling. He found himself thinking about her life and caring about it and, at the same time, berating himself for feeling that way.

One day he found something in his school mailbox that caught his attention, and he could hardly wait to share it with the class, Kelly in particular.

"There is a student writing contest, three levels, elementary, middle and high school. There are prizes for each. They want students to write a story, based on a real event in your lives or the lives of friends or family. They want at least a thousand words, but no more than three thousand. It's state wide, and there are several prizes."

"What's the big prize?" Kelly asked excitedly.

"The grand prize is a five hundred dollar savings bond. That's something you keep for a few years while the money grows, and then cash in, for you, about the time you start looking for a college. Anyone interested in trying this?"

Three hands went up, Kelly's being the first. "Fine, come by after school today, and we'll talk about how to get started."

Robert carefully went over all the things he'd been teaching them these last two months, explaining how important the beginning is and how they should be aware of their writing style and how to maintain that throughout the piece. He told them to get started at home and be ready to come in with part of a first draft on Friday.

The other two had written a few paragraphs, but Kelly had produced an entire first draft. She made it a point to say, "The story's finished. What ya think?"

He took them home, opening a beer after dinner and working on the others first, saving Kelly's for the last. He made extensive comments and suggestions, correcting spelling and grammar. Then he read Kelly's, putting down his blue pencil after the second paragraph. He read it through to the end, closed the binder and sat back. This thing could win, he thought.

He spent time with each student on Monday, talking about the corrections and suggesting the next step in the process. While he talked to the other two, Kelly paced around the back of the room, glancing at the world globe, watching the fish in the class tank, staring out the window. Finally the others took their stories and left, and it was Kelly's turn.

"Well?"

"Excellent; more than a first draft. A few minor touches and this will be ready to send."

"Think I could win the money?"

"I think there's a very good chance of it. You have what it takes to be a professional writer."

"That's what I wanna be, Mr. S. I want to write books like those we read in class." Then she looked at him quizzically, as if she'd just remembered something important. "What about you? You teach writing. Do you write stuff and send it places?"

"Sometimes. There are a couple of literary magazines I send to, and I edited the one at the university. I like to write literary criticism."

"Criticism? You mean you like to say mean things about books?"

"That's not it. Criticism means discussing the book, what's good and bad about it, what you think the author is trying to do, how

12

the style works, stuff like that."

"Kind of like you do with my stories."

"Kind of." Then he had to broach the one problem. "This is supposed to be based on a true story, and you have yourself coming to this school, leaving your good friends behind at the other school, feeling lonely and unhappy until meeting your new best friend, Roberta."

"Yeah?"

"You come in here almost every day. There's no Roberta in class, and I have yet to see you with anything like a best friend. Are you lonely and making up a friend you don't really have?"

"No." Her lip went out in a pout. "It's all true. Don't you get it?"

"Get what? I really don't understand."

"Duh, Mr. S. Roberta? Robert. Don't you see?"

"Me. I'm Roberta?"

"Well, yeah." She shook her head and rolled her eyes in an exaggerated manner. "I couldn't say my best friend is my teacher. Nobody would believe that, and I wouldn't win, so I changed it to a girl in class."

"Ok, but I can't be your best friend."

"Why not? Do you hate me or think I'm just some dumb little kid?"

"Don't be silly. It's just that a best friend is a peer. That means someone more like you, your own age, probably another girl, but you're a kid and I'm an adult, and I'm your teacher. It's not like we can hang out together, share favorite songs and all that stuff. Best friends have things in common." Robert was having a hard time explaining the fine points of this to a girl who could be deliberately obtuse when it benefited her, and her blank expression didn't help.

"We do have stuff in common. We both like to write, and we share stuff. Like you told me about your mom and how she is divorced from your dad, and I told you about how we moved here after my father left."

Robert didn't realize, until that moment, that in their long conversations, he'd related so much of his life to her, far more than appropriate for a teacher to share. It was like that first day. She seemed to be able to control the dialog, to get him to keep talking about himself, even after he'd said too much. If she changed her mind about writing, she would make a great TV interviewer.

He changed his approach. "Look, I am so flattered by you consider me your best friend, but it's only fair to you that you have someone your own age to pal around with, share kid stories, go to movies and all that."

"Well, I don't have that. Would you rather I had no friends at all, that I just sat home at night crying in my room because I'm so lonely? I mean, if you don't like me and don't want to be my friend, just say so." Again the pouting lip.

Feeling cornered, Robert corrected her. "No, you know I like you. I'm your friend, but I'm also your teacher, and I'm just concerned that you have friends your age to play with."

"You do care about me. I knew it. Don't worry, sometimes I hang out with some kids, but you're my real best friend. What about you? Do you have another best friend?"

"Well, I, actually not a best friend. I have a small group of guys, college friends, and we catch a movie sometimes, go to a club, take camping trips. But we're a group of friends, no best about it, and we don't hang out all the time. We each have busy lives, new jobs and all that. I also am friendly with some of the bike club people."

"You spend more time with me than with them?"

"Sure. I'm here with you all day and after school."

"OK, then. I am your best friend. We hang out together all the time. We tell each other stuff."

"Kelly, please. Let's just change the subject."

"Sure. Did I ever tell you about what happened with my dad."

He was going to tell her that it was OK, that he didn't need to know, but she launched right into it. "One day he just left. I mean, he went off to work, and we never saw him again. We hear he ran away with some girl, but who knows. That was a year ago. My mom couldn't afford to keep the apartment, get a sitter for me, you know, so we moved back here and moved in with my aunt, who doesn't work and watches me while my mom works at the beauty shop. So that's how come this is a new school, and my use-to-be best friend is like two hundred miles away, and I can only afford to call her once in a while."

"I bet you miss your father and are hurt that he left."

"I did and I was, until I met you, and now things are better."

Somewhat relieved, Robert asked. "Oh, so you think of me sort of like a substitute father?"

"No, no. Just like I said, you're my best friend. I gotta go. Let me know how I can make my story better."

When Robert told the story to his mother, she responded with a strange comment. "Wow. It's a good thing you don't teach junior high. You'd be in serious trouble."

While Kelly's story was very good, Robert found a number of awkward sentences, and some confusing paragraphs. He didn't, however, find any spelling mistakes. Kelly was not only a good speller, she was also religious in her use of spell check, now that she wrote on a computer. After finishing his comments, he read it over one more time with a sense of pride in his star student. But that soon morphed into a negative feeling. This little girl was becoming far too important in his life. He realized that he'd canceled other activities, such as meeting his friends for happy hour, in order to work with her after school, even on Friday, when every other teacher almost trampled on the students on their way out.

As much as he objected to her casting him as her best friend, deep down he felt flattered by her feelings. He'd read about teachers obsessing over students, and he never wanted to be that kind of person. Even though he was sure that she'd put him in the role of father, he was going to draw a strict line and not let her draw him deeper into her life.

She didn't move when the bell rang, and as soon as the others left, she demanded. "What about my story? Let me see." Without responding, he simply handed it to her.

She talked out loud. "OK, I should change that. I can fix this. Oops, I didn't see that. Oh, no. Not this. I won't touch that."

"What? Let me see." He took the paper back from her. "This just doesn't sound right. I don't think it fits the character. It's forced, you know, like a square peg in a round hole. Now, my suggested change is just that, a suggestion, and you should adapt it to fit your voice."

"No. That's exactly how I feel, what I said, everything. That's

15

my favorite part. I won't change it."

"Suit yourself. Here's the envelope addressed and stamped and the entry form. I filled out my part. Just fill in this part, sign it and put in the finished version."

She took it all up and started for the door. Then she stopped, turned quickly, ran back to him, gave him a big hug and was out the door before he could say a thing.

On Tuesday, the day Kelly never stayed, her mother walked in after school, after making an appointment over the phone to discuss Kelly's writing. "I'm Lauri O'Mara. Thank you for seeing me on short notice."

"I'm glad you want to discuss your daughter's writing."

The woman, a fairly attractive blond, full bodied and a bit overdone in hair style and make up, sat down and frowned. "While I would like to talk about the writing, that's not the main reason I'm here."

Her expression made Robert feel uncomfortable, and he sat down opposite her at the table. "Yes?"

"Kelly has been talking about you for weeks, but now she says you are her best friend, and that seems a bit weird, her being a child. I'm frankly a little concerned about your motives and intentions."

"Mrs. O'Mara. I guess you read her story. That I was the Roberta character, that came out of the blue. I tried to explain how a best friend should be a peer, one of the girls in class, but she almost threw a tantrum. I tried to tell her I could be her teacher and a friend, but that I couldn't be what she wanted. I was trying to be delicate because of her father."

She sighed and leaned back. "I kind of suspected something like that after hearing her side. So, I guess she told you everything, the whole sorted family history. Apparently, she wouldn't listen to your explanations?" Robert nodded.

"She can be like a dog with a bone. I'm sorry I was suspicious, but what I'm hearing makes sense. She's kind of fixated on you, maybe as a substitute for her father, who reminds me just a bit of you, looks wise only, that is."

"Well," Robert stammered uncomfortably. "I'm sorry about your marriage and how it must have hurt Kelly."

"I should have known better. He was young, nineteen when we

married and not ready to settle down. Couldn't keep a job more than six months. My salary kept us going. Right after he left, Kelly blamed herself, mostly because she could be every bit as stubborn as he was, and they butted heads constantly. But, after a while, she did a 180, deciding that he was a jerk who deserted his family and wasn't worth thinking about any longer."

"Well, I guess I need to be some kind of model of a dependable adult male, and I will. I told her I'd give her all the help she wants, four afternoons a week, even if it means arranging my schedule."

Mrs. O'Mara reached over the table and placed her hand over his. "No. This isn't your responsibility. I appreciate all you've done for her, but don't put your life on hold. She'll continue to make demands until she's taken over your life."

Robert patted her hand and tried to reassure her. "In just over two months the school year will be over, and she'll move on to sixth grade, and soon she'll forget about me and go on to something or someone else."

"I hope you're right. I'm trying to ease my new boyfriend into her life. I wised up. Neal is ten years older, forty-one, a very stable man with his own insurance agency. I'm walking on eggs here, afraid that Kelly will drive him away."

Robert smiled. "I wouldn't worry. Your daughter is very personable. She'll win him over, and," he smiled again and winked, "Turn him into her best friend. Oh, and about her writing: it's brilliant. She's a natural writer, and if she keeps it up, she could well write for a living."

As much as he enjoyed Kelly, her excellent writing and her treating him like he was the greatest thing on two feet, he made an effort to keep things as formal as possible, resisting her attempts to get him to talk about himself and his personal life, trying to change the subject when she related personal information. She was shameless about sharing anything that came into her head, like the afternoon she came in and almost demanded. "Do you think I'll be pretty when I grow up?" He said he was sure she would be and then tried to change the subject as she pressed him for a more detailed answer. It was a fencing match, and it took his best bobbing and weaving to keep from getting drawn in.

17

3

In the following weeks, she became much better at understanding literature, and her writing continued to improve. He started to realize it wasn't some natural genius, but her absolute, single-minded dedication to the process. She had become, in every fiber of her being, a writer, no nonsense, no ifs, ands or buts.

If she was obsessive before, the letter that proclaimed her the winner in her age division clinched it. "I will write best sellers for a living." She announced in class one day, and that same day, after school, she asked, "What other contests can I enter, other places I can send my stories?"

Robert promised to do the research for her, feeling proud of the writer he'd created.

Every other Monday morning was drudgery. Being a late start school, they held staff meeting at 7Am on Monday. Normally, it was just something to get through, but one morning he sat next to another new teacher, one he'd noticed but hadn't really talked to yet. Sandy Barnes was about his age and rather cute in a petite brunette kind of way.

"I'm Robert, fifth grade." He put out his hand.

"Yes, I know. Sandy, fourth grade. You never socialize with the staff. You always seem to be in your room. Scoring brownie points for a regular job?"

"Maybe that, and I'm giving extra help to some student."

"Dedicated too. I like that."

The meeting interrupted their conversation, and as he sat there, stealing glimpses of her, he realized that he'd been so involved at school that he hadn't been on a date since before he started. After the meeting, he invited her to get a drink with him after school, actually, after five, remembering he was committed after school.

I need a girlfriend, he thought as he wrapped up the after school session, one of the rare ones that involved two other students besides Kelly. Got to get my life in balance, he thought as he locked up his room.

After chatting a bit about where they'd gone to college and what they enjoyed doing in their spare time, and while observing that she liked white wine and always cocked her head when she was listening, the subject drifted, as it often does, to their mutual profession, and soon Robert was talking about his star student and how she'd won the contest, and he must have been getting carried away, because she put her finger to her lips. "Let's not get into the students, or that will dominate the evening."

"You're right. What do you like to teach? I love teaching writing, my university emphasis."

"Math. Fourth grade is such a pivotal year for math."

"Yeah math is good. I like to incorporate a story when I do math, like early traders trying to figure out how much to charge. Like to write?"

"Not really. Like to read, but I write only when I have a need."

Robert was disappointed, but he pressed on, looking for common interests. He asked for another date, a movie and dinner.

He liked Sandy, enjoyed her company, and she obviously enjoyed his, but that was pretty much it. There wasn't the fire, the anxious waiting for the next evening together. Even the sex, which was delightful, was just sex, not great passion. It became clear to both after a few weeks that they were simply dating, filling in the gaps with each other until someone magical came along. It wasn't going to lead to a committed relationship, some long term thing where couples end up having the discussion about "is this the real thing or not."

By late May they had drifted from regular dates to infrequent to just friends wrapping up the year together, each with separate summer plans.

He also started hitting the clubs regularly each Saturday night with some of his college friends, and occasionally he met a woman, went out with her or maybe just had a one night stand. On weekends, he do at least one long ride with the bike club. The rest of his life was the classroom. He simply wasn't meeting women who interested him, but once in a steady teaching job, he planned to go to grad school, where he would meet loads of women who shared his interests. For now, he'd bide his time.

While the other kids weren't as pushy and therefore not too

easy to get to know, he'd learned quite a bit about many of them, as most of them would stay after school on occasion, asking for help in all subjects. Although writing was his thing, he took pride in being able to make any subject interesting, always creating a story to put the material in context, remembering how boring it was to get fed information in a vacuum.

Kelly got into writing short stories, stories about kids her age, and she sent them off to all the places Robert came up with, after first soliciting his praise, something she seemed to need before she had the confidence to submit. One of her stories was published before the end of the year, no money, just recognition, but it was enough to keep her creative fires burning.

With less than two weeks remaining in the school year, Kelly came in and said, "I've got a great idea. Why don't you teach sixth grade next year, so I can have you again."

"That's nice." He said with a smile. "But, I don't even know if I'll have a job here next year at all, and I certainly can't be picky."

"You have to come back. I'll go tell the principal how important you are, and how good you are at teaching. I'll talk her into keeping you."

"That's sweet, but you'll talk her into not keeping me. Relax. I hear that the teacher I replaced doesn't want to come back, wants to spend more time with her new baby, so I might have this job again next year, provided, of course, that you don't try to help me."

"If you do, can I still come in for extra help?"

"Of course. You're always welcome."

Another kid, Kevin, who came in for help now and then, raised his hand. "If you are teaching fifth next year, you'll have my little sister. I told her about you. It would be cool if she were in your class.

It was then it finally hit Robert. He'd been successful. The kids appreciated him and had learned from him. He was becoming hooked on teaching.

Two days before the end of the year, Kelly came to class with some envelopes, handing some out to the kids she spent some time with, and then she came up to his desk and gave him one. "What's this?"

"Invitation to my eleventh birthday party. July first." Then she sat down, but that wasn't the end of it.

After school, she stayed as usual, even though the books were all checked in and the grades registered. "Well?"

"Well, what, Kelly?"

"Well, you're coming, aren't you?" Her hands were on her hips, and she had a scolding look, probably learned from her mother.

"Listen. I don't think it would be appropriate, me coming to a kid's birthday party. That's for your family and friends." He was trying to be calm and matter of fact.

"You're my friend, remember?"

"It's still not a good idea." He knew the value of staying on message.

"I told my mom and my aunt and the other kids you'd be there. Am I just some dumb, pesty kid you had in class, and two days from now you'll forget you even knew me." She puckered up as if she were about to cry. "It'll be like, 'Kelly who? I don't remember any dumb little Kelly'."

"Kelly, stop that. You know that's not true."

"Yes it is. If you don't want to be my friend, fine. I'll tell my mom to cancel the party. I don't want to bother if you're not there." Her voice had gone up in volume and pitch.

"OK, Ok. I'll come. I'll be there. Now stop that wailing." He knew he was being handled, but she put things in such a black and white way that refusal would simply crush her.

Almost immediately the tearful look stopped and a broad smile filled her face. "I'm so glad. The address and time is on the invitation. Don't be late."

She also said she was so glad he was coming back, even if he wouldn't be her teacher. Then she asked him if he wanted to be a teacher forever, and that caught him off guard.

"Well, yes in a way. Someday I want to teach at a college, a big university, but I have to go back to school before I can do that."

"That would be cool, but wait for a while. I don't want to lose your help."

Robert at once was flattered that his attendance at the party was so important to her, but also annoyed that she was heaping obligations on him that were not part of his teaching relationship with her. He

21

decided he'd make a quick appearance, and that would be that. Next year, new teachers, new students, clean slate.

Robert found out just how wrong he'd been when he attended Kelly's party. The mother, Lauri, greeted him. "Glad you are here. Kelly's been impatiently waiting for you. At least after today you can get a break from her for the rest of the summer." She handed him a glass of punch, and he walked into the back yard, filled with kids, balloons and tables of treats and presents.

She ran up to him, smiling, and was about to hug him when he put his hand out and shook hers. "Happy birthday, Kelly." he handed her a package, wrapped in colorful birthday paper.

"Oh, oh, oh. What is it?"

"Something every young writer needs. There's a thesaurus, dictionary and a writers' guide to publishing for children. Now, you have to dedicate your first best seller to me."

Kelly squealed with delight, grabbed him by the hand and introduced him to a number of relatives in a rapid fire rotation, referring to him as her favorite teacher and best friend, which made him uneasy each time she said it.

Robert stood around for what seemed an appropriate length of time, than gave his rehearsed excuse for leaving early. "Great party Kelly. I had a nice time, and again, happy birthday, but I have to run. My friends and I are leaving for a camp trip in a couple of hours."

"Oh, too bad. I'll walk you to the door."

As he was saying goodbye, and needing something to add, he said, "Have a great summer, and maybe we'll work together on your writing in the fall."

"Oh, yes," she almost shouted. "And we can write together forever, after we get married."

Robert froze, a cold wave of panic running through him, and he couldn't think of a thing to say. He just stared at this little girl who was beaming at him. He desperately tried to put what she said in some context. Was it an accidental burst, meaning nothing, a joke, or did she really believe that he was going to marry an eleven-year old child.

Finally gaining his composure and his voice, he asked. "What did you say?"

"I guess I shouldn't have blurted it out. I mean someday when we get married."

`   "Kelly, I don't know where you got that idea. I hope I never said anything to make you think. I mean, you're a ten, eleven year old kid. I can't marry you, and when I do get married, it will be to a grown up woman, so please drop this idea."

"Oh, silly. I know you aren't going to marry me now. I'm talking about when I grow up. I guess I'll be old enough to get married when I'm eighteen, and that's exactly seven years from today. So, that's when we'll do it. I'm going to write that date in my diary."

He put up his hand and almost shouted. "Stop! You are not hearing me. I have something to say about who I'll marry and when. I don't know what will happen in the next seven years, but I might meet someone I care about. And, you are a kid. There'll be lots of changes in your life as you grow up, changes in how you are, what you want. You'll have lots of boyfriends and you might even fall in love with one. You can't just make this grand plan as if the world is going to stand still while you grow up."

She was standing there, stone still, face blank as a mask, eyes hard but with a hint of tears. "You don't think I'll be good enough for you, pretty enough, smart enough. Is that it?"

"No, no, no. Kelly, you are smart and pretty, and you'll be even prettier when you get older, but you have your life to live and I have mine. Six months from now, you'll feel silly thinking about what you're saying now. You have to trust me. By next year you'll have a crush on some boy and this will be forgotten."

She shook her head slowly from side to side. "Oh, no. I've known from the first. Sometimes you just know things. When I grow up, you'll want to marry me, you'll see we belong together. I just want you to promise you'll wait."

Her determination was sad. She had no idea how many changes she'd go through in the next few years. He didn't want to hurt her, but the last thing he wanted was to allow this fantasy to continue, if even for a short time. "What if I meet someone over the summer and fall in love?"

"You can't. You won't. Remember, you have to go back to school, get a job in a college. You can't do all that and just go around falling in love with any dumb girl that comes along."

23

I'm not planning on running off any marrying just anyone, but I'm trying to tell you that who knows when I'll meet the right one. I can't make promises to you for the distant future. Don't you understand?"

"Ok, look. Just go out with all those girls, but you don't want to get married until you finish all that school and get that job you want. I just want you to wait seven years, and then if you don't want to marry me, just say so. Is that so hard?" Now she was starting to cry, just a trail of tears starting down her cheek. It was breaking his heart to watch her. "I just want you to give me a chance. I can't help it if I'm just a kid. I'll grow up as fast as I can. Just wait for me. I promise we'll be happy." And now, without the drama or the loud accusations, she was crying, silently, heart-wrenchingly, pitifully, crying.

He wanted so much to be out of there, but he didn't know how to leave her without destroying her. She had always seemed so self-assured, so strong, but now she was vulnerable, a desperate, pleading child, and he was at a loss. He also felt deeply for her. They had become friends, and he truly cared for her. If she were grown, she would be just the type of girl he would be interested in. She had so many qualities he admired and respected. And here he was, trying to escape, wondering what he could say to her.

She looked up at him, her eyes pleading for some reassurance, and in that moment, he took the coward's way out. "Ok, Kelly. I'll wait. I won't get married, but when you become eighteen, one or both of us can call it off. Is that fair?"

"Yes. And don't feel like you have to sit home. Go out with other girls. I'm not worried."

The tears started to dry and a smile slowly came over her rather expressive face. Then she moved to hug him, and he stepped away.

"I don't feel comfortable doing that. Let's save that until you grow up. Now I really have to go. See you in the fall."

The urgent camping trip was just an excuse, but that evening he did join some of his friends for drinks. The conversation with Kelly was weighing heavily on his mind, and he simply had to tell someone, even though it felt so damn weird to talk about it. After the second beer, he mentioned it as casually as he could.

Flynn, a tall skinny man with a hawk-like face, a new middle manager at a local software company, was the first to react. "Damn. Rob's gone and got himself engaged."

Ted, fresh from passing the bar and about to start his first professional job, chimed in. "And he likes them young. I think you could be my first client 'cause you're gonna need a good lawyer."

They all got a good laugh at Robert's expense, but Robert wasn't seeing the humor in it. "How the hell am I going to handle this? Come on guys, say something constructive."

Chip, the last member of the foursome, and the only one still in school, now working on a masters in history, wagged his finger as if to signal that he was formulating an idea and finally spoke up. "Don't worry about it. You put her off for, well, for a kid that age, forever. I assume she can't contact you over the summer, and by the fall, she'll be like the proverbial baby duck, waking up in a brand new world."

Then Flynn, ever helpful, added, "You'll run into her next year, and she'll break you heart, 'cause she won't even remember your name." That got another round of laughter.

Ted broached the untouchable subject. "It's not that unusual for an adult to fall in love with a lovely child. No accusing here, just asking you to consider if that's what's going on."

Robert felt his face flush. "No, that's silly. I mean, I like the girl. She sweet and smart, and I enjoy helping her, listening to her and all, but she's just a kid."

"That's right." Ted observed. "A kid on the cusp of puberty. If she was a couple years older, you could be really compromised."

"Well," Flynn added. "She's not in your class next year, so you won't be around her. No problem."

Robert, with a pained expression on his face, flagged down the waitress by waving his empty glass, before turning to Flynn. "Not as simple as that. I told her she could come in any time after school for more help."

"Jesus!" Chip was shaking his head. "You may just have a problem."

"Flynn pulled out his Blackberry and start to make like he was entering something. "There, I've got your wedding date saved. At least I'll have plenty of time to find you a present. Actually, I'm thinking of a cake with a file to help you get your sorry ass out of prison." This time the laughter was more an uncomfortable snicker, as Flynn had hinted at something they were all thinking.

Robert was now on the verge of tears. "One more thing. I need to tell her mother what went down, that is before Kelly tells her side. But if I call, I might get Kelly."

"Have your mom make the call, run interference." Ted was the practical idea man.

The next morning over breakfast, and it took all his courage to do it, Robert told his mother what happened at the party. Her face dropped, and it looked all the world as if a dark cloud had come over it. "Good god, Robert. She's eleven, and she controlling the situation. If she doesn't grow out of this, and if you don't stay far away from her, she'll have you so tightly bound up, you'll never break away."

"Oh, come on mom. You act as if the adult, child roles have been reversed or something."

"They have. She knows how to handle you, and she's doing a damn good job of it. You're right, I'll call the mother, and when I get her, you lay it out and have her get control of that kid." She reached over, pulling the kitchen phone from its cradle and giving Robert a questioning look that meant, the number, now.

Sure enough, Kelly answered the phone. "I'd like to speak to Lauri O'Mara, please."

"OK. Who should I say is calling?"

"Ah, I'm, I'm one of the mothers from school."

Robert was sitting at the kitchen table, hands clasped together, leaning forward as if he would be able to hear both sides of the conversation., while Pat sat calmly, waiting for Lauri to pick up.

After what seemed an interminable time to Robert, Lauri came to the phone. "Mrs. O'Mara, I'm Pat Spagnolo, Robert's mother. Please don't say anything yet. Is Kelly gone?"

"Yes, I think she went to her room. What's this all about?

"Robert needs to talk to you. Here."

Robert looked at the phone as if it were a snake, picking it up carefully and taking a deep breath before saying, "Mrs. O'Mara, we have a problem. Did Kelly tell you what she said to me at the party?"

A long pause. "I don't think so. She said a lot of things, but perhaps you should tell me."

Robert felt his throat constrict. How can he start this. "Kelly stopped me on the way out of the party, and..."

"And what?" She sounded impatient.

"She told me she planned to marry me." There it was said and hanging in the electronic void between them.

"Oh, God!" The reply came after a nerve-wracking delay. "She's been saying she wants to marry you, and I've been telling her she was being silly. She actually said it?"

"More than said it, she even has a date, her eighteenth birthday."

There was a dry laugh before she answered. "Well, at least she didn't say her twelfth birthday. What did you tell her?"

"I tried to tell her she couldn't just come up with that. I tried to explain all the reasons."

"Tried? Tried? You make it sound like you didn't get through to her."

"She wouldn't take no for an answer. Wanted me to promise to wait, to not get married before she grew up."

"And of course you laughed at her or dismissed it as some childish nonsense."

"Not exactly."

"You didn't tell her you were going to wait for her? No, you didn't do that?" Her voice sounded pained.

"I just told her I had no plans to get married and she should just wait, and that she would probably forget the whole thing soon."

"You can't do that with Kelly. You have to say absolutely no, no in no uncertain terms, coldly and emphatically, no!"

"I didn't want to hurt her. She was starting to cry. She's such a sensitive kid."

"She's playing you." Lauri's voice was a anguished shriek. "Whatever you said, she heard it as a promise from you."

Robert was getting frustrated by her tone, as if it were all his fault. "Look, Mrs. O'Mara. She's your kid; you need to lay down the law. Demand she drop this crazy idea."

"Oh, you can count on that, but she's not going to listen if you get all soft on her. She learned she can get her way with men. My ex couldn't tell her no. Neither can my brother in law or my father. They all spoil the little princess. You're the adult; she's the child. I'll set limits at home, and you have to set them at school."

When he put down the phone, Pat asked, "What?"

"She kind of chewed me out, like I was some fool kid."

"Good for her. You're acting like one. Does the kid have this number?"

"I don't think so."

"Well, if she gets it and calls. I'll pick up and deal with it."

"Sure, but don't be mean to her. She's really just a sweet kid."

Pat groaned and walked out of the room, leaving Robert wondering how females could be so insensitive to each other, and thinking that while Kelly was a bit mixed up, she was a very misunderstood young girl.

4

As far as Robert knew, there were no calls from Kelly that summer. On the two times he brought the subject up, Pat didn't want to talk about it.

Kelly only moved silently around the dim edges of his mind that summer, always there, but never an issue to be addressed. He had other things on his mind. For one thing, he'd been assured of a job for one more year, same grade. Being new to the profession, he would have to spend some time planning lessons, gathering materials, and, just before the new term, setting up the room to be an optimal learning environment.

Also, the camp trip he lied to Kelly about was actually one that was planned, but planned for a week later than the party. The guys were going to spend a week in the high country of Yosemite, doing day hikes, cooking over the camp fire, swimming in mountain lakes.

On their third day two young women set up in the next site. Kate, a big boned, rangy blond, came over to say hello, and she seemed to fasten her attention on Robert. They pooled their supplies and wine and had a communal dinner around the fire. Her friend, Bette, a short, husky woman with a sweet face that didn't seem to match her powerful frame, seemed to take an interest in Ted.

As the night and the wine slipped away, Robert learned that these two were avid outdoor women, having backpacked the Muir Trail, the Lost Coast and the Grand Canyon. Robert considered that kind of sexy, but intimidating. He was wondering if he were up to hauling a sixty or seventy pound pack over eleven thousand foot passes. There was something about woman who made him feel he had to push his limits that really fascinated him, and Kate was the type. Watching her through the camp fire was mesmerizing.

The next day, they hiked into the Tuolumne canyon, down the stair step stone terraces to the bottom. On the way back up, it was all Robert could do to keep up with Kate. He knew he had to see more of her.

Kate lived in San Jose, close enough to Robert to making dating feasible, so numbers were exchanged and vague promises made.

He hadn't so much as unpacked and cleaned up before he was on the phone to her, setting up a date. It was set for a Saturday night, and there was the hope that he would not have to drive home.

They had a great time, talking about the outdoors, travel, sports and the like. Fortunately, they only touched lightly on their professions. She was a software engineer, very much no nonsense and technical. He knew almost nothing about her job, but was curious and asked many questions. As her explanations started turning technical, he was having trouble following her. However, there was the requisite magic, and the evening was moving flawlessly.

After some long, lingering kisses in her condo, she invited him to stay, and she made love like a wild woman. She was the perfect cure for a semester of almost all work and no play. They parted in the morning with promises to get together soon.

Kate worked long, hard hours during the week, relaxed with wine with her friends after work on Friday, hiked and played tennis during the days on Saturday and Sunday, leaving only Saturday night free. Robert was disappointed, wanting to see her often, having this vague feeling she was a lifeline to or from something. He tried for some mid-week time, offering to do all the commuting, but she wasn't interested, and Robert instinctively knew that if he pushed it, he'd seem needy and push her away. In the end, he feigned contentment with the one night per week, a night that was on his mind the rest of the week.

After three weeks, Robert asked himself the inevitable question, was he in love with her? He tried the fantasy that he actually was, but it didn't have the impact he expected. It was a great relationship, and she made no demands on him, and perhaps that was it. She enjoyed him, but didn't need him, didn't want to get entangled, to make commitments, to start making long range plans. Kate's life was compartmentalized, and Robert was just one of many compartments.

This realization really came home to him one night at her place, over a meal and glass of wine. They were talking, but it was about travel, places they've hiked and camped, writers they both admired, the future of e books and a series of other, impersonal topics. They never discussed their relationship. Every conversation fairly shouted, "We are just dating."

Another thing Robert reluctantly realized was that this mattered much more to him than to her. It was obvious that should the relationship end, she would move on without looking back, but he would be devastated. In the beginning, he didn't want to seem needy, but he soon realized that he was needy, and that not seeming so was just a cover for his true feelings.

Being so wrapped up with Kate, he wasn't thinking of Kelly, concerned about her or concerned about her plans for them. It was a relief to have that off his mind, and, while he didn't dwell on it, it was strange that she hadn't contacted him. Perhaps her mother got through to her. On the odd moment he stopped to reflect, he felt sorry for her, vowing to be extra nice to her during the coming school year.

The drama that children create seemed less pressing on him now that he had a real relationship with an adult woman, a bright, attractive, sensual woman.

Late in the summer, Kate called him, saying that she planned to take three weeks to go traveling in Lapland. He glanced at his calendar and realized that the trip coincided with the last of his summer vacation, so he hinted that he was free to travel. That brought an awkward silence to the line.

After a few moments, Kate responded. "I'll be going with Bette and another friend. This is a buddy trip, not a couples kind of thing."

Robert said he understood, but he knew he didn't sound convincing.

And then she added that after school started, would he still feel like driving to her place every weekend? He assured her that it wasn't a problem, but she said, maybe he should think about it. After all, she felt kind of selfish having everything on her terms.

He started to protest, saying he didn't feel that way at all and that he enjoyed going to her place, and there was so much more to do there. He felt himself rambling, trying to put off the inevitable next part of the conversation.

"Bobby," And she had opted to call him Bobby from the start, "You know how hectic my life is." He didn't answer, realizing it was a rhetorical question. "Long hours of work, the gym three afternoons a week, Tuesday evening yoga, professional association meetings and talks on Thursday, happy hour with the girls on Friday. I'm realizing I don't have a minute to just relax, read some mindless novel, take in a movie, even watch TV."

"But," he injected weakly, "It's only one evening."

"That's it. Everything is just one evening. I need some down time. I think we should cool it for a while."

Even though he had no doubt about the answer, he had to ask how long was awhile. And, of course, her answer was vague. Awhile, was simply a while.

"So," he said, and his voice sounded leaden to him. "So, you'll get in touch whenever the time is right?"

"Yeah, that would be best. You understand?"

Well, he didn't understand, not one damn bit, but what could he say but yes. Awhile was permanent, something he felt from her tone, perhaps something that arose from his own insecurity, his poor record with women, and she was breaking up with him, and he with no choice but to be agreeable. And, he thought, it was ironic that his new apartment, his first, not counting dorm rooms at the university, was picked out with her in mind. He wanted a place she would feel comfortable in, should she ever visit. He wanted her to see the damn place at least once, hopefully for a night of passion. He'd paid more than he wanted, mainly because he felt it was attractive to a woman, and since he had deep doubts about his own attractiveness, the apartment was to be his alter ego.

When he put the phone down, the silence in his place was devastating, and he felt hollow. He was hit hard, and his first thought was that maybe he was indeed in love with her. Why else would the break up feel so bad? He was confused, not really knowing his feelings, but knowing he really looked forward to their evenings together and that he would miss her terribly. And the sex too; he would miss that. Thinking back, he realized that there was always a fairly long dry spell between his infrequent sexual relationships. Now with school about to start and him having to impress the principal if he hoped to gain tenure, he'd have little time to develop a new relationship.

His new apartment wasn't a total waste as far as romance. He did hit the local clubs often the last weeks of summer, like a desperate coyote after the first snow, and on occasion he'd met women with

32

whom he'd hit it off. One went home with him for a night of exhausting sex and a leisurely breakfast, the breakfast giving him the pleasant illusion of having a girlfriend. They both new, from the onset, that it wasn't a serious romance, but out of that night they formed a loose friendship, and for many months considered each other their backup, during the sexual dry spells, a friend, in the current slang, with benefits.

Aother woman gave him her number, and they had two or three dates, finally ending in sex. But without a spark, they were both just killing time, and, with the sexual curiosity satisfied, neither had the energy to continue things.

On the first day of school, after looking around for Kelly, Robert faced new rows of smiling fifth grade faces, lovely little kids all, excited and anxious to find out what was in store for them. He poured himself into his work, and within days, he'd gotten to know them all and basically liked them all. It was going to be a good year, he could tell already, and unless something went totally awry, he'd have his tenure, and then perhaps he could start considering taking a night or two per week for graduate school.

It was a good class, but it lacked that special high octane kick that Kelly had given last year. Even with all the problems, demands and uncomfortable crossing of boundaries, Kelly had made the year special. She had that fire, and she was a gifted student. He doubted he'd have a student like that again, and he wondered how she was doing in Ms. Harmon's sixth grade class. In fact as the second week of school started, he began to wonder why she hadn't come to see him, considering her talk of marriage at her birthday party. Perhaps her mother had set her straight, maybe even demanding that she stay away.

While he had been afraid to deal with her after the summer break, he found himself hoping she wasn't bruised too badly. Beyond that, he was really curious; had this temporary childish crush simply gone away and made room for whatever was next on her long list of interests. Oddly, the thought of her totally forgetting him bothered him. He wanted it over, but he really didn't want her completely out of his life. He loved being her mentor, watching her enthusiasm over a subject that he also loved.

That evening he met his friend, Flynn, for a quick drink at

happy hour in a sports bar half way between the school and Flynn's work. When in the course of catch up on work, and for reasons he could not explain, he'd mentioned about Kelly not coming by and how he felt about that, his friend gave him a sharp look, a look Robert demanded to have explained.

"Rob, do you hear yourself? You want a fan, a lovesick little girl to follow you around and stroke your ego."

Robert blushed, spinning the idea around in his mind as if he were examining a fine diamond, and just as quickly rejecting it. "No, it's not that way at all."

"Fine. Than what way is it?"

Like a drowning man, Robert thrashed around for the words that would save him, keep him ethically afloat. "It's concern, for her feeling, her talent, her..." And he trailed off, not sounding convincing, even to himself. Finally, eyes cast down, he mumbled, "Good god. Maybe there's something to that, although I hope not. I'm not that emotionally stunted?" And then, after a long pause in which Flynn failed to respond, he weakly added, "Am I?'

Flynn came to the rescue. "What the hell. We all want to be needed, admired, and with your recent run of luck with women, your ego, well, you've been pretty badly deflated."

"Still," Robert reluctantly observed, "No excuse."

"Well, no." Flynn admitted.

The topic slid in to the conversation a time or two again that evening, and Robert said he'd taken a good look at his subconscious and was not going down that road, not going to use a child to make him feel better, more secure. He said it, and he meant it.

The following Tuesday, having exorcised Kelly from his thoughts, Robert was grading papers after the bell when the door opened and in stepped a uncharacteristically timid Kelly. Robert looked up, unable to suppress a broad smile. "Kelly. How have you been? I hope you had a good summer. How's sixth grade treating you?" He seemed to want to keep up a line of chatter to avoid the something uncomfortable floating in the air between them.

As soon as Kelly could get in a word, she said, "Is it OK for me to come in here? I don't want to bother you. My mom said I was being a pest."

34

Robert looked at her, with her head down and hands behind her back, and he felt himself deconstructing, turning into a pile of random emotional parts. "Oh, my, Kelly. No, no, not at all. You're not a pest, and I'm glad to see you." And then, before he could stop himself, "I've missed you."

She immediately brightened. "Really? I thought you were mad at me, sick of me, never wanted to see me again. And I missed you teaching me all that cool stuff about writing and all."

"Kelly, sit down. You are always welcome here, and I'm always willing, anxious to help you with your writing." And as if he needed to be more convincing, he added, "You can come by every afternoon if you'd like."

"Really?" Her face showed a mixture of shyness and pleasure. I thought you were mad at me, you know from the party."

Kelly was sitting in a chair in front of his desk, and Robert moved over to a chair near her, putting him on the same level, taking down the barrier between teacher and student. Then softly, "Please understand something. It wasn't anything against you. Having a ten, I mean eleven year old girl talk to me about marriage, well it was kind of a shock. I mean, even to have that conversation, me being a teacher, forget teacher, just adult, well, that would look bad. It's something they'd fire me over, thinking it was my idea."

Kelly's eyes seemed to stop down like a camera lens as she looked at him. "I'm sorry if I scared you."

"Well, you didn't. Actually that was pretty scary." He smiled. Then, to lighten things up. "I pictured your mother walking in right then and calling the cops on me, screaming at me to leave her little girl alone."

Kelly realizing the humorous note, laughed and said, "I'm sorry. I won't say the M word again, at least until I'm older and it doesn't look so bad."

With that, Robert's light mood started to waver, as he wondered where the conversation was headed. "So, you haven't given up that idea?"

Her smile was almost patronizing. "Oh, no. That's all settled. It's just that we don't have to talk about it yet. We have almost seven years. Later, when you're comfortable, we can talk about our future."

"Kelly, this future thing is what's making me uncomfortable."

She nodded and made the motion of zipping her lips, and then said, "Can I show you the new story I'm working on?"

Now he was back on familiar, comfortable ground, and he took up her paper and read it without looking up. It was good. It would have been good for a fourteen year old, better than average for a high school senior, astounding for a sixth grader.

"Kelly. You've brought your character to life. This is a nice piece of writing, no of literature. I think you've found your future career. This can't be a first draft."

She confessed that she'd been working on it all summer, revising, editing, trying to remember everything he'd taught her, hoping he would like it and would be willing to help her again. She also wanted to know if it could be published, so he went through the youth fiction mags he kept for his classes, finding one that he thought would fit the bill and handing it to her, reminding her that they pay in copies, not money, but reminding her that everything published gives her future credibility.

And there he was again, the mentor, the man behind the eventual literary success of this girl, the, and this only flashed uncomfortably though his mind, ego behind the talent. But, the fact was that because of him, for whatever reasons, she had put in the effort to make this a good story. If his approval was what motivated her to be a good writer, he could live with that, take credit for it.

There was a ghost in the wings, something he noticed on the periphery but turned away from before it could come into focus, the idea that he actually enjoyed her attention, her attachment, her admiration. To acknowledge that would be to question what kind of adult he was, how emotionally secure and mature, to need the adoration of a child. The conversation with Flynn came back verbatim.

Now it seems as if nothing had changed. He was busy at work trying to be a creative teacher, and his social life revolved around the occasional date or drinks with his pals. On weekends he would ride his bike with the local club, good folks, but none who were becoming either good friends or steady girlfriends. There was nothing remarkable in his life.

5

Kelly was on the cusp of becoming remarkable, her enthusiasm, her dedication to perfecting her writing, her eagerness to have him approve the words she put to the page. It was as if, he mused, that she thought that should she produce a great work of literature, he would have no choice but to marry her. Naturally, that was unspoken, as was anything about her future marriage plans. She was respecting his feelings, but it was obvious by all the subtle interactions that she was still focused on the subject, focused with a bulldog determination.

Whatever the reasons, and he was sure they were many and complex, she was producing writing that was way beyond her years, writing that was being sent out and published in children's magazines. She was also becoming a regular contributor to online children's literature sites. She was a keen observer, and she could take the small childhood dramas and turn them into interesting fiction.

She was also back to her old routine, coming in almost every afternoon after school, often acting very impatient should one of his students be there, asking for help.

She was again suggesting that they bike ride home together or take weekend rides, and he was continually stressing that it would be inappropriate in a teacher/student relationship. He never rejected her suggestions, but he never accepted them either.   Rebecca, the young woman who he'd met at a bar before school started and who he was having a casual relationship with, was now more available to him, her recent part time boyfriend having moved away. They, not being wildly passionate or in love with each other, established a convenient routine. The had a standing date on Saturday, usually dinner and then either a local music venue or a film, always topped off with a night at either his or her apartment. It was a good relationship, a warm and comfortable relationship, a tender and friendship-based relationship, and it served to remind him that he was still capable of interacting with adult females.

Naturally, Friday night was, as always, reserved for his close pals, that is until Ted announced one night, after the second or third martini, and during the rock band's break, that he was engaged. Since he had only mentioned the girl a few times, mostly in passing, the news came as a surprise to the others. "His only response, and typical for Ted's level of communication, and luckily he was a corporate, rather than trial lawyer, had been, "Well, it just happened, kind of unplanned."

Although he assured his friends that they would still get together, it was obvious to the others that the bachelor buddy routine would be seriously disrupted, and that if Ted believed his wife would let him spend every Friday night was the boys, along with a weekend camp trip per month in the summer, than he was even more innocent and naive than they'd long suspected. Ted was a nice guy, an intelligent guy, but at his core, he was still a college kid.

Robert had a few too many that night, and when he got home, he considered the slow dissolution of a long time core of friendship, a core that gave him a secure foundation, a connection, an excuse for not forging new connections. One by one, each of them would move on, start a family or move to another town. With his head spinning from too many drinks, Robert stretched out in the dark and looked at his future. He enjoyed his job, but his dream was always to teach at a university, that and be a serious literary critic, one with the right credentials after his name. He also wanted a real relationship, not these casual dates, these women who seemed to come and go through his life like disembodied spirits. He thought, almost absently, how nice it would be to meet an adult version of Kelly, someone with whom he could share the passions of his life. He vowed to himself to enroll in grad school the minute he got tenure with the district.

For now, Robert had a full curriculum to teach to a bunch of fifth graders, kids so used to TV, computers and cell phones that concentrating on one thing for more than five minutes was an alien concept, a form on ancient torture. Each day he gathered himself up, hopped on his bike and settled in to try to stem the rising tide of contemporary indifference, and each day, just when he felt he felt he was losing ground, Kelly burst through the door, filled with inspiration, excitement and the urge to communicate.

Head figuratively down, the moments of his day filled, Robert walked the treadmill of his life, watching the days turn into week, as the school year passed the half way mark.

His mother had invited him over for his birthday, a day that had slipped up on him, almost before he noticed, and since he realized he had no date for the evening, her offer was more than welcome. However, as he was organizing his desk after the last of his students departed, the door swung open and Kelly walked in with a cake, complete with twenty-three candles.

"Happy birthday. I made this at home this morning, and I talked mom into bringing it down after school."

Taken by surprise and deeply moved, Robert was speechless for a few moments, during which time he wondered how she'd even known his birthday. When he found his voice, her standing motionless before him, cake in hand and a wide grin on her face, he gushed with thanks, telling her how much he appreciated it. While he was expressing his thanks, she put down the cake and stood right in front of him. Without thinking, he gave her a hug, and then, as he reconnected thought to action, he pulled away, uncomfortable and slightly embarrassed. She was still standing in the same place, grin even wider, looking very much as if she'd extracted a commitment from him.

She urged him to light the candles and make a wish, and while he did light them, no firm wish formed in his mind. He blew out the candles, and pulled out some paper plates left over from the class Thanksgiving party, cut two larges slices, to which she added two cartons of milk she'd saved from lunch.

They sat and ate, and they had a pleasant chat, not about writing or school work, but just about the general small talk friends engage in. Despite her age, he realized, she could hold her end of a conversation, provided it didn't venture beyond what an eleven year old could be expected to experience.

She didn't pull out any writing, having not come in the role of a student. As he looked at her, he realized that she was starting to change, was in a growth spurt, had lost much of her childish roundness and was in the process of turning into a gangling adolescent. He also realized that she was already has tall as his mother, and she was still growing and would probably be close to his height when she leveled off.

In another year she'd start turning into a woman, and he was

39

glad that she'd be in junior high school and not here testing her new feminine charms on him. That would be really uncomfortable.

She took another piece of cake home, and he brought the rest with him to his mother's, who it turned out also had a cake.

"What," Pat asked, as he walked in with half a cake. "You buying your own birthday cakes now?"

"Kelly." He added a shrug.

"Oh, yeah, the future wife." Her look, sarcastic.

"Stop that. She's not going to get me to marry her. In fact she didn't even bring the subject up." He felt strangely proud after saying that. Then he added, without sufficient conviction, "I'll probably be married with a couple of kids by the time she graduates."

"Not if she has anything to say about it, as I'm sure she will. Still, probably not a good idea to be alone with her over cake." And then to add to the fun she was having at her son's expense, "Also, probably not wise to be alone with her over cocktails either." With that she couldn't help laughing.

Over dinner, Pat asked, as mothers often do, how he was feeling, and he confessed that he felt his life was on hold and that perhaps it would get unstuck when he got tenure next year. "I just feel like I'm in a tight routine, on a treadmill. All those plans I made, all still on the shelf."

Since the local paper was one of those who carried his book column, a daily paper's version of a book review, he decided to talk to the editor about getting Kelly in the weekly student and school section, suggesting that she could write about school life from a kids' point of view. It was an impulse, likely as a response to the birthday cake. Naturally the editor was skeptical, wondering what a kid so young could write that would interest readers. Robert assured him, saying that if he didn't love her first submission, he'd drop the subject.

Kelly crafted a beautiful piece about the social aspects of lunch, who pays, who doesn't, who brings lunch, who sits with who and how all those things affect your social position. The editor thought it was outstanding and offered her a weekly column.

6

As the year wound down, Robert was feeling like the positive version of Doctor Frankenstein, a man who has created a writing monster, a word warrior. He had the uncomfortable feeling he was getting on with his stuck life though her, an idea that came to the surface on a spring day after the last bell.

As she walked in the door, he looked up and asked, "Want me to see your next column?"

"No. Don't need help, but I have a question. You told me you wanted to teach at a college, but you needed to go back to school so you could do it."

He looked over at her and responded with a slow, almost drawled, "Yes."

"Well, when are you going to do it? You're getting older. I'd hate to see you get too old for college."

After reassuring her that there was no age limit on college and emphatically stating that twenty-three isn't all that old, he explained that the first two years teaching is stressful, both because he was learning the fine points of the job and because he had to look good in order to get tenure. When that didn't completely satisfy her, he told her he planned to start taking evening graduate classes in the fall.

Then she asked an interesting question. She wanted to know what college he would like to teach at. He thought for a minute, and responded with, "If I had my choice," To which she nodded.

"Berkeley," he announced. "That's the University of California at Berkeley, one of the best universities."

She immediately wanted to know where it was, and he said that it was close to San Francisco, which she knew because her mother had taken her there for the weekend a couple of times, and she'd been to Fisherman's wharf, Pier 39 and Golden Gate park.

He explained that the university was at the base of a hill and that upper campus, along with the nicer neighborhoods are high enough for a view of San Francisco, across the bay.

Kelly was so curious, she got on Robert's computer and opened a map program.

"Wow. What a cool place to live. You gotta hurry and get back to school, so we... you can move there."

As graduation started looming up, Robert had to do a double take, apparently having his head down as he plodded forward and not noticing how quickly the year went by. Is this my life? He wondered, picturing yearly nine month blurs, broken up by summers.

Kelly, who was putting in at least an hour a night writing, was submitting to any magazine open to kids, plus the newspaper and internet sites. As she approached her twelfth birthday, she could, without hyperbole, call herself a writer.

Naturally he attended graduation, afterward telling Kelly how much he'd miss her. But she laughed and said, "The junior high school is only a few blocks away. I'll be coming to see you." The she looked him in the eyes, a slightly mischievous look on her face and added. "Don't be sad."

Robert expected to be invited to her birthday party as he had last year, and he felt that she understood not to make the embarrassing marriage scene again, but as the date came around, he heard nothing. Even though a kid's birthday party felt awkward and he would only go because it was expected, he felt a twinge of disappointment at not being invited. It was only later in the summer, when he received a card from Denver, that he realized that she hadn't been home for her birthday, but was instead visiting some relatives with her mother.

He was not to see her again until after the start of the next school year.

However, his professional life was in flux. At the end of the year, the principal had called him in and said that enrollment was down, and that they didn't need three fifth grade teachers. His heart sunk, thinking he was going to get laid off just before getting tenure, but, and there always seems to be a "but," there is another opening, should he be interested.

The principal knew he also was credentialed to teach single subject English, and there was an opening at the high school. Unfortunately, it was only an 80 percent contract, which meant less hours and less money. The idea of making less didn't excite him, but he realized that with rent being his only real expense, he could swing it if he cut out much of his entertainment budget. Accept it now, he thought, and if another district came along with an offer, he'd jump ship. Also, the idea of teaching writing to older kids excited him. He agreed to meet with the high school principal.

As soon as the high school principal made the connection between Robert and Kelly, the weekly column being something he looked forward to each week, he was hired. "Anyone who can teach an eleven year old to write like that is a keeper. Welcome to high school."

Before leaving, Robert asked if there were any opportunities to supplement his 80 percent, and he told him that many of the schools have after school programs, and that once school got underway, he might be able to pick up a day or two.

Figuring Kelly would be looking for him in September, he dropped her a note, letting her know where he was teaching and that he would probably pick up an after school assignment, so he wasn't yet sure when he would be free to work with her.

As both Robert and Rebecca's other action dried up about the same time, they found themselves in a more or less steady relationship by default. Robert realized that she was a friend as well as a lover, and it occurred to him that he'd had lovers and female friends, but never the two in one package, and when he broached that idea, one late night in bed, after energetic sex, she, after a few moments of reflection, said that it was true for her as well. It was becoming as comfortable as a well broken in marriage, and he was content enough. In the process, he had started learning to enjoy jazz, her favorite music, and she had bought a good bike and was starting to take regular rides with him.

Being able to teach high school, with a more specific language arts program and having a steady, fairly secure relationship, along with signing up for that graduate program, should have made Robert's life happy, or at the least, complete. But there was something missing as he started school. Kelly had, whether he wished it or not, become a part of his life. She was a reflection of his passion for words, for the well-turned phrase. Her small successes were also his, and he was getting to enjoy the high pedestal she'd put him on. Moreover, he was concerned that without his support, she may start to slip away from her writing talent.

Some of the high school kids were bright and some liked to

43

write, but it wasn't quite the same. However, he didn't have very long to mull over these feelings.

He'd put out a couple of feelers for after school jobs, but most of what was out there was helping elementary school kids with homework, which seemed kind of boring.

Then, just three weeks into the fall semester, he got a call from the junior high, the after school coordinator, a guy he hadn't even contacted. "Robert, I hear you're an excellent writing teacher."

Robert was surprised, surprised that the man had even heard of him.

"If you're interested, it's been suggested that you might be a good choice for a school paper. With the tight budget, it isn't done during the day any longer, and it's been suggested that it would be a good after school program."

Robert was floored. It couldn't be more perfect, more so when the coordinator, Miguel, said he could only schedule it two days per week, and neither were the day he took his first grad class. Of course he was interested, he insisted, but then, remembering that s Miguel houldn't have even known his name, and remembering about this job being suggested, he had to know where it was coming from.

"Strangely enough, it was a student, a new seventh grader. She came in to see me a few days ago, and believe it or not, she brought tear sheets of all the stuff she published last year. Well, according to her, you just about walk on water. She suggested a literary journal, a year book or some kind of newspaper. The paper idea sounded good, and she begged me to get in touch with you as soon as possible, as you had lots of other offers by now."

"Kelly!" Robert blurted out.

"Kelly, indeed. I tell you, if she wasn't so hot to become a writer, she could make a fortune in sales. She wouldn't let up until I actually promised to talk to you."

Robert got off the phone feeling both terrified and exhilarated. He was thrilled to have an interesting after school job, thrilled to be doing something he loved and actually thrilled to be working with Kelly again. And yet, that this kid, a girl barely twelve, was able to have such control over his life was scary. She was moving his career forward, and when he stopped to think about it, he might have put off

44

grad school for another semester if not for Kelly's persistence. She was either one of the most manipulative people he'd ever met or the most enthusiastic fan a man could ever have. What scared him the most was that he had no idea which scenario was true.

From a practical point of view, it was perfect. Miguel was willing to accommodate his schedule, so his day job, his afternoon job and his grad class didn't conflict with one another. He was making as much money as he'd made full time at the elementary school, was doing stimulating work, had the energy for the university class and was, with Kelly on his team, certain to have a good newspaper.

The following week he made the quick trip from the high school to the junior high and found the room Miguel had acquired for his use. Within minutes the students started wandering in, but when the bell rang, Kelly wasn't among them. A wave of disappointment came over him for a moment, and then she made her usual dramatic entrance, announcing, as she stormed through the door ahead of two boys, "I found two more reporters for you, Rob... Mr. S. Ok, Mr. editor, tell us what to do."

She had rather jumped the gun on his little speech, but he motioned everyone to sit down, and he started in telling them that his role was adviser and publisher. He'd set the plan, get things started, but it was the students' paper, and one of them would be the editor. Naturally, he knew who it would be before even bringing it up. In fact, one girl, probably both recruited and primed by Kelly, spoke up. "Kelly got this whole newspaper idea going, so she should be editor."

The others kind of looked around and nodded, some likely not knowing what an editor is or what she does. And since no one else asked for the job, that part was done. They discussed the other jobs, and Kelly helped pick out the people, reporters, photographers, sports writers and all the rest. Kelly obviously had been thinking about this, as she seemed to have a good idea how it should run, and she wasn't shy about filling the role of editor.

Soon everyone grabbed the job they wanted, and the kids started to talk about their first issues and what stories everyone wanted to do. This was feeling too easy to be true. Robert was sitting back, making suggestions but letting them run with it. And then, able to stop talking and to observe, he couldn't help noticing subtle changes in Kelly, changes over the few short months since he saw her at graduation.

She had grown taller, and she was starting to develop a figure. Where she'd been pretty much straight up and down, she was now starting to get curves. And then in one of those moments of self-awareness, a moment when he caught himself thinking about thinking and seeing the implications of what he was thinking, he felt his face flush. He was aware of her, aware that she was starting to grow into a woman, and he was painfully aware that he, as a teacher, wasn't supposed to even think of a student in those terms, particularly a student who is fixated on marrying him. He tried to put the whole idea out of his mind, but the more a person tells themselves not to think of something, the more they can't manage to think of anything else.

At one point, she turned to him and gave him a smile, perhaps, it seemed to him, a knowing smile, but how could she know what he was thinking. It was guilt, he decided that made him interpret an innocent smile the wrong way. Whatever passed briefly between them in that moment, Robert was sure it foretold a very stressful year for him.

Within a week the paper staff was getting organized, Kelly settling people to the jobs they wanted to do, while she took on attending the school board and city council meetings. While other kids were happy to write about school sports, dances and the lunch menus, she was looking at the wider world. To Robert, it looked very much like ambition, but since she was always so full of ideas, the object of her ambition evaded him.

His high school students were also starting to get motivated. He started a writing contest among them, with other English teachers to do a blind judging, and as the writing came in, looking better than he'd hoped, he sounded George, the principal, out about a possible literary magazine. He was now, without a doubt, something he'd always wanted to be, a writing teacher, and he found that he was able to motivate students to like writing, not all of them of course, but a respectable percentage.

He also discovered that his work could and would be the subject of his project for the grad class. Everything was falling into place, with one exception.

He really wanted a real relationship, and the closest he'd come was Rebecca. He really liked her. They were good friends, a worthy foundation for a serious relationship. He also wanted something that would totally exclude Kelly from his life outside the classroom. It wasn't, and he was uncomfortably concerned about the possibility, anything like attraction with Kelly. There was nothing of the sexual predator about him. There was an emotional connection. He cared about what she did, how she felt and even how he appeared to her. Two years ago she had called him her best friend, and she had managed to entwine their lives to the extent that she was growing closer and closer to being his best friend, and he knew how terrible that would be for both of them.

He'd learned early on not to talk about Kelly to Rebecca. A harsh, "Don't obsess over one of your students," was enough to remind him that talking about the kids was both weird and perhaps a bit creepy, and it did sometimes feel creepy when he thought about her outside of class.

One night, after a nice meal and comfortable conversation, they were lounging on his couch, music in the background, glasses of wine in their hands, and Robert started thinking of taking it to the next level. "Rebecca, do you think our relationship has any future?" He'd tried calling her Becky, but that had totally turned her off.

"Future? Do you mean like marriage and family?" Her tone hinted at the idea being far too premature.

He ran his fingers absently through her long brown hair, and the wine was making him mellow and a bit romantic. "I'm not trying to rush anything. It's just, well, do you see us as a couple, a steady thing, an item, as they say."

She turned to him with a very earnest look on her face. "I'm really comfortable with you, and, well, the sex is nice. But," and she hesitated for a moment, studying him, "I'm not actually in love with you. I mean I love you, but not in love, if you know what I mean. And I don't think you're in love with me."

He had actually rehearsed this scenario in his mind, so he was ready. "Maybe or maybe not now, but this friendship is deepening, and friendships can, do actually, grow into love, and everyone says to be friends first."

"I guess," she said. "And, you're right about the friendship. It's kind of an organic thing we have, and I think it's too early to start trying to put labels on it. I'm for riding this very pleasant wave and seeing where it takes us. Are you good with that?"

He was, and he said so, but in a way that masked his disappointment. It was a relationship in progress, and as long as it was going the right way, he felt comfortable enough. He had something, a real relationship with a real, interesting, vital woman, and that helped put his job and his students in perspective.

It wasn't until he had Rebecca and his mother over for Thanksgiving dinner and then a few days later, helped both of them put up Christmas lights, that Robert realized that his first semester at the high school was just about behind him. If his life was routine, this was an excellent one, one filled with accomplishments as well as challenges. It was being said that his paper was the best in the district, better than the high school paper. He had run two literary contests at his school and published the best writing, selling the journals them to students for enough to pay for the printing. George, his principal acted as if he walked on water, so his tenure was in the bag. His relationship, while not at a deeper level, was still working out nicely and comfortably. To top it off, Kelly came into the last newspaper meeting of the semester waving a check.

"I'm a professional," she shouted. The fifty dollar check was from a youth magazine. She had actually sold a story, not recognition or copies, but payment. Strangely, Robert almost felt as if he'd received a check, a check for hundreds.

"Kelly, I'm so proud of you. Keep this up, and you'll have a best seller before you graduate from high school."

She blushed. "Thanks, but kids can't write best sellers."

"Oh, yeah. What about S.E. Hinton?" When he saw the questioning look, he added, "Look her up on the internet. You might even read her first best seller in high school."

Robert was later to characterize that statement as pouring gasoline on a fire, as Kelly now had both a goal and a deadline, to have a book published by age 17, preferable before.

Robert declined Kelly's offer to have Christmas dinner with her, her mother and aunt, saying he had other plans. What he didn't mention, taking the coward's way out, was that he and Rebecca were going to spend a week in Hawaii, the first romantic get away in their relationship. This, Robert thought, could well be the turning point, the time when they define the relationship, perhaps even make plans to live together.

Approaching the San Jose airport on New Years Day, tired and content, Robert looked back at the week with a sigh of delight. It was almost all he could have asked for. It had been romantic, warm and balmy, lots of sightseeing, great accommodations. The only thing missing was that next step. Caught up in moment, he'd even told her he loved her. She told him she loved him too, along with a kiss on the cheek. It was clear that "I love you" meant only that and not "I'm in love with you." Backpedaling, he tried to make it sound like he'd meant the same thing. There it was, love without a capital letter, comfortable love, dating into the foreseeable future love, shake hands and part friends when it finally ends love. And by the time he landed, he decided that it was also how he felt, that the heat of the moment on a warm beach was only that.

7

Robert rode his wave of success through the second semester, taking another interesting grad class, continuing to make the paper even better, inspiring more high school students to love writing and cementing his relationship with the principal. Somewhere during that semester, his tenure became a done deal. He had a job teaching there as long as he liked, and he was tempted for a time to just settle in and become a big fish in a small educational pond.

For some reason he couldn't explain, he related that to Kelly one day after the other newspaper kids had gone home. It was innocent enough. "Things are going well for me here. I'm happy teaching high school and doing this paper. I could make it my career."

Kelly did that hands-on-hips thing she did before taking an unmovable stand. "No!" She shouted.

"And why not?" He almost snarled. He was annoyed that she should presume to tell him his business.

"You have a dream, just like I do. You are going to teach at that big university on a hill in Berkeley, with that view of San Francisco. You're not going to waste your life teaching a bunch of high school kids in this dumb little town."

"Settle down Kelly. Even if I have the endurance to finish a doctoral program, there's no assurance I'll even get an interview with Berkeley, let alone a job. Besides, it isn't your concern."

"Oh yes it is," She insisted. "Because you and I. Well. Well, you made me believe in my dream, so I have to make you believe in yours. If you don't believe, than everything you told me was a lie, and I'm never going to be a writer, and I'll just be a beauty operator like my mother, and you'll teach here until you're old, and neither of us will ever be happy." By the time she finished, her face was red and her hands trembling. She was almost in tears.

Robert was struck dumb. The passion and conviction in her voice, the power in her words came from out of the blue, came from someplace that didn't match up with the twelve year old kid trembling before him. He had spent two years talking the talk to her, and now she was demanding, yes demanding, that he walked the walk, and he frankly had no response.

Weakly, he attempted to answer. "Adult decisions are complicated, and I have to think of all my options, weigh them."

"You did all that. You're taking those classes so you can teach college. You're like around twenty-four. Aren't you grown up enough yet?"

He was being scolded, like his mother scolded him when he was in high school and changed his mind almost weekly about his future plans. How can this kid make him feel like a foolish little boy? How can she know which buttons to push to get a response? He put his hands up and said, "Stop. Look Kelly, just because I encouraged you with your plans, I'll discuss this with you, not that I owe you any explanation. No, don't say anything until I'm finished. I was only saying that this job, this life, isn't too bad. I could live with it. However, I'm not dropping out of grad school, and I'm not giving up on my dream. Now, unless you want me to get very angry with you, you'll drop the subject. OK?"

She nodded sheepishly, and since she was sufficiently cowed for the moment, he bid her good night and she quietly left.

The complex relationships between people sometimes progress imperceptibly, but often move incrementally, in sudden jolts. An adult, child relationship becomes an adult, adolescent, and then an adult, young adult relationship before becoming one of peers. That afternoon in the newspaper class was one of those turning points. While there was still a hint of tantrum in her outburst, it was more a manifesto. She had established her future plans, not childish wishes, but a real plan, and she was demanding that he stand up and declare his.

Almost a teenager, she was crossing that line between child and young woman, and she was, without articulating it, insisting on a new relationship, insisting on being taken seriously. Robert understood that she would not be denied, nor would she be patronized. She was strong enough to set her basic rules of interaction and smart enough to know when they were being ignored.

For the rest of the school year, their respective levels were not quite as far apart. She was growing figuratively as well as physically closer to his height. He found himself talking more to her than at her or down at her. She had become a confident enough writer that they could discuss her work much as an editor would with a writer, less like teacher with student. They discussed the newspaper, a few safe tidbits of personal issues and occasional updates on future plans. She always wanted to know about his grad school class, if it was interesting, if he were getting good grades.

One day she came in with an acceptance letter, one from a fairly well known youth magazine. She had a story accepted, and these folks paid. He decided to celebrate by ordering a pizza and sodas delivered. He shared his latest piece, published in a university literary journal and his latest book reviews, adding that he could hardly wait to review her first book.

She held up three fingers. "Three years. Give me three years. I want to have a book finished by the time I turn 16."

"And," he asked teasingly, "What will this book be about?"

"Not sure yet, but like you taught me, it'll be about something I know, probably school kids and their relationships."

And as the school year wound down to a close, Robert realized that they had a good relationship. She had avoided the uncomfortable topic of marriage, and they had become good friends. It was an easy, comfortable relationship, born of two years of working closely together. Robert was sure that they would remain friends, even after she'd grown up, established her career and they both had families. In ten years, he thought, he'd still be in his early to mid thirties and she'd be a college graduate, and they would be two adult friends with common interests. Somehow, those thoughts gave him a measure of comfort.

In fact, the comfort level was high enough that when Kelly had her mother invited him to share her birthday dinner, he didn't hesitate to accept. Working closely with her for so long put him in frequent contact with her mother, with whom he'd developed a casual friendship.

All he needed to do was grad stacks of writing, design and give a final exam and post grades, and he could start his summer, one in which Kelly's birthday was a minor celebration.

Lauri was more than just a beauty operator. She was a smart and somewhat ambitious business woman, having recently quit working for someone else and opened her own salon, which seemed to be doing well. She was also considering marriage to Neal, the man she'd been dating for the last year, and who had joined them for dinner. A strong woman who knew what she wanted, she'd obviously imparted that to her daughter. He respected the both of them, and he enjoyed Neal, who wasn't much for small talk, speaking only when he had something worth saying.

That was a summer of changes. Kelly went off to Denver again to spend a good part of the summer with family, and Robert's relationship with Rebecca turned the corner. Apparently, the other man she'd been dating when Robert met her was out of her life but not her mind, until he'd contacted her to tell her he was getting married. This seemed to clear the slate for Rebecca, and he told Robert she was ready to take the next step, perhaps move in together.

Rebecca, being a cautious and practical person, opted to bring some things to Robert's apartment and to semi inhabit the place, keeping her own place just in case and as a place for some down time. This was perfect for Robert, who, try as he might, always fell just short of total commitment. Slowly invading his consciousness was the notion that in all the times he'd been in love, he'd never been head over heels, never without the shadow of doubt, the "but" clause, as his lawyer friend Ted would say. Rebecca was almost Ms. Right, but how could he tell, how could he say that the next one might be all she is and more? Did this make him immature? He asked himself that question often, but never dug for an answer. Naturally, he concealed his doubts from her. Immature, he may possibly be, but foolish, never.

It was almost a perfect summer. She was a nine to fiver, and once the work day was over, it was over and she had loads of energy for fun. For his part, school was out, and his only obligation was the grad class one day a week. His only time away from her was the ten day annual camp trip with his buddies. It was almost like a honeymoon, but all honeymoons eventually come to an end, as theirs did when school started.

Walking into that junior high classroom where he had his newspaper class jolted him back to the reality of being a teacher, those pale green walls, desks with the wood grain laminate, dull, gray linoleum, the green chalk boards. He wondered how anyone could learn in a place that looked like a third world jail. Still, he took that day before school started to arrange a space for his program, to find a way to coexist in a small room with the day teacher.

While teaching high school was still ostensibly a stepping stone to his eventual career, there was nothing in the way he attacked it that gave the slightest clue. He launched into his teaching, an expanded literary mag at the high school, the junior high newspaper and his grad school class, each with total commitment and focus.

It wasn't deliberate, but he was ignoring Rebecca much of the time. He'd compartmentalized his life before she moved in and had thus filled his day, and it was a routine that left little room for a relationship, other than dinner together and sex every other night.

Rebecca wasn't taking it well. Sure she was spoiled, spoiled by months of Robert's twenty-four hour a day attention. The change was too sudden, too abrupt for her to adjust. On the outside, she was still smiling, while apparently pouting on the inside. And, it was always, "I have to do this paper, and then we'll have time." Or, "I've got to edit the literary submissions, and then I'll be free to play." Everything enjoyable was just around the corner, just beyond the next deadline.

One day, in an attempt to bridge the gap and share in his world, she suggested that she come by during his after school class to see what he did, saying that since it wasn't the formal day program, it shouldn't be a problem.

Robert started to say it would be OK, and then he corrected himself. "No, I don't think you should do that."

She was taken aback. "Is it against the rules?"

"No, but it would be hard to explain you to the students."

"What's to explain? I'm your girlfriend. The kids are old enough to understand that."

"Well, yeah, but there's one who would not take it well, a kid I've been working with for a long time."

"What? Some kid would be jealous or some damn thing? Oh, wait. You're not talking about that girl you've been mentoring for two or three years?"

"She's sort of attached to me, kind of proprietary." He was stumbling. "I think she sees me as a father figure and all."

"Oh, no you don't. There's this young girl you have a, how

shall I put it, close relationship with, and you can't introduce me as your girlfriend because she'll get jealous."

A wave of panic rolled over him. "That's not how it is." After he said it, he realized how weak it sounded.

"That's how it sounds. I don't supposed you've ever mentioned me to your little jail bait." Her eyes burned into him. "No, I didn't think so."

"There's nothing going on."

"I don't suppose so, at least not yet. I don't think we can do this. I don't know what you want, but clearly it isn't me, and I'm not going to compete with some fucking preteen. I'm beginning to understand why you have less and less time for us."

He sat in his chair, face in his hands wet with tears. He didn't want to lose her, and he didn't want to parade her as his girlfriend, and he certainly didn't want to seriously consider her accusations. There was no way he had some predatory interest in Kelly. He just knew how she was and how she reacted. Was keeping the peace so damn bad? In the next room Rebecca was packing the last of her stuff, and then she marched into the room and said, without slowing her march to the door, "Good bye, Robert, and don't call me."

He was alone, and the silence in the room was palpable and painful. He missed having her there, but did he actually miss her. He thought about her, about the times they had about the great sex they'd enjoyed, but something inside of him was somehow numb. Then, thought willing himself not to, he thought of Kelly, who had changed over the summer. There was no denying that she was maturing, looking more and more like a young woman, a very attractive. Oh, my God, no. Don't even think that. She's thirteen, a kid, a student. He asked himself point blank if he desired her sexually, and his honest answer was no. No it wasn't sexual. He admired her, respected her, cared about her as a friend, but without any lustful thoughts. Thinking of Rebecca excited him, but there was nothing like that when he thought of Kelly.

8

The following week, he was still down from the break up, and Kelly apparently noticed. "Mr. S. what's wrong?"

"Oh, nothing. Just a rough week."

"Come on, it's more than that. I'm your friend. Talk to me."

He tried to evade the subject, but she stood in front of him, persisted, almost nagged, until he blurted, "My girlfriend broke up with me, ok?"

Kelly suppressed her broad grin almost as quickly as it engulfed her face, and she forced as sad expression. "I'm sorry. You're a really great guy, and you'll have another girlfriend before you know it."

It was hard to work with her after that, not that her quick betrayal of her feelings was a problem. It didn't surprise him. It was the fact that he was now aware of her as a rapidly maturing young woman, and that awareness made him uncomfortable. The jeans which were almost a part of her daily outfit, were form-fitting now, showing that her waist and hips were diverging from their former monotonous uniformity. Casual conversation with her became difficult, almost impossible, as he felt that his only defense against implied impropriety was to be as cool and formal as possible. It was difficult because they'd spent over two years building a working relationship, and that she was sensitive to the change.

She put it frankly one day, several weeks after his break up with Rebecca. She sat on the edge of a desk and looked him in the eye. "You're acting kind of unfriendly. Is something wrong? Are you mad at me?"

"No, no. I still think you're my best student. It's just that I have to remember the teacher and student relationship. It's not good to be all buddy-buddy with my students." He was having a hard time meeting her gaze.

"But, after school, we were always kind of friends and all."

He patted her hand and then quickly pulled his away. "We are, you know that, but here at school. I don't want anyone to get the wrong impression."

The sudden jerk of her head told him she wasn't going to let this go. "Anyone? Who? The other kids? Another teacher who might come in? Me?"

She'd put him on the spot. "Everyone, including you. I, I have to be only your teacher."

"So, you can't be my teacher and be friendly?"

"Of course I can. I just have to remember that there's a line." He made a motion with his hand as if to draw a line between them.

The sign of a good writer is to be able to read people, and she had no lack of that ability. There was a gleam, a rather sneaky gleam, in her eyes. "Are you saying that you're having trouble remembering the line? Is it that you want to be more than my teacher, but you're like afraid?" She drawled out the last word as if she were tasting it.

He looked quickly around to see if any of the other students were listening in, but they were either at a computer, working on their stories or chatting. In a rare moment of social brilliance, he got his answer. "No, you see, it's about not having this conversation, not sitting in a classroom trying to make it personal. As a teacher; as an adult, this kind of talk makes me uncomfortable, and that's part of the reason I'm acting cool."

She slipped off the desk, turned and picked up a piece of paper. "I got it, Mr. S." She thrust the paper in his hand and said, "Here's my story on the school board meeting. Please check it and let me know if I need to fix it. And, now I promised to help Becky with her school food story." She turned and walked away, and Robert felt like a real shit, even though he was in the right and did what he had to. Don't let her manipulate you, he told himself, but that didn't help much.

Interestingly enough, this was the year he had all seniors, kids damn near adults, and some of the girls would probably be less likely to be carded in a bar than himself, and he was often carded, with his baby face. Some of these girls, only seven years younger than him, openly flirted with him. Many were very attractive, and several dressed provocatively, and while he, being a normal man, noticed, he never considered or even fantasized about any sexual relationship. Had he met some of them on the street, not knowing their ages, he might well have hit on them, but he had this internal control, this censor that shut those thoughts down even before they could arise. Yes, there were many young high school teachers who had affairs with students, and while he didn't blame them for being tempted, he did blame them for crossing that line.

With all that in place, he could work with these girls, sit next to them and critique their work, without any discomfort. So, why did Kelly, only thirteen, make him so jumpy the minute she got close? The now unspoken business about marriage was likely the hurtle he couldn't get over. Although she never mentioned it any longer, it hung there between them, underlined by that half smile out of the corner of her mouth whenever they were in the middle of a long conversation. He was certain that she was still checking off the days to her eighteenth birthday and was likely collecting brochures for romantic honeymoons.

One night, having dinner at his mother's and having a few glasses of wine, the urge to have a sounding board pushed it out of him, and he related the whole inner conflict.

With the exception of a few facial expressions that seemed to show concern, she sat and listened passively until he had gotten it all out. And then she sat, maddeningly quiet for the longest time, finishing her glass of wine, deep in thought, with Robert poised on the edge of his chair as if it were a cliff.

Finally, "To begin with, you're afraid of her." He started to scoff, but she waved him off. "I think you're convinced that she's got your life planned, and that your only hope is to get her to change her mind, that the decision about some eventual marriage is hers to make."

"Don't be silly, mom. She has no control over my life. She's just a kid, and there's no way she can make me marry her if I don't want to."

"If you don't want to? Interesting that you should add that. Robert, you know in your head that you're in control of that, but there's an insecure young boy in there." She reached over and tapped him on the chest with her forefinger. "And, that little boy isn't all that sure of himself, all that much in control. Somewhere deep inside, you're telling yourself that since she's so damn positive about this, that it's somehow carved in stone, somehow your fate to either accept or struggle against, like a fish on a line. And now, I've finally put my psychology major to use. Call your grandfather and tell him all that tuition money wasn't wasted." She laughed, breaking the tension her words had strung.

"Jesus! Look, I'm not going to marry the girl."

"Great. Now say it over and over with more conviction. This kid has given you something, and it sounds like you've become a bit addicted to it. You don't want it, but you can't leave it alone. I've raised a good son, a moral and ethical one. Some guys would take advantage of a girl like that, but that would never occur to you."

This was one of those rare evenings where it wasn't just small talk between family members. They talked for a long time, and Pat recalled a crush she had on a boy when she was in school and how she'd constructed all these scenarios about them and their future, and at one point they became almost reality. After he assured her that this was different, she agreed, but pointed out that there are all kinds of relationships that can suck you in and shut out the real world. Her final advice was what stuck with him. "Be openly friendly with her, but keep your emotional distance. In your head, pull back and look down at what's happening."

Amazingly, that tidbit of advice made the difference. Starting the next newspaper class, he was his old self around her, knowing that he was a disinterested observer, immune to any emotional roller coaster rides she might have in store for him. And, for months it all worked out wonderfully.

She was working on a story about a junior high girl who had a crush on a high school football star, the sexy older guy thing, and it was a good story, but he saw something autobiographical hiding between the lines. To his credit, he didn't react to that or even hint that he saw it. He focused on the fact that it was a very good story, probably the best she'd written, and he knew just the magazine she could send it to.

"Do you think they'll buy it?"

"Kelly, you've read the magazine, right?" He reached in his briefcase and pulled out a copy. "And, you know the quality of the writing." He handed it to her. "Spare me the false modesty. Now, I think you know if your work is good enough or not, but you always wait for me to say it. This time you tell me. Is that story good enough for this magazine?"

She lit up. "You darn right it is." Then she gave him a high five.

"That what I want to hear. You can't always have me handy to reassure you, and you don't need it. You know how talented you are."

"Yeah," she shyly admitted. "But, I so trust your opinion. You're the expert."

"Ok, hire me to be your editor when you start writing those best sellers. Now, we've got a newspaper deadline, and I need to know if all your reporters have gotten their stories in."

Later, he remembered something practical and called her aside. "Have your mother take you to her bank and open a savings account for you. Deposit that check and others, put them aside for college, which is getting more expensive every year."

Christmas break was almost upon them, and with it his twenty-fifth birthday. Kelly came into the room with a small package, handing it to him while wishing him a happy birthday. "Kelly, you shouldn't have done this."

She didn't answer, but just pointed, indicating that he should open it. It was a watch, not an expensive one, but a nice one. Kelly added, "I noticed your old one was looking pretty lame."

He was touched, but it wasn't right. "Kelly, I very much appreciate the thought, but you shouldn't be spending all this money on me."

"Rob... Mr. S. It's money I earned writing, money I'd never have if you hadn't taught me everything I know. It's happy birthday and thank you, so don't argue with me about it."

And he didn't, knowing that arguing with her was like trying to pull a bone out of a starving dog's mouth. He thanked her and was so touched that he felt tears welling up in his eyes, which she obviously saw, as that familiar sly smile crossed her face.

The next day he got the strangest Christmas card, in it was a wedding announcement. Ted was getting married New Years Eve in a small ceremony with just a few close friends and family. Since his engagement and Flynn's new live in girlfriend, the old gang wasn't getting together very often any longer, and Robert felt sad about that. He was the kind of man who liked consistency in his life, likely one of the reasons he preferred a steady relationship to casual dating.

When he called his mother to tell her the news, she informed him that she couldn't talk long, as she was meeting Lauri for Christmas shopping and lunch.

"Lauri, as in Kelly's mother?"

Pat confirmed that, and he asked, "But when, how did you two get to be friends?"

"Well, our kids kind of pushed us together, and we seem to have a lot in common, enjoy each others' company and all. Why, what's the problem?"

He stammered a bit before she added. "Contrary to your self-absorbed ego, we really don't talk about you too much, beyond having an innocent laugh at your expense."

He picked up a gift for his mother, as well as token gifts for his three buddies. Then, as an after thought, he decided to get something for Kelly, and that was a problem. He didn't want to get anything too personal, but he didn't want to get something that didn't have some meaning. Spending too much would send the wrong message, but some cheap, token gift would seem insulting. All the other gifts took a hour or so combined to buy, hers took several days. As an avid reader and writer, he naturally gravitated to a book store, remembering how he'd bought her a dictionary and thesaurus set, which she had said she appreciated. A thick volume caught his attention, The current *Writer's Market*.

Since Pat was having Lauri over for dinner on the twenty-third, presumably bringing Kelly, Robert had it wrapped and ready. She shrieked with joy and moved to give him a big hug, when she looked around at two moms and seemed to think better of it. Instead, she shook his hand and handed him a small flat package, which turned out to be a CD. "Some of the kids are starting a band, and I talked them into recording some Christmas songs with me. Now when you play this, you'll always think of your best friend."

Sitting around the table felt both comfortable and weird to Robert. On one hand, it was a close group of friends and family, but then it was like dining with an implied future wife and her mother, something that should freak out all three adults. Oddly, the evening seemed mundane. It was a mix of small talk and plans and aspirations.

Lauri talked about her hair salon and all the unexpected problems involved with owning a business, along with that great feeling at the end of a profitable month. Pat, who usually didn't discuss her work, talked about how she'd gotten a real estate license after Robert's father left, and how she's worked her way up to one of the top salespersons. Naturally, Robert was anxious to talk about how great his classes, literary journal and newspaper were coming, remembering to give Kelly credit for being an outstanding student editor.

Kelly, almost shyly, talked about the few stories she'd had published, the ones she was working on, and her plans to try writing a novel when she got to high school. She also talked about the paper and journalism, and as Robert listened to her, he thought that this didn't seem like an odd assortment of people from forty-five to thirteen, but more like a group of friends, professionals all, discussing careers and ideas, and for a moment, Kelly wasn't just a kid, but an adult friend. It was just a moment, and then he was again looking at a young teenager.

After the evening, he told his mother about how things seemed kind of weird. Pat said it was, but, "Friendships are funny things, even very bizarre ones. I actually like the kid now. Thought she was a terribly manipulative little princess at first, but I see she's a strong willed young girl with some solid future plans and a surprisingly level head."

"So, you're now longer bothered by the marriage thing?"

"No. I think she'll outgrow that. She's growing up fast, and she'll be adjusting her sights as her work and confidence grows."

"In other words, you're saying she'll outgrow me." That unexpectedly hurt his feelings.

"No, honey. This isn't anything against you. I just think she'll grow in her own direction, grow apart from you or from what you represent to her. It's back to what I thought when you first told me about this."

"Well, I guess that's good. So, when do you think all this will happen?"

"I'm guessing it'll be in high school, when she gets a real boyfriend and puts away her fantasy, like she's probably put away her dolls. Little girls live in make believe worlds, big girls take on the real world."

He wanted to argue with her and the implication that he somehow wasn't good enough for a woman in the real world, that he was some kind of vacuous "Ken" doll that only little girls played with, but he realized that he'd be arguing against his own positions, his own protestations. Still, his ego was bruised. Just because she might grow into a successful writer and a strong woman, that doesn't mean she'd laugh at the thought of once wanting to marry dull old Robert, the plodding high school teacher. Then he realized where his thoughts were leading, and he silently laughed at his own foolishness.

9

One day, shortly after the second semester started, Kelly came into the newspaper classroom with a boy, dark skin, big brown eyes and shiny black hair. "I found us a new reporter. Mr. S. this is Sib, short for Sibbatha. He's from India."

A polite little boy, he put out his hand, said he was glad to meet him and called him sir, all in that delightfully lilting Indian accent. Robert liked him.

Turns out he only been in the country a couple of years and still hadn't manage to fit in anywhere, gather a circle of friends, and it was clear that Kelly was taking him under her wing. She spent the rest of the session huddled with Sib, hardly speaking to Robert.

Good, he thought, she has a friend, and then he realized that he'd never seen her that close with any of the girls, and he wondered if she really had any close girlfriends.

After that, they always seemed to come and go together, and he started to wonder if she had her first boyfriend. Naturally, at her age, that concerned her, realizing that she was too young for a real relationship.

Thinking about that on the long drive to the university one afternoon, he had to laugh at himself about having any realistic views on relationships, with all of his failed and nothing on the horizon. As it turned out, he was a bit premature in his thinking.

A young woman in his class, one who usually sat on the other side of the room, came in late that evening, and, trying not to disturb a class already in session, spotted the empty chair next to Robert. They nodded at each other before getting back to the day's topic. Then, as they got up for the break, she put out her hand and introduced herself. "Hi, I'm Sandy Brenner. Gonna grab a coffee. Join me?"

While he hadn't paid much attention to her before, he was now very aware of how attractive she was, a tall redhead with a wide jaw and pale eyes. Striking, was the word that came to mind. She was almost finished with her M.A. degree and hoped for a career in publishing. He told her he was going for the doctorate and a teaching job at a university.

She wrinkled up her nose at this, saying, "I've been in class-rooms for most of my life, and I'll be glad to put them behind me for good."

In just a few minutes, he realized how many common interests they shared, both in love with good writing, both considering *Elephants of Style* one of their favorite books.

After class they walked to the parking lot together, and as he drove away, he was looking forward to seeing her at the next class, already planning to invite her to have a drink afterward.

He was nervous, thinking she'd reject the offer, but she acted pleased, saying she was hoping he'd suggest it. Over a glass of wine, they shared their ideas and passions, discovering they'd read many of the same books, had the same views on composition and style and had the same general goal of improving people's taste in literature, him through teaching, her through publishing works of literary worth.

As he made the long drive home late that night, he couldn't help thinking that Sandy might just be the one he'd been waiting for all his life. He could, he thought, fall madly in love with her.

They arranged to go out after class again the following week, and over a glass of red wine in a cozy Italian restaurant, Sandy confided that she'd deliberately sat next to him, that she'd noticed him, but, "It was clear you didn't know I was in the room."

"Not true." He meant that, but she countered with the fact that he'd never talked to her or even smiled in her direction, thus proving she was invisible to him.

Finally, he had to confess something. "I noticed you from the first day of class, wanted to talk to you, but..."

She leaned forward and looked him straight in the eye. "Come on, but what?"

He felt himself flush. "OK, I figured you wouldn't give me the time of day. I thought you were way out of my league. That was hard to say, OK?"

Her eyes went wide, and her expression went from surprise to a slowly widening smile. Then she took his hand, leaned further over and gave him a warm, wet kiss. She followed this up with an invitation to come to her place.

Once in her apartment, there was only minimal small talk before

65

she lead him to her bedroom and pretty much took the lead for two hours of foreplay and some of the most exciting sex he'd even had.

To get home in time to change and get to work, he was up at six, after not falling asleep until almost two. The next day was close to sleep walking, and by the time his after school newspaper started, he wanted nothing more than to crawl into bed.

Kelly asked if he hadn't slept, and he mumbled some answer, so she told him to relax, as she had everything under control, and was expecting all the stories to be finished by the end of the day. He slumped in a chair and watched as a room full of kids busily knocked out their stories. And true to her work, just before the final bell, Kelly presented him with a travel drive containing all the stories, something he could proof and lay out over the weekend.

The weekend, at least as much of it that he had for himself, for work, was limited to Sunday, Friday night and Saturday spent with Sandy, walking, eating, talking, making love. His bike never came out of the garage.

An immediate pattern formed. He would stay over one night after class, and he'd spend either Friday or Saturday night, often both, with her. He forced himself to double up on his grad class and school work on the other nights. He had become the modern young American man, every minute of every day accounted for. He normally would have balked at this, but Sandy was simply everything he could imagine in a woman. In fact, after a bit of prodding, she promised to pick up a bike, claiming that she'd rode almost daily as an undergrad, but was short on extra money for non-necessities.

One of the bike club group was selling an old bike cheap, cheaper still, since Robert was going to pick up half the price without telling Sandy.

Unfortunately with his time accounted for, biking became a two hour activity every Saturday afternoon, but it was, he figured, better than nothing.

That Spring was becoming a blur, and he was wondering where it would all lead. The problem with grad school was that they both had career plans, and these might not lead to the same town. That was a nagging fact, that being totally wrapped up in her, in the heat of passion and all the promises for an incredible life ahead, he managed to put out of his mind. In a reversion to adolescence, typical of young men who are either in love or in lust, he simply told himself it would all work out for the best, as if the universe was tuned to his needs and desires.

While he was still aware of Kelly and spoke to her extensively during those two newspaper sessions each week, he was, probably for the first time, ignoring her emotionally. Oddly enough he felt bad about this, feeling almost as if he were betraying her. Yet, she wasn't complaining, as he'd expected her to do.

He did notice that he never saw her without Sib by her side, and that made him vaguely uncomfortable. In fact, the more he paid attention, the more it bothered him. She was thirteen, and to his mind, too young for whatever was happening.

One day, after class, he asked her to stay a couple minutes. She told Sib she'd catch up with him, and came back in the room. "What's up? You haven't talked one on one to me for a while."

"I know, and I'm sorry about that. Have a lot on my plate right now, paper to grade, the newspaper to get out, a major paper due for my class, and finals right around the corner. But that's not what I wanted to talk about."

She didn't answer, just cocked her head and looked at him, the way she does when she's giving him her undivided attention. Now that he'd committed himself to this conversation, he was having misgivings and some difficulty getting started.

"It's about you and Sib. You seem to spend a lot of time together."

"Yeah, he's one of my best friends."

"I'm just concerned, you know, because of your age." Her answer was a blank stare, so he stumbled on. "I know you have big plans for your future, and I don't want to see make any mistakes that could jeopardize that." Again, nothing but the blank stare, nothing to show him he was on the right track. "There are things you are too young to deal with."

She opened her mouth to speak, hesitated, and started in with, "I'm not sure what you're getting at, what my future has to do with Sib." And then she abruptly stopped, her mouth opening wide. "Ohmygod! You mean, like sex, like getting pregnant!"

Robert stumbled in with, "Well, that's a concern. Young girls can get caught up in the moment and make a decision that can affect their whole lives."

Mouth still open, she put her fists on her hips. "Robert Spagnola, you have a dirty mind. Sib and I are just friends. I'm honestly insulted." She exhaled loudly, spun on her heel and stormed out of the room, slamming the door behind her, leaving Robert feeling lower than pond scum. She was an innocent child, and he'd tried to make something sorted out of a simple friendship, and he wasn't sure he could make things right and restore the relationship. He'd been scolded, made to feel like a little boy who had been caught with porn by an adult. He was both ashamed and angry that this kid could switch roles with him.

The bad taste in his mouth from the encounter even took some of the magic out of his weekend with Sandy, who almost immediately picked up that something was wrong, but it took the whole weekend to pry in out of him, Robert still smarting from the final incident with Rebecca.

As he told it, Kelly was "the student he'd been mentoring for years," something Sandy was aware of, as he'd shared some of Kelly's writing with her. He explained that he was concerned that she'd get in a relationship too young and waste her talent.

He imagined a number of reactions from Sandy, most of them unpleasant, but he didn't expect her to laugh. "Men can be so dense. You figure if you're friends with a woman, there's sex involved, so you figure every guy feels the same way. So, you're being like the overprotective father who asks a guy on his first date with the daughter what his intentions are. I know about that; my father was one of those."

Robert tried to defend himself, but only managed to make himself look more ridiculous. Finally, he demanded. "Ok, if you know so much, is this something I can fix, because I feel like a real shit about it?"

"Give her a week or two to cool off and then just apologize, letting her know what a jerk you were. Being contrite will go a long way."

It didn't take a couple of weeks, within a week Kelly walked up to him, smiling and asked how he was doing. Surprised, he asked, "You're not still mad at me for those stupid things I said?"

"Naw. It took a couple days, but then I figured out what was really going on, so I'm cool with it."

"What's really going on? I don't know what you mean."

"Oh, yes you do. You're just jealous of Sib. You're afraid he's going to steal me away from you. Don't be so insecure. I'm not going anywhere."

He felt himself flush, his face on fire, and for a moment he wondered if what she was saying was true, but he knew he loved Sandy, not little Kelly. "No, no, that's not it at all. I was just being overprotective, playing father and all that. It was just stupid."

"She waved him off, turned and strutted off, chanting, "I made you jealous; I made you jealous."

It was maddening the way she could inject a tiny virus of doubt in his mind. No, of course he wasn't jealous, not of a little kid, not over a student barely in her teens. But, for some reason, when she said things like this, said them with that matter of fact tone, he always crawled inside himself, questioned himself, doubted even the things about himself he was absolutely sure of.

He certainly wasn't going to mention that little exchange to Sandy, even though she wasn't jealous of the kid and didn't take the whole thing seriously. There's a limit, a point where any normal woman will start to question this very, and yes, he had to admit it to himself, very abnormal relationship.

But the school year was winding down, and summer with most of his responsibilities and quite a bit of Sandy's erased for nine glorious weeks. They would finally have time, time to plan, time to build the routines of relationships, time to find their areas of compatibility, areas of comfort, areas of bonding. Sandy would still have her part time jobs, and Robert would be spending some time prepping for the following school year, but compared to the back breaking schedule of the last months, it would be like a holiday for both of them.

His high school students were working on their final writing assignments of the year, reading the last novel, getting ready for finals. The after school class was researching the articles for their last edition, and his relationship with Kelly was as smooth as it could be, the two of them busily working together, like members of a team, friendly but businesslike. The only hint of the recent incident was the occasional crooked smile that spoke of some knowledge that in reality she didn't possess, but that in her mind was carved in stone, the belief that she had him emotionally locked up and that he was jealous of any male she spent time with.

Robert wanted to plan a trip to Alaska over the summer, contingent on Sandy getting time off of work. It was hard, him having a career already, her working on whatever paid the bills while she worked toward her career. Getting these degrees, while something he wanted and kept after, wasn't the urgency it was for her. He actually liked his day job, and if it took an extra year or two to get through grad school, it wouldn't be the end of the world. It was all comfortable, a routine made of challenges just big enough to engage him, but not so big as to intimidate him. He was, he felt, intellectually challenged, while emotionally comfortable, the best of both worlds.

It was a beautiful, sunny, warm day in May, a day when most of the students, and, if truth be known, most of the teachers, had a case of spring fever. The final edits of the school paper were coming in, and soon Robert would be laying it out, showing the final version to the class and sending it off to the printer. Kelly, who had been working with another girl on her piece, suddenly walked up to Robert. "Will I be in your class next year?"

His mind elsewhere he could only respond with a vague "what?"

"I'll be in high school." She stopped to make hand gestures that proclaimed that what she was saying of obvious. "You teach high school?" A rhetorical question. "You know I want to be in your class. After all you're the best English teacher in the district. I figure that if anyone deserves a seat, it would be me. Right?"

"Wow, Kelly, I hadn't even thought that far ahead. I'm not sure what I'll be teaching next year. This year it was freshmen and juniors, but the year before it was almost all seniors, so who knows."

"I believe, Mr. S., as my biology teacher says, humans are mammals, which means they are also vertebrates, meaning we all have backbones." And when Robert didn't respond, she continued. "If you actually have one," and she touched her own spine for emphasis, "walk into the principal's office and ask for freshmen. You do want me to grow up to be a famous novelist, don't you?"

"Kelly, I can't promise anything, but I'll mention it to him."

"Can't promise? I've been asking around. Seems you are like some kind of teaching super hero. You tell him you really want ninth graders, and I'll bet you get them."

"But, there's no guarantee I'd have you in my class. Big school, at least two, maybe three people teaching that class. I'm assuming you're talking about college prep."

"Straight A student, yeah, college prep. You teach the class, I'll worry about getting in."

All of a sudden the incongruity of it all hit him, and Robert began to laugh, a laugh he couldn't stifle. Puzzled, she demanded to know what.

"This conversation. I mean, 'You teach the class, I'll worry about getting in.' Those are words I'd expect from a university junior, certainly not a junior high kid."

"I'm not a kid, and I'll be in high school in a few weeks, and I want the best teacher the school has to offer."

Afterward, he thought about it, and it seemed natural that she'd be in his class again. He'd worked with her in one capacity or another for over three years, and he was just egotistical enough to love the idea of grooming a writing superstar. On his next prep he caught the principal alone in his office. In a very off hand way, he said how much he'd like to work with freshmen again, college prep being his preference.

"Rob," and George called him Rob, "You've done a great job with every grade. Let's see, you've had different grades each year, so. I wouldn't have a problem with that. And, I guess you'd also want juniors again, rather than do a new syllabus."

"Not necessary. Freshmen and whatever. I start over each year anyway."

George reached over and patted him on the shoulder. I've got to admire you. Most teachers would like to do the same grades a few years running, rather than making all new plans. You obviously intend not to let yourself get stale, get in a rut. I like that. Frankly, I haven't even started on the schedule yet, but I'm thinking three freshmen classes, the rest, whatever, I guess."

He waited a week before casually mentioning it to Kelly on almost the last day of school. "Kind of looks like I'll be getting mostly freshmen next year. If you're in one of them, that would be great, really pad my scores for the year." That last delivered with a wink and a smile.

Robert wouldn't know for some months that Kelly had already talked to her mother and was priming her to almost demand that her little girl get the "best" college prep Language Arts teacher in the school. With the usual Kelly planning, she was already putting the finishing touches on the structure that would be her high school career.

10

"I'd love to attend the junior high graduation with you." Sandy sounded sincere, even a bit excited about it. "I'm dying to meet your teen prodigy. Perhaps I'll end up her editor one day."

Robert had asked her, feeling much more secure than he had in the relationship with Rebecca. He wasn't going to worry about Kelly's reaction or to the jealousy nonsense. Kelly would see that he was in an adult, committed relationship, and Sandy would see that, even though she already knew it, Kelly was just a kid and not a threat. In fact, as promised, they would all go out to dinner afterward, his mom and Lauri already pretty close friends. This would be the moment everything would be both very adult and unambiguous. Kelly, moving into young womanhood, would drop the foolish idea of them getting married, and everyone would be, for want of a better word, cool. It might even mark the turning point in his relationship, perhaps leading to an engagement. Robert was always a big one for symbolic moments.

The event wasn't fancy, being held in the gym, family and friends on fold up chairs between the basketball hoops, students on the stage, a representative from the district office there to make a generic speech, one that was probably almost taken verbatim from one given in almost any past year. It was all the same routine formality with the cap and gown, but for the kids, who had never experienced it before, it was a special tribute to them, to a very special class of graduates, a group unique in all the classes in all the junior high schools in the history of the world. It was as it should be. For the most part, they would have a lifetime of feeling ordinary, but only few moments of feeling special.

When Robert and Sandy entered the gym, the soon to be graduates were already on the stage, squirming and watching the audience for family. Robert spotted Kelly before she saw him, and there she was in full make up, hair all fixed up, looking very proud and grown up.

When she spotted him, she winked and gave him a big thumbs up, and then she saw Sandy, looked at her for several seconds and smiled broadly, for what reason, and she always had a reason, Robert couldn't fathom.

73

As the graduation ended, Kelly rushed up to Robert and his party. She moved as to hug him, but with her mother, his mother and this new girl staring at her, she looked to be doing a quick reevaluation, ending with a warm handshake.

Then Robert introduced them, saying, "This is my friend, Sandy." As soon as he'd said that, he looked closely at the two and it seemed they were sizing each other up, probably his slightly paranoid imagination.

The Sandy smiled broadly and said, "You look a lot like me at your age."

To which Kelly replied, almost as if she'd been reading a prompter, "If looking like that is what I can look forward to as an adult, can't happen fast enough."

At first Robert thought, with a twinge of panic, my god, they're going to be friends. But then it hit him, the comments about how they looked alike. Odd that Robert had never noticed, never made the connection. They could be sisters, similar faces, similar figures, if he used his imagination to age Kelly a decade. And the most obvious, both flaming redheads. Does this mean something, he asked himself.

As if she'd read his mind, Sandy noted, "He's true to a type, isn't he?" With this all the women, his mother included, got a chuckle at his expense. At that moment he felt naked, emotionally naked, with four predatory females circling him, getting ready to draw blood. What were they thinking? The scenarios that crossed his mind made him wince, made him feel like some kind of deviant.

Feeling he needed to change the subject, he proclaimed, "Lunch is on me today. Where shall we go?"

The adult women all suggested places that were little more than coffee shops, but Kelly, always one for layers of complication, insisted that since she was only going to graduate from junior high once, she wanted something to remember, which obviously meant expensive, so they set off for the best steak house in town.

With a beer for Robert, wine for the women and iced tea for Kelly, they ordered and settled in to chat. Breaking the ice, Sandy asked Kelly, "So you plan to be a writer, a novelist?"

Kelly looked kind of sheepish. "You know about that. Well, I'm just getting started. I've got a long way to go."

Sandy held up her hand to stop Kelly rambling. "Nonsense. I've read your work, and you're good, more than good."

Kelly flashed a look at Robert, surprise, perhaps a bit of anger at him sharing her work without asking, violating something personal between them, but it was just momentary, just a look, and then she turned back to Sandy, blushing slightly. "You really liked my writing? It's only some short stories now, but I want to write a novel."

"I do like your work. Robert has shared it with me. He's really very proud of you, you know. Writing is our field. We love good writing and know it when we see it, and you are exceptional, and I don't mean just for a thirteen year old. You'd be exceptional if you were eighteen."

Kelly leaned across the table as far as she could, as if trying to go nose to nose with Sandy. "Thank you. He," and she nodded at Robert, "tells me that, but you know, he kind of invented me, like Frankenstein and his monster, so he's kind of biased."

"Well, biased or not, he's right, and you are a monster, a monster talent, getting better all the time."

That launched an animated conversation between the two about writing in general and her writing in particular. Kelly, was soaking up the praise like a big sponge, when suddenly Sandy stopped. "It sounds like no one else is telling you this stuff. What about your girlfriends? What do they say when you share your work?"

Kelly's face changed instantly from enthusiasm to consternation, and she shook her head. "I don't know what you mean. Who would I share my work with, besides mom, Robert and the magazines I send stuff to?"

"Your close group of friends, girls, a best friend perhaps."

Kelly pointed to Robert. "He's my best friend."

"You've got to have some girls you laugh with, share secrets, hang out with."

She shook her head. "No, none of that. I know some kids in class, kids from the newspaper, and we talk about stories for the paper, school work, but that's all. I really don't hang out with any of them. There was a boy from India I hung out with for a while, but he thought he was my boyfriend, and when I told him he wasn't, we kind of stopped hanging out."

75

Hearing this, Sandy seemed very surprised, almost shocked. Then Lauri, who had been listening attentively, spoke up. "It's true, and I worry about it. Before we moved, when she with in fifth grade, she had lots of close friends, kids she'd known since kindergarten, but at the new school, she never seemed to connect, except for Robert, but none of the kids."

Sandy looked at Kelly with an expression that could only mean, "Why?"

Kelly, looking like she didn't really want this attention, frowned for quite a while before saying anything. "You know, kids. They're just kids. It's all games, TV, silly gossip, clothes and stuff. I've got plans. I got a future, some goals, not a lot of time to waste on kid stuff."

Lauri shook her head, and Pat had a "I suspected as much" smile on her face, but Sandy said, "Hold it. I've got at least ten years on you, and I play a lot. I've got girlfriends, and we sit about the local club with a glass of wine and gossip and laugh and just act like a gang of girls hanging out. Trust me, you're not too old or too busy to be doing the things young women do."

Kelly just shrugged, as if to say "that's who I am, and I can't change."

Girl talk not to the typical man's taste and the beer working its magic, Robert excused himself and headed for the restroom. When he came back the subject had changed, and everyone was making small talk, something Robert could be comfortable with.

Back at school, Kelly and Lauri headed home, as did Pat, and Robert and Sandy went off toward his place. There are certain burning questions in the minds of insecure people, so before he unlocked his door, Robert asked as casually as possible, "So, what did you talk about when I was in the bathroom?"

"You." She waited just a bit before elaborating, perhaps out of just a touch of sadism. "Actually, as soon as you left she blurted out, 'Are you going to marry Robert?' I obviously didn't see that one coming."

"Oh god," he groaned. "I'm sorry about that. She can be, well, what can I say."

"That's fine. I could see where she's coming from, and I think I

76

know why."

When Robert's eyes widened in surprise, she continued. "That conversation about girlfriends, girlfriends she doesn't have but should at her age. Then what Lauri said about having friends at the other school, but just you since moving. You see where this is headed?"

Robert didn't have a clue and said as much.

"She's fixated on you. That's the whole thing about planning to marry you. You became her mentor and friend, and it was reinforcing and safe, and she allowed herself to drop out emotionally with kids her age. Emotionally stunted, I think they call it."

"So, if she had girlfriends, she wouldn't obsess over me?"

"That's what I'm thinking, but it isn't about you, my dear. This really isn't normal for a kid her age. You can't be all things to her, and you shouldn't. It's bad for her, and it's bad for you. She's got you so off balance. Well, it's sad."

"So, I should push her to make more friends? I get it."

"Yes, but don't reject her in the process. You need to wean her off you, get her involved with kids her own age, and soon, you'll just be her writing mentor."

"Easier said than done. She's a stubborn kid. Oh, yeah, and what was your response to her question?"

"I equivocated, naturally. Basically, I told her the truth. I said that we were both taking classes toward our careers, which might lead us to different parts of the world, so it was too soon to even think seriously about questions like that."

"That satisfied her?"

"Probably not, but it left her nowhere to go."

After an hour of passionate sex that night, and just before he fell asleep, he thought how he might push Kelly into relationships with peers.

Over breakfast, something he prided himself in, along with fresh ground coffee, Kelly once again crept into the conversation, as she always crept into his life. "Were you perhaps a bit over the top in praising her writing yesterday?"

"I've told you before I think she's damn good. In fact, if she ever writes a book, and assuming I have a job in publishing, I want first crack at it."

Kelly's birthday rolled around in early July, so Robert had a twofold reason to give her a call. "Happy fourteen." And after she finished gushing about how sweet he was to call, he added, "Sandy says that she wants first crack at your first book, sight unseen. That's high praise."

"Mr. S. My mom is taking me out to dinner tonight, and I'd love for you to join us. Bring your mom. You can even bring Sandy if you'd like."

Sandy was working, plus living forty minutes away, and Pat was busy, but he decided to go, thinking it was a good chance to talk about the friend issue. Apparently, it was to be that steakhouse, a place that had become Kelly's favorite, but Robert opted not to ride with them, freeing himself up to leave when he wished. Then he remembered that if he were going to celebrate her birthday, he'd need a gift, always a problem considering their relationship. He drove down to the closest beach town to a little cooperative gift shop, a local artist place, hoping he'd browse his way to an idea.

He knew it as soon as he saw it, a pair of silver earrings, open books crossed with pens, perfect for a young writer. As soon as she opened the gift, as they waited for dinner, and with no one else around but him and her mother, she jumped up and threw her arms around his neck, giving him a hug that almost stopped his breathing. Oddly, it didn't make him uncomfortable, but the notion crossed his mind that she wasn't growing into a young woman, but rather a young bear.

Lauri and Robert shared a bottle of white wine, and Kelly almost absently remarked, "On my eighteenth birthday, which will be a really special occasion, even though I'll still be too young, I'm going to toast with a glass of good wine."

By desert, everyone was relaxed and mellow enough for Robert to bring up the uncomfortable subject. "I'm concerned that you don't have close friends, girlfriends. I was thinking of the conversation on graduation day. You're really missing something important."

"I don't see you with a lot of friends." She was going to make it difficult.

"You don't see me when I'm out with my friends." Strictly speaking that was true, but he realized that his friends were all drifting into careers and family life and they really weren't getting together often. Then he added. "But this is about you, and at your age it's even more important."

"Aw, come on. I know lots of kids. I knew half the kids in that last school."

"Knowing kids and having really close friends are two different things, and you know it."

She leaned back in her chair, fists on hips, a sign he was getting defensive. "So, what am I supposed to do, put an ad in the paper, 'desperate loser teen seeks friends?' Maybe I should offer to pay by the hour."

"Kelly, if you're going to act this way, I'm going to leave." He pushed his plate away from him to dramatize the point, and it worked.

"Look, I'm sorry. I'm kind of sensitive about this. Don't you think I know this? Don't you think I get lonesome? Crap. I'd have a zillion friends if I knew how."

With Kelly, when she got dramatic and emotional, Robert was never sure how sincere she was. She did have a flair for acting. But, giving her the benefit of the doubt, he soldiered on. "Make an effort. Talk to the girls in your class, small talk. See if you have anything in common. Offer to study together. Ask them to join you for a soda or snack. Exchange emails or whatever."

She sucked up a deep breath, as if ready to debate him, and then she just exhaled slowly and paused for a moment. "Yeah. And there's this girl who was in the paper. She always acted like she liked me, wanted to be friends and all. She gave me her number. I could call her. I think she'd kind of like that."

"That's a good place to start. Maybe she has a group of friends, and you'd be one of them. There's nothing to lose. After all, she made the offer."

As Robert was getting up to go, Kelly asked, "Are we going to hang out this summer?"

"You don't want to hang out with a boring old man. Besides between a summer class at the university and some travel plans," he carefully avoided adding, with Sandy, "I'm going to be pretty busy, but I'm always available to talk about your writing. Still, you have friends your own age to gather, and I have to plan to teach some pretty savvy college prep freshmen. If I'm not ready, you little geniuses will eat me alive."

It was all pretty lame, but it kept him talking until he was on his feet and backing away from the table.

In the phone chat about Kelly's lack of friends he'd had with Lauri, She'd agreed to follow up on any suggestions he made over dinner, both of them concerned, for both similar and vastly different reasons, about her lack of close friends. Between discussions with Sandy and his own reflecting over the three and a half years, he was convinced that if he continued to be her major social outlet, that one day, as she matured, she would resent him, maybe hate him for stealing her childhood, even though he wasn't deliberately trying to do it, to monopolize her time, to passively feed her marriage fantasies. There'd come a day when hindsight would distort these years, and he'd be the guy who vicariously lived his own literary aspirations through her, leaving her successful but emotionally stunted.

Naturally, having that horribly analytical mind, he had to review the past few years and do some serious soul searching. Yes, he is and was a scholarly writer, a respected local book reviewer and a frequently published essayist, but outside the rarefied atmosphere of the writing snobs, he was unknown. Could it be true that he latched on to Kelly, spotting her talent from the start, grooming her to be something he could never be, a potentially best-selling novelist? Was he living a fantasy life through her? He didn't think so; everything in his self-conception shouted no, but was he self-conscious living out this little drama, the man who created a literary star?

Thoughts cascade, one running over the next in a rush to pour out of an overstimulated brain, and his logical next thought was, could I write a great American novel? One voice inside laughed at the presumption, but another voice argued that he had all the writing skills, was familiar with the subtle techniques of many important writers, could construct sentences and paragraphs that would take an idea or theme and build on it. After all, that's pretty much what writing a novel was all about. That was indeed all, all expect inspiration, the germ of an idea that would grow into a piece of literature that would draw people in, make them incapable of putting the book down.

Perhaps his life wasn't that interesting, or perhaps he lacked enough imagination, but that huge inspiration never came. Kelly, on the other hand, could take some small incident from her life, sometimes only some interactions she happened to observe at school, and craft them into a compelling story. She was a natural storyteller, and he'd supplied the technical tools she needed to tell them with style. She likely would have acquired those tools, through trial and error, eventually on her own, but what she had was a gift, one Robert felt had not been given him.

He actually tried, in the late hours when he was home alone, to write a novel. Taking his own advice, he wrote about a young single teacher, but what came out was a nicely crafted narrative, but not a novel. He thought about writing about his relationship with Kelly, but the idea was both uncomfortable and too close for any perspective. He realized that if someday he tackled his autobiography, it would only have appeal if he were famous, and not for the riveting account. That was it at the core. He could write well, technically well, but his best efforts weren't riveting. His writing simply lacked feeling. He was emotionally a C student.

He consoled himself with the knowledge that he was smart. Everyone said that about him. It was one of the things Sandy liked about him, and it was something Kelly constantly reminded him of. He was always the leader in any discussion in his grad class, and his professors treated him as an intellectual equal, often being won over by his arguments. Finally, turning these ideas over in his mind in bed, very late one night, he fell asleep with a phrase echoing in his head, "Smart but dull."

He was driving himself crazy with this downward spiral of introspection, so when he ended up at Sandy's place that Friday, he went through the whole line of convoluted reasoning with her, and to her credit, she listened without interrupting, only cracking an occasional smile.

When he finally asked her opinion, she started with, "Did you ever really want to be a novelist?"

After a moment's hesitation, she answered, "Well, not really. I wanted to be a journalist as a kid, the romantic stuff, traveling to war zones, exotic places, covering things as they happened."

"But you didn't."

"When I graduated from high school, I spent a summer traveling. Found out that I didn't like living out of a suitcase, not having my stuff with me, no routine. Went to college and realize how much good writing sucked me in, and bad writing, no matter how exciting the story, left me cold. Actually, while I read a lot of fiction, I'm pretty addicted to non fiction. I guess I read for information, but no matter how important the info, the writing keeps me reading or not."

"So that's when you picked your major, your direction?"

"Yeah, I wanted to read good writing and also write it. I fell in love with conveying information in a way that made people care about it, about reading it. Then it sort of occurred to me that I wanted to teach others, and here I am."

"So, you've answered your own question."

"I guess so, unless there is some subconscious desire to be a novelist that I'm not owning up to."

"Don't overthink it," she demanded. Before continuing, and as if for effect, she got up slowly and walked back to the kitchen, actually sexily slinked back, returning with the bottle of wine. Only after she refilled their glasses did she continue. "You love good writing; you love to teach others how to do it and you discovered the prefect pupil. She's your Mona Lisa, and that's pretty intoxicating."

That was the perfect thing for him to hear, and he thanked her and kissed her, and when he sat back down, soft background jazz rolling through his now untroubled head, she added, "And you are not dull. You are an exciting man, a complex thinker, an exceptional teacher and an astute grad student. Just because you don't write novels or report from the trenches in some war, that doesn't make you boring."

If there were any words that could arouse him sexually, those were them, and he responded by lifting her from her chain, almost spilling her wine, and kissing her lips, ears, neck and chest, and within minutes they were in her bed, skipping dinner, the movie and all the other plans they'd made.

11

Sandy was able to work her schedule around a week's trip to Alaska, a quick flight to Vancouver and a few days on the inland ferry, with stops along the way to hike rent kayaks and explore a few glaciers. It was romantic, the little cabin, just big enough to sleep in, the long days, lasting until almost eleven at night, the cool northern rain forests, walking on ancient ice. They flew home late at night, and she had to get back to her daily grind the next morning, back to work, back to making ends meet on part time jobs, as she got ready to start her last semester as a student.

Robert was using this together time to cement the relationship, hoping that whatever happened after her last semester, they'd still be together. On the last night on the boat, cuddling in the tiny room, he asked her if she could see a future for them together.

"If you're asking if I love you and want this to last, the answer is yes. It all hinges on where I get a job. I'm not going to serve coffee and do part time accounting for the rest of my life."

Desperate, knowing that she'd been sending resumes to New York publishers, he asked, "How about San Francisco? There are publishing houses there."

"Very few, and I've looked. Very few jobs in these small houses." And, anticipating what might be his next question, she continued. "I've also looked at L.A. Not much there either, unless you specialize in screen plays."

"Well, that would be a foot in the door." He tried not to sound desperate.

"Feet get broken shoving them in doors. Besides, L.A might as well be New York. What, we'd meet for weekends in the middle, maybe Pismo Beach. That wouldn't be a very permanent relationship. Of course, assuming someone down there would hire me, you could try to find a job in LA Unified."

That was a possibility, he thought, but he knew that new teachers down there, even if he could get a job, are usually assigned to inner city, crime-ridden, violent schools. Did he, he wondered, love her that much.

Robert, with his aversion to sudden changes, opted to put the question to one side, assuming, rather hoping, that it would all work out, that someone local would offer her a great job, that no one in New York would respond. Now, that last thought made him feel guilty. Would he really want to see her career dreams dashed for his benefit. The more he thought about it, the more he felt like a cad. Her happiness came first, and all he could do was hope that he would somehow fit somewhere in that happiness.

There was a message on his phone when he returned. It was from the principal, George, telling him that the schedule was set, and he did have three sections of Freshmen, plus two of juniors. Robert thought that Kelly probably already knew about it and that she'd probably already pushed Lauri into getting her enrolled in one of his classes. Kelly was single-minded that way, as she was when she landed him that newspaper job.

And that reminded him. Now that he was at the high school full time, plus the grad classes, he really didn't need the after school class any longer. Also, he had to admit, without Kelly as editor, he'd be working much harder. In a moment of honesty, he also admitted to himself that without Kelly, he simply wasn't inspired to continue. It really was more for her than for the money and for the sense of accomplishment. This was a hard realization, as it brought back that same old question about his relationship with Kelly. Why was she such a big part of his life, a part he couldn't let go of?

But the summer was on the wane, and with the future of his relationship holding its breath, Robert was determined to make the most of every day. Part of this was a gathering of his buddies, all either married or in long term relationships. This was the first time they had all gathered as couples, his first time with a serious date, the first time Sandy met them. It was a wonderful evening, a prelude to what the next stage of life might be, no longer the guys who either camped together or met for beers at happy hour, they were now mature men with careers and significant others. It was fine wine, soft background music, a dinner around a formal table, talk of career advancements and investments in the future. They were all now as close to thirty as they were to twenty, and Robert was the only one still a student, if you'd count a part time grad program as being a student.

Sandy was a social success, charming, witty and a sparkling conversationalist with a curious mind and eclectic interests. His friends loved her, and hoped that she would be the one to perpetually round out the group.

"I like your friends," she said, as they got ready for bed. "They're a nice mix of boyish playfulness and maturity. They also made me feel like one of them."

"And you are," he said as he wrapped his arms around her and leaned in to kiss her. "The wives and girlfriends like you too. Maybe we'll all end up old married couples together."

She laughed lightly. "Well, that's always a possibility, and not a bad future at that."

Then August ambushed them as they reveled in their endless summer. Classes were starting, and Sandy had a thesis to write, a thesis class and one other minor class, plus the comps to study for. She was on schedule to walk away with an M.A. before Christmas, and she was still sending out resumes, determined to get the job she's worked her ass off for.

His classes were starting also, and the start of the school year was close enough to motivate him to start on a syllabus, knowing that college prep classes would make this a challenging year. So the leisurely play and love making, the sunny days walking in the woods or on the beach were over, and the business of life was back on track.

His principal, a very fit forty-two-year old tennis player, had joined his biking group and had been riding with them off and on for several months. As a result, the two men were becoming more than coworkers, moving toward being close friends. They'd often ride together on a Sunday, stopping afterward for lunch. George had made it clear that he respected Robert's expertise and commitment in the classroom and considered him one of the better teachers at the school.

Like most people fairly new in their profession, Robert needed occasional validation, a pat on the back, an "atta boy" to let him know his best efforts were appreciated.

George, remembering his own early days as a teacher, understood this and always believed that praise worked better than a raise and was easier to give. Still, while it may have started as a mentor and new teacher relationship, it was now closer to professional equals, as George knew that he could not motivate students to want to write. Robert had a gift or perhaps just an over-abundance of passion, but whatever it was, his students did well, particularly last years' seniors who tested way above the state average.

So, with school starting the following Tuesday, the two men joined a 50 mile loop ride on Sunday morning, with breakfast as the midpoint. "Are you geared up for the coming year, Rob?"

"Absolutely. I think this will be the best year so far. Syllabus is done, first two weeks of lesson plans already written. College prep kids: gotta be ready for them."

"Oh, yeah." George started with a chuckle. "I remember facing kids like that on the first day, sizing me up, ready to eat me alive if I started to bore them. And you've also got your little super star this year."

Robert was taken aback. George obviously meant Kelly, but how did he know that she was his super star. His surprised look must have given him away, because George continued. "The kid's got quite a reputation. Published often, earning money as a writer, star of that junior high newspaper and your biggest fan." He paused for Robert's reaction, which was still surprise.

"Don't you know? She tells everyone who will listen her story about the struggling little girl who was taught to be a successful writer and honor student by the world's greatest teacher. You have no idea how many teachers in this district are frustrated by the comparison with the teacher who literally walks on water. If you ever run for city council, she'd be your campaign manager."

Robert felt his face flush. She always told him how he'd taught her everything she knew, but he had no idea that she'd been spreading this gospel to all her other teachers. He knew how outspoken and insistent she could be, and he could only imagine how she'd built him up, deflating the other teacher by comparison. The fear of facing all these colleagues crossed his mind, before he answered. "I know she thinks I'm responsible for her writing success, but I had no idea that she was blabbing about this to others. It's embarrassing. The kid tends to be dramatic, to go really overboard. I'm going to have to have a talk with her."

"Don't worry about it, Rob. While it can get annoying after a while, the other teachers understand. You're her hero. Hell, how many kids have the start of a career at fourteen, and it's obvious that she'll make a comfortable living at this by the time she graduates. She tells everyone she's planning a novel, and I'm sure she'll write one and make some serious money off it. You started her down that road and kept helping and encouraging her, and you've got the right to take a bit of credit, to take the occasional bow."

"I'm surprised you're so familiar with her. She hasn't even started high school yet."

"Oh, no. I've already had the full treatment. She and her mother didn't go through channels, they made an appointment with me, and spent the time giving me a laundry list of the reasons she had to be in my class, even after I conceded their point. I was to understand that, under no uncertain terms, I destroy her life or her career by having her spend even one day in another teacher's class."

"George, I'm so sorry about this."

He leaned back and laughed so hard the other patrons turned to look. "Don't be. It's so refreshing. Most students and parents don't give a damn, and if they do it's about the negative, as in anyone but teacher so and so. To have a kid and her parent come in with this level of concern and commitment is wonderful. If every mother and child felt that way, we'd be entering the golden age of education."

The conversation wandered through and around education, but there was still a question in Robert's mind, one he wanted to but was afraid to ask. It took finishing lunch and a second beer before he could get the courage to interject it as casually as possible.

"George, you know that whole thing with the kid. Does it make me sound like I'm obsessed with her writing career or anything?"

He shrugged. "I was a coach for a while, in my early days in the classroom. Had a kid, a natural quarterback. Got all involved in him, got him a scholarship to UCLA. Kid stayed with me one summer, while his folks were out of town, so he wouldn't miss practice. Short answer; those of us who are dedicated, sometimes, we obsess. I don't know, maybe we always wanted to be a star football player or writer of popular fiction or a science wiz, and we live these dreams through exceptional students. Hell, you're weird; I'm weird. Comes with the territory."

That conversation made him feel a world better. Getting wrapped up in a student's life, well, that's just what really dedicated teachers do, teachers perhaps with unfulfilled dreams. Riding his bike home, he laughed out loud when he thought of the old saying: Those who can, do; those who can't, teach.

The next time he went to Sandy's place, she was in a dark mood. Her favorite publishing house, the one she most eagerly wanted, rejected her resume. No openings, they said, but she, in an attempt to read between the lines, saw it as, "You're not good enough." It took Robert most of the evening to convince her that no openings, most likely meant just what it said. After all, he reasoned, how many resumes do they get each week? They probably fill an opening the day it opens. "They said they'd keep it on file, so maybe next month, you'll get a call."

It worked to ease her mind a bit, but it didn't ease it enough to put her in the mood for sex, so they spent the night curled up like spoons, and it was fine, as these nights would become common when they were an old married couple. They were comfortable with each other, something more important in the long run than momentary sexual pleasure.

12

First period of the first day of school, and the first one in the door was Kelly, looking very much like a high school kid, which meant she looked very nearly grown up in her faded jeans and Lake Tahoe tee shirt. She grabbed the seat front row center, crossed her legs, pulled out a writing pad and a pen and nodded her head, as if to say, "Ready when you are."

For just a moment he contrasted the girl before him, with the one, dressed up, full makeup and styled hair on her birthday and graduation, the glamorous look that transforms a young girl into a cover girl. The classroom Kelly, no makeup, red hair pulled back, loose clothes, intense, pale eyes focused and waiting. Robert realized that he liked this Kelly, this real, getting down to business Kelly, best.

Robert asked her how she'd been over the summer, small talk. She mentioned in passing that her new friend seemed stuck to her like glue, always wanting to spend time together. According to Kelly, that was sort of a mix of good and bad, nice, but sometimes a bit too much.

During class, a couple of boys were talking in the back as Robert explained the lesson, and Kelly turned around and scolded them. "This is the best teacher you're ever going to have, so listen and learn something." It was so out of the blue that the whole class was taken aback, and the two boys, looking sheepish, quieted down. Kelly then nodded, as if to tell Robert it was OK to continue.

Naturally, Kelly, being Kelly, she popped into his room immediately after the last bell of the day. His first comment, before she was half way to his desk was, "You don't have to be my bailiff. I can keep order."

"You're too nice. I don't mind being mean. You know; good cop, bad cop thing."

Robert was curious about the new friend, only getting a tidbit before class, so he asked her for details. Apparently, this girl, Karen, thought Kelly was the greatest, acting so happy to be her best friend. "She kind of gushes, and that's weird."

But another thing about Karen that bothered Kelly was the affection. She always wanted to hold hands and kiss Kelly on the cheek when the met up or parted.

Robert was out of his depth here, but he ventured a guess, based on his own observation. "It's kind of strange to me too; guys don't do that, but I've seen girls walking hand in hand, hugging, even kissing, so I guess it's a normal girl thing."

Kelly seemed a bit skeptical. "I saw it a lot when I was younger, you know,fifth, sixth grade, but you don't see much of that in high school."

Robert ventured that some kids go through stages at different times, and in his case, he didn't really get interested in girls until he was perhaps sixteen.

"A late bloomer. That's kind of sweet." She smiled coyly.

As usual, Kelly had said something that made him want to end the conversation, make him uncomfortable being in the room alone with her, so he made some excuse about having lots of work to do, and she left. Given enough time she always managed, through a subtle shift in their roles, to move him slightly down from the adult and her slightly up from the kid. Whatever their relationship, she obviously wanted to control it.

Robert looked at the recommended reading list for the class and thought it was bullshit. He had to include it, but he put out his own list, saying these were some of the best examples of various styles of writing, and that he didn't expect the students to read all of each book, he suggested checking them out of the library and reading at least a chapter, adding a fun project he'd planned, writing like a famous author. Kelly beamed at the idea, obviously already sketching out some parodies of the people on the list. Robert got some guilty pleasure thinking about what she might come up with.

Robert threw himself into his work, his grad classes and especially his relationship with Sandy, feeling that at any moment they might shift to a long distance relationship. In the back of his mind, he thought about all the places she might work and the ways they could see each other, planning meetings at charming resorts and figuring how much he could afford to spend of travel. The one thing he wouldn't do was assume that her career would end what they had. It was unthinkable.

Everything in his life fell into a routine for two months. The

90

kids were getting into his program, and some of them wrote some creative stuff, particularly his "bad Hemmingway" assignment. Kelly showed a side of her writing he'd never seen, her gift for satire. She was not just getting better every year, she was getting better with each assignment. She did stop by after school two or three times a week, ostensibly to talk about a piece she was writing, also to ask how his classes were coming and if he had applied to teach at Berkeley or maybe some less interesting university. She seldom mentioned her new good friend. Then one day she dropped a bomb on him, walking in after school with a travel drive, handing it to him and demanding, "Read this and tell me what you think."

"What is it?" He ventured.

"Just read it and we'll talk tomorrow." She smiled, turned and walked out.

That was just like her, issuing edicts, making demands, not out of rudeness but out of her feeling that certain things are expected of him and that she had historic rights to his time and attention. He would have resented it in any other student, but his curiosity was hard to contain, and he popped it in his school computer and started to read, not able to wait until he got home.

What he read both mesmerized and shocked him. The writing was outstanding, but the subject matter was totally unexpected. It was about a friendship between two young girls that one wanted to pursue to a more intimate level. The friendship progressed to affection and finally to sexual experimentation. She'd carefully avoided being graphic and pushing it toward the pornographic, keeping it tender and thoughtful. In the end, one girl wanted a romantic relationship and the other said she couldn't do it, that she was heterosexual, but would like the friendship to continue, which, after having progressed to an intimate level, couldn't really go back and so started to dissipate.

It was a great story, a story of teen sexual discovery and the lines between friendship and intimacy. It was also obviously Kelly's story, and he'd been instructed to discuss it with her the following day, something he was totally uncomfortable with.

The next morning during class her eyes burned into him, huge questions implied in each look. He felt like the damn bell would never ring.

Another student stayed after school to ask a question, and Kelly stormed in before she was finished. Kelly's impatience was palpable, and the other girl felt it, getting her answer and quickly departing.

"Well what do you think?"

"Of what, the story or the situation?"

"The story, naturally."

"You handled it with style and delicacy. It could have been, let's say in poor taste, but you made the characters sympathetic. And as always the writing was flawless."

That made her smile, but before she could say anything else, he continued. "This is obviously about you and your friend Karen."

"It's a short story. Just fiction."

"I doubt it. Is there something you'd like to talk about, not that I'm trying to pry anything out of you?"

"OK, this friendship stuff sucks. There's always some hidden agenda. And you know, now she's friendly but pretty cool toward me, like be my girlfriend or you're not my good friend any more."

She was hovering over him, so the first thing he did was point to a chair, and once she sat down, he took a moment to compose himself, as she sat upright on the edge of her chair. He put his hands up, moving them back and forth as if to frame his ideas and slowly started. "To begin with, you have no idea how difficult this is for me, an adult man, a teacher, to discuss this subject with a teenaged girl. This is why the world provides mothers and female counselors. So, do you want my input?" She nodded vigorously.

He took a deep breath and continued. "This relationship is obviously uncomfortable for you, and I'm sure it is for her also. She's not only exploring her own sexual identity, but it's one that many people are biased against. It must have been stressful for her to want to express intimacy with you, probably fear of rejection. And in the end you did reject her, but if the story is accurate, you did it with delicacy and attempted to keep the friendship part."

"Right, but she doesn't seem to want to continue being a good friend. Oh, she's friendly enough, but she doesn't want to hang out, call all the time and all that crap."

"Kelly, put yourself in her place, and imagine how she feels. It

92

sounds like she had a crush on you."

"Well, she said she loved me, and that was the weirdest part."

"Still, it sounds like you let it go," and this is where a choice of words was difficult. "Let's say, it sounds like you let it go farther than you would have wished."

Kelly actually blushed, unusual for someone who normally seems immune to other people's reactions to what she says. "OK, it was, whatever, you know, exciting. I got caught up in it. I actually had an, you know." She looked away.

"I understand." He was glad she didn't say orgasm, as that would have made them both far more uncomfortable than they already were.

"And, you know, it took weeks to build up to that, cuddling, kissing. It was kind of thrilling, and well, I'd never been like that with anyone before. But, then when we did it a couple of times, I felt kind of weird after, and I told her that I liked her, but I wasn't like that, that I really liked guys and I probably couldn't do that any longer. Her expression like changed suddenly, hurt looking, sad. I tried to make things better, telling her what a great friend she was, but I just seemed to make it worse."

"Kelly, there's probably no really good way to handle something like that, and it sounds like you did the best possible under the circumstances. But don't judge all friendships on this."

"Acquaintances are fine, but this best friend thing is a mine field. Besides I've already got a best friend, one I can always count on. You."

That sounded to Robert like a judge pounding his gavel and sentencing him to a long prison term. She'd put all her friendship eggs in one basket, his, and her happiness or total despair depended on him, a burden no one would want to shoulder.

"Don't let one thing turn you off. There are people out there who will want to be your friend, people who will love you just for who you are. Don't ever close yourself off from that."

"Sure, whatever you say. But, is it good enough to publish?"

The opening up of her feelings lasted under ten minutes, and now it was all about getting her story published. It was scary how she managed to compartmentalize her life, almost as if she had multiple personalities, a sensitive, insecure little girl and a ruthless self-promoter. "I can give you three publications right now that would likely take it, depending on how you slant it. Make it sound academic, and there's a mag that deals with teen issues. More of a story, kind of like what you have here, and I think another publication might take it. Write two versions, and we'll send them off."

"Thanks, Rob... Mr. S. And, don't tell anyone about this conversation."

"Do you really think you have to ask? Obviously, it doesn't leave this room."

Well, he thought, Kelly is growing up. She experimented sexually, so it's only a matter of time before she experiments with boys. Robert hoped she'd show the same maturity in her sex life as she does in her writing. She was a bit of a free thinker, and it wouldn't take much for her to become a wild child. He was worried about her, feeling protective. After all, he had four years invested in her, and that had forged a pretty strong bond.

13.

Kelly's story sold, actually sold for some good money. The editor basically threw the door open to her, one more publishing avenue for her. Still a high school freshman, and she was making more money than the kids with after school jobs at stores and gas stations. And, more and more, each time he talked one on one to her, there was this obsession about writing a novel. "I'll be fifteen in a few months, and if it takes a year to write and polish a novel, I'll be lucky to have it ready to publish by sixteen."

She was sitting on the edge of his desk, and it was after school. She'd come in ostensibly to ask about the paper she'd turned in, wondering if she'd gotten a good grade, knowing in advance that she'd gotten what she always gets, an A+. It looked like she had adopted her official high school uniform, faded jeans and a baggy t-shirt. She had different jeans and shirts for different days, but it was always the same, and her hair was always pulled back and tied, and she never wore makeup, expect on those rare occasions when she dressed up and went out to celebrate something, like her graduation from junior high.

"Sixteen isn't some kind of deadline." He reminded her. "Very few people have a finished novel by sixteen, let alone one fit to publish."

"That Hinton girl did it. If she could, I can."

`   Robert was sorry he'd pointed out to her that Hinton had published while still in school. Now it was a goal, more an obsession, with Kelly. "But, you know, if I remember right, she wrote it at sixteen, but I don't think it was published until she was seventeen."

"Maybe I could like do it earlier, be the youngest. I'd like that."

"Damn, Kelly, why don't you start a fortune 500 company while you wait, and maybe cure cancer and solve the world hunger problem in time to graduate." Her obsessions were driving him up the wall.

"You're a teacher. You're supposed to be encouraging me to be everything I can be. What about my self-esteem?" She was playing, teasing him.

"You have enough self-esteem for the whole school, and

maybe I've encouraged you too much over the years. You're a good writer, but you're becoming an egomaniac."

She put the back of her hand to her forehead and sighed. "Ah, the burden of greatness. I have to go sign autographs now. See you in the morning, Mr. S."

He sat back and smiled as she left. What a kid, he thought. Even her arrogance was endearing. But, with all the hype aside, he was sure that she would at least try a novel, and if she didn't try to adhere to some arbitrary time table, she'd probably do a damn good job of it.

Competition is good, and with Kelly being so competitive, that first period had become a dream class. There was an unspoken notion among many of the students about trying to outdo Kelly. The literary discussions were as good as in any senior class, possibly almost as interesting as in a college class. Being AP, all the classes were above the line, but that one was quite frankly intellectually stimulating.

Actually, it was a dream year, with five sections of AP, three freshmen and two junior. He had to actually keep on his toes, attempting to keep these kids challenged. He actually found himself considering staying in the high school, even after getting his doctorate. Many have done that. Teaching young minds at any level is exciting.

Once, and he knew better the minute he said it, he mused about that to Kelly.
She'd come in after school, as she often did, to discuss writing, literature and whatever else her hungry mind had come upon. She asked him how the year was going, and he told her what a great year it was and how he could easily spend the rest of his career doing this.

She jumped to her feet. "No, no, no. You can't waste a mind like that on a bunch of dumb teens. You belong at that UC Berkeley college, a place where real talent goes to learn. Promise me you'll teach at Berkeley."

As a quick way to end the conversation, he replied, "I can only promise to apply. Beyond that it isn't up to me."

"Well, you gotta be so great that they can't possibly pass you up. We'll work on that."

Before he could ask her just what the devil she meant by that, she headed for the door, saying she had to get home and help her mom.

He pictured her deluging the university English department

with letters demanding that the hire him. With her around, life was never easy.

At least life was easy with Sandy, particularly with her classes ending and her thesis wrapping up. The M.A. after her name was now just a formality, which gave her more time to play, and as his classes were also wrapping up, he had a bit more time too. It was all just too good to be true, which, he knew meant that it wasn't true.

She showed up at his place unannounced one evening, looking very excited and with a letter in her hand. He was in an old pair of shorts and a tattered shirt, relaxing with a cold beer and some old movie on TV.

"I got it!" She proclaimed.

"You got what?" He asked, but he was pretty sure he already knew.

"That job. The job. The one I wanted. They want me in New York in two months. They even have a place I can stay temporarily until I find an apartment. They want me, really want me."

Waves of mixed emotions washed over him. He was happy for her, knowing how much she wanted that job, but he was devastated, knowing she was actually leaving, actually moving clear across the country and for all intents and purposes, out of his life.

He hugged her and said all the right things, things he meant at one level. But finally he had to admit that it was breaking his heart to know she was leaving.

"Robert, I've said this before. Come with me. I'm sure you can find a job at an agency or a publishing house or even a teaching job if you'd like. You'll love it, and we could move in together."

"Sandy. There's no sure thing for me there. You've been applying for these jobs for over a year, gearing your classes and work toward this. I'm on track to be an academic. And teaching jobs are hard to find in this market. Remember, I have a California credential, and I'm sure I'd have to take some courses, tests and all that to get one there. I have security here, a good way through a grad program, the best teaching year I've ever had. I'd be walking the streets of New York, looking for a job and likely living off of you. I think you'd get tired of that damn soon."

"Robert, Robert. Don't always be so cautious. Just go for it.

97

Things will manage to work out."

He had finally guided her to the couch, and she was sitting reasonably still. "It's easy for you to say, honey. You have the job, the job you've always wanted. I'd be giving everything up for a maybe, and maybe if I didn't find a good program or a job I liked, I'm afraid we'd end up resenting each other. I so wish there was a publishing house like this out here for you."

The excitement went out of her in one long breath. "This is what I really want, but you're also what I want. Don't make me choose."

"Sandy, darling. We've had this discussion. You've already made your choice. But, I'm close to finishing my doctorate. With that, I could get a job back east. It wouldn't be that hard."

"That leaves apart for a year. But, look. We can have a long distance relationship until you finish your doctorate. Then, there are lots of great universities in the New York area that would be thrilled to have you. We can do this."

He so wanted to believe, even though he pictured her settling in, dating, finding someone to share her new lifestyle, eventually relegating Robert to a an old friend, a flame that has become a warm ember.

Hope is something always worth nourishing, keeping alive, even when it seems on life support. Robert would hurry through his doctoral program, call and write, and during the summers, travel to New York to spend time with her. It could work. He'd make it work. However, that was in the future, and for now they had a few short months to enjoy, to create memories, to cement the relationship, to make it survive a separation.

The first thing on the agenda was his birthday, and Sandy, Kelly and his mom all wanted to help him celebrate. Pat decided the best thing was a dinner party at her house, with all the important people in his life invited, meaning Sandy, Kelly and her mom and Flynn, Ted and Chip, along with their wives.

By now, all the people in his life had, at one time or another, mingled, so they all were well acquainted, and the party went well, all enjoying some good wine, except for Kelly.

When Kelly heard that Sandy was taking a job in New York,

she seemed to brighten for just a moment, and then a cloud of sadness seemed to come over her, and Robert understood that the girl really cared about his happiness, even if it came at the expense of hers. Naturally, Kelly wanted to hear all about the job and listened in fascination.

At one point Sandy remembered a comment for Kelly's birthday party. "Are you still thinking of writing a novel?"

Kelly nodded eagerly. "Yeah, and I've been playing with some ideas, started a couple of times, but it's just not coming yet."

"Well, don't push it, but based on the writing Robert shared with me, as soon as you finish one, I want to see it. No other publishers, no agents, just have Robert read it, and if he gives it a thumbs up, I want it. Deal?"

Kelly looked as if she'd squirm out of her chair. She could hardly sit still as she shook hands with Sandy and swore that absolutely she would be the second person to see it after Robert.

Later that night, in bed, after exciting birthday sex, Robert's mind turned to the evening celebration. "You didn't have to say that to Kelly, you know."

Sandy was snuggled against his shoulder. "Say what to Kelly?"

Almost dreamily, Robert replied. "About wanting to see her first novel. Sure you made her feel good, but now she'll be a maniac about getting published."

Sandy slid up, back against the pillow. "I didn't say it to make her feel good. It might not be for a while, but I know she's got it in her, and when she does. Well, when she writes something you approve of, I've got myself a best seller and a jet propelled career."

"Seriously, you think she's that good?"

"I think she's potentially that good, and you've trained her well. If she writes a novel, it will be excellent, and if she's true to form, it will be a young adult, relationships thing that will sell to every teen girl who reads. In other words, a best seller."

"And you'll have discovered the next super star."

"And she will be too busy being successful to obsess over you. Everyone wins, right?"

Naturally, the next time Robert talked to Kelly in school, she asked him about Sandy's comments. "Yes, Kelly, she was dead serious. However, don't just go out and throw words on a page. Remember, I have to say it's worth publishing, and I want you to be ready, have some solid idea. In short, don't just write anything, thinking you're going to have a hit."

"Of course. Sure. I know that. Oh, the bell. Gotta go."

Robert knew that absent tone. She heard him, but he doubted she was listening.

Somewhere during the Spring semester, when the school year starts to gradually wind down, things get busy for teachers and students. There are grades to get and grades to give, and for some students, colleges to apply to. Added to that, Robert was counting down the final days before Sandy departed, trying to spend every possible minute with her, hanging on to each moment desperately, as if it were not only the last for them, but the last for him. They had researched plane fares and schedules, planning for his trips to New York, but not a trip for her. Clearly she would be too busy to get away, but with summer coming, he'd have the time to visit her, and that was the plan.

Also, he wasn't seeing as much of Kelly lately. She seemed to be involved in another project, probably writing more stories. She always seemed a bit distracted in class, as if she were deep in thought. In a way Robert was curious, but he was also a bit relieved, being able to concentrate on Sandy.

And then the day came for Sandy's flight. Even though he'd had weeks to prepare himself, he couldn't help crying as they embraced at the airport. Then, sitting in the bar, nursing a draft beer, he watched her plane take off, carrying his hopes and dreams with it. She had flown out of San Francisco because of a better departure time and better price, so Robert found himself in the city for the first time in many months. Not wanting to go home to an empty apartment, he took a motel near Fisherman's Wharf and the Marina, showered and walked the few blocks to the wharf for dinner.

He ate listlessly, looking out the window at the boats on the bay, seeing the sun sink low over Marin, sipping a glass of wine, a more expensive one than he would usually consider. When he finished, he walked over to the bar and ordered another. The stool next to him was empty, but the next one was occupied by a fairly attractive woman. He glanced over and tried to smile. She returned the smile and greeted him. After a few moments, she turned to him again. "You look kind of down. Bad news?"

"Just saw my girlfriend off. She's moving to New York for a new job. Not my best day."

She sympathized with him and started chatting, asking him about his girlfriend and his job. She told him she was in the hospitality business, at one of the downtown hotels. It was clear after a talking for over an hour that she was hitting on him, and under normal circumstances she would have been worth having a fling with, but with Sandy on his mind, he couldn't work up any enthusiasm. He finally said he just wasn't feeling all that social at the moment and just wanted to crash. She gave him her card and he took her hand, squeezing it to let her know there was some interest and to thank her for helping him through a rough evening. He pocketed the card, thinking that the day may come when he'd call.

14

After a couple weeks Sandy called to say she was settled in her new apartment and job, and things were going well. The people she worked with were great and they were helping her get up and running. She had already read a promising manuscript and had called the author to set up a meeting. She said that by mid-summer, things would be settled enough for him to come out. They picked a day, and he went on line to get a deal on a ticket.

Now he had something to hang on to, and the work of winding down the school year didn't seem as much like drudgery. And, with a freer mind, he turned his attention back to Kelly, catching her as she started to leave after the bell.

"Hang on a minute. We haven't talked much. What's up?"

She looked at him sheepishly, reached tentatively into her backpack and then hesitated. "I've been working on something."

"Another story?"

"Novel. But I've only got the first five chapters."

"I'd love to read it."

She hesitated again and then pulled out the stack of paper. "It's really only a draft."

"I understand that. I know your work well enough by now."

She handed it over. Then, as she turned to go, she added, "There's something else I'd like to talk about, but in private."

"After school today?"

"Can't. How about tomorrow?"

"Deal. I'll have read this by then."

It was the first thing she'd even written that was a disappointment. She had started with a rather vague idea, something that might have worked well as a short story, but then she'd tried to pad it into a novel. It rambled in a way that told him she'd been counting words. He was going to have to be honest with her, but he wasn't looking forward to it.

When she came in the following afternoon, he noticed for the first time that she was dressing differently. Gone were the sloppy tee shirts and loose jeans. Her clothes were form fitting and flattering to her nicely developed figure. In a moment, his image of her as a little girl was permanently shattered. She had been dancing on the edge between girl and woman for some time, but she was no longer on the edge.

With her typical hands on hips, she asked, "Well?"

He shook his head, and she added, "I was afraid of that. Why?"

"You know why. You wanted to write a novel, but you didn't have a novel to write. You're talented, but not talented enough to just throw words at the paper and expect them to stick."

"So, I'm not a novel writer?"

"That's not what I said. Wait until you have a solid idea for a book, something you know and that you're enthusiastic about. Then you'll write a good one. Remember, an eighty thousand word short story is just a short story with a bunch of extra words."

She smiled and nodded, adding that he was right and she knew she was trying too hard. Then she just stood there, and the two of them just looked at each other, wondering which would speak first. He did. "There was another matter you wanted to talk about?"

"Well, yeah, but maybe I shouldn't bother you with it."

"After over four years, there's nothing you shouldn't bother me with. Come on."

She took a deep breath and sat on the edge of a desk. "Well, I'm... I'm having, well an affair."

The first thing that stuck him was her choice of words, odd of a teen. She didn't say she was in a relationship, being sexually active or even having a boyfriend. It took him a minute to respond, fishing for the right words. "So, you're dating, have a boyfriend, that sort of thing?"

"Kind of. There's this good looking football player, and I figured that, well…"

This was confusing. "I'm not sure I'm following you. What kind of relationship are you talking about?"

This time she settled into a chair, exhaled with emphasis and started fumbling for an explanation. "Well, after the thing with Karen, people started to talk, rumors, you know, the whole lesbian thing, is she or isn't she. I was getting this gay label, not that I have a problem with gay, but it made me start to doubt myself. Maybe I was gay and just not admitting it. I knew I wasn't but, you know, it was all kind of mixed up." Then she just stopped talking.

As she stared at him, things started falling into place, like falling dominoes, and it was looking kind of strange. "Are you telling me, you're having a relationship with this football player just to prove to yourself and others that you're not gay?"

"It's kind of that, but not just that. He is a good looking guy, and I." At this point, she stopped and blushed before starting again. "I like sex. I'm enjoying it."

"You are talking about it, kind of impersonal, but what about the guy. You like sex; so you like him, love him, have a crush, whatever." At this point he was feeling at least as uncomfortable as Kelly seemed to be. This was not the conversation a male teacher has with a teenaged girl, particularly given their history. He was, in spite of his discomfort, anxious to know what was going on and hoping he could give her some meaningful advice.

"I guess I like him well enough, but he's not that interesting, you know, to talk to. His idea of reading is the sports magazines. I can't have any real conversations with him. I guess I'm doing what they call experimenting. But, you know, as a writer, I kind of have to have experiences, personal stuff for my writing."

"Doesn't sound like this is going anywhere, and it doesn't sound like very good reasons for a relationship. How about him? How's he feel about you?"

"Don't have a clue. He says we're having fun together. That's about it."

"You make it sound like you've lost interest. Are you thinking of breaking up?"

"Yeah, but I hate doing that. That thing with Karen didn't go all that well. And, you know guys. If I hurt his ego, he'll probably bad mouth me to the other guys."

"And, you know guys." He was mocking her. "Come on Kelly, not all guys are like that."

"Dumb jock high school guys usually are."

"So now I'm seeing what you really think. Look. Make up some excuse that doesn't put him down. Say your mother is after you to spend more time studying. Say you realized you're too young for a steady relationship, something like that. Part friends."

"Yeah, you're right, and the next time, I'm going to look for someone I can relate to, not just a hot body."

Robert felt his face flush with the hot body comment. A comment like that from a fourteen year old.

She saw his reaction and closed the topic. "Well, you've helped me. School will be over soon, and I don't want this to go on during summer, so I'll have to come up with something." And, he suspected that it was said more to make him squirm than anything else, she added, "But I will miss the hot sex."

Then she turned and left.

That night Robert dreamed about Kelly for the first time. In the dream, she came into the classroom, but it was late at night, and she was wearing a nighty, hair fixed up, lots of makeup. She was talking to him about her writing, but she was stroking his hair and talking in a soft, husky voice. Then she pushed him down, ran her tongue over her lips and said that she had writers block and needed some hot sex to free her mind. He woke up both nervously sweating and somewhat excited. He couldn't go back to sleep, or rather he was afraid to go back to sleep. He spent the rest of the night grading essays and other late semester papers, trying very hard to forget the dream.

The next few days in class he found himself avoiding eye contact with her. It was crazy, he thought, just a dream, but it was making him paranoid. He was, however, happy that she wasn't coming in after school.

But then the following week she showed up after the last bell, looking up and down the hall before closing the door behind her. Robert felt a wave of panic come over him, but he forced himself to hide it and smile. He asked a feeble, "What's up Kelly?"

"Damn him. He broke up with me." She had an expression like she was going to bite someone.

Robert was relieved that it wasn't about him. "But, Kelly, isn't that what you wanted?"

"No. I wanted to break up with him. He just discarded me, and I'm better than that. Can you imagine, he just said he was tired of being with just one girl and needed to be free. What? He thinks he's such a great catch. A pretty body, but, but... vacuous. That's the word, vacuous. Imagine him tired of me." She emphasized the words by point both index fingers at herself. "Damn, I was past tired of him, but I was being nice. I'm going to be one of the girls he talks about to his dumb-assed friends."

For once Robert had the right things to say, and he suppressed smiling at her indignation. "It's all part of relationships. Things can end, and you can be the dumped or the dumper. Trust me Kelly, I've been dumped plenty of times in my life, and I've been on the other end a few times. It happens. He was never the right one anyway, and you knew that. Caulk it up to a bump on the road to growing up."

She smiled slightly. "I guess you're right, but he's such a shit. You wouldn't let a girl like me get away. You're too smart for that. And you won't either in three years and six weeks." She flashed him a devil smile, and he was going to say something, but realized that the remark was better left unacknowledged.

Then she changed direction so quickly, he got mental whiplash. "Sexual relationships, I see, are necessary for a novel, at least my novel. That was the problem. I was too innocent. I need some worldly experience, something to build a novel on." She had her fists clenched as if she were about to try to conquer a mountain.

` "Kelly, stop. You don't have sex just to fuel your writing. Relationships are about people, about relating, about some connection. You can't just go to bed with someone thinking about how you'll write about it."

She looked rather sheepish, as if she'd just listened to what she was saying. "Well, of course I'd have like the guy, at least a little."

He shook his head. "I'd hate to see you become promiscuous."

She smiled. "I guess you want me to save myself for my husband."

The implication was clear, so he chose to ignore it. "You're not even 15 yet; there's plenty of time for sex and for marriage." And he knew he had to add something he really loathed to say. "I hope you're using protection." Without answering, she just nodded.

Then she leaned forward with a look that said she was now getting serious. "I write about what I know. You taught me that. I've been writing about people my age, people who are going through kid issues. Well, I'm growing up, and one of those issues is sex and relationships.

I have to know something about it to write about it."

"You're talking about selling out a very deeply personal, emotional part of your life in order to write about it. Doesn't that sound over the top?"

"Writing is who I am, all I want to be, almost. I know there's a good novel in me, but I feel like some innocent kid without the worldly experience I need to write it. Sure, there's a chance I'll mess up my head, but I'm pretty strong, and I've got you. I know you'll always be there for me."

"Always, but I'm not superman. I can't save you from drowning if you've already drowned. I'm afraid you'll get hurt."

"You mean, like get my heart broken or something? Not going to happen. My heart is locked up for three years and some weeks."

"You may find that it's not that easy to control the future or your feelings."

She shifted, as she so often did, from serious to casual, almost flip. "Well, anyway, it's all, how you say, academic. I had one short thing with a guy, mostly to prove I'm not gay, and I really don't have anyone in mind. It's all talk right now. Besides, I picked that last guy for looks. Next one will be for brains or personality. Anyway, gotta go home." She got up, spun around and left, putting an exaggerated swing in her walk, perhaps to tease him, possibly to demonstrate that she was one up on him in some way.

15

The end of a school year is like an oncoming car, approaching slowly and then suddenly upon you, causing you to panic. Without Sandy, Robert was able to grade everything without waiting for the last minute, and then he woke up one day and it was final exams. His grade ledgers were all done except for the final grade, and he graded the exams quickly, filled out the report cards and was done for the year. Kelly, naturally had an A+ in the class, her understanding of literature almost as good as her writing, likely resulting from her writing.

With the start of summer, he made his final plans to visit Sandy in New York in July. Before his trip, there was something that seemed to have become a tradition: Kelly's birthday. In the last five years Robert has missed, maybe one of them. He hadn't really been keeping track. This time, Lauri, who was doing quite well and had bought new furniture, decided to have a big party, inviting all of Kelly's friends. Robert wondered about that, knowing that she had so few her own age.

Actually, there were more kids there than he'd expected. Karen and her new girlfriend stopped by for a short time, as well as that Indian boy from the middle school paper, and a couple kids from the English class. None of the kids stayed long. Several of Laurie's friends were there. Also, one of the math teachers, Polly Moat, a middle aged woman who Robert had only a few brief conversations with. He was obviously curious, and Moat told him that Kelly had been one of her favorite students and had asked her to come.

So there it was, mostly adults. Robert thought that it was sad. Here's a girl turning fifteen and no gang of close friends to help her celebrate. Yet, Kelly looked pleased, walking around, engaging everyone in conversations, being the charming hostess. It was as if she were determined to get all this kid stuff behind her and start to live her adult life. Was it dysfunctional or single-minded ambition? Whatever it was, the twig that started to bend in elementary school had grown into an oddly shaped tree. And whatever she was, she was no longer a kid, but a young woman, sure of herself, dancing to her own music. It was a compelling picture, and she was compelling, charming, attractive. There was also something slightly dangerous about her, something he felt but couldn't articulate.

His gift to her that year, a subscription to an important university based literary journal.

Then it was time to fly to the east coast. He locked up the place, asked a neighbor to come in and water the plants and collect the mail, and he was off to the airport.

Sandy met him at the terminal, and because of the traffic and parking in the city, they took a cab to her apartment, with a stop at a charming little bistro in the village. She talked almost non-stop, all excited about how quickly things were moving at her job. She had a minor author on board and perhaps another almost signed. She was still on the bottom rung of the ladder, but she was working long hours to impress the partners. She was consumed with work, and Robert tried very hard to sound excited about it.

She stopped long enough to ask him about work and grad school and about Kelly, and she also stopped long enough to make love. After that, in bed, she lit a cigarette, which surprised him. She'd never smoked before, and he didn't have the heart to tell her he didn't like the smell. She smoked and talked about work, a bit about how exciting the city was, although, she admitted, she'd been too busy to really explore.

He was dying to ask if she had dated since moving there, but he knew it was the wrong subject, wrong question, even the wrong thing to think about.

She was up at 6, in the shower and making breakfast as he was getting up. They ate quickly, she looked at the clock, handed him a key and told him she be home around six or so. He was left to wander the city, checking out Wall Street, the Empire State Building and other New York tourist draws. He found a nice restaurant a couple blocks from her place and made reservations. She was pleased, having brought home some work and not wanting to cook. Dinner and talk of work was followed by a quick session of love making, and then he watched TV while she reviewed some book chapters. Bored, he offered to read something and give her his opinion. She brightened at that, and that's how they spent the evening.

She worked long hours, even needing to go in half a day on Saturday. They wandered the city for the rest of the day, stopping to

109

eat. On Sunday, they caught an off Broadway play. Mostly she was either talking about or concerned about work. There was little discussion of his life in California. By the time he left, he doubted the future of the relationship. She said something about the next time being hopefully less busy, once she'd had the time to get really settled into the job. She added that she was sorry she couldn't have spent more time with him. They vaguely discussed plans for the Christmas holidays, but she added that she'd only get that day and half the twenty-forth off.

She was clearly really busy, having a harder and harder time focusing on him, and he knew when it was time to leave. However, since he'd traveled cross country, he wasn't in a hurry to catch a plane back to California. After their goodbyes, along with promises to get together on winter break, he caught a cab to the Amtrak station and took a train to Washington DC. He picked a room a short subway ride from the capitol and spent the next week playing tourist, including visiting all of the museums. Then, on impulse, not wanting to get back to his life, now a lonely one, he rented a car and headed to the Shenandoah Valley, checked into a rustic lodge and spent a few days hiking in the mountains. Finally, he'd managed to kill all of July and the first week in August, and it was time to get back, get ready for the reality of work and try to figure out if he still had a relationship.

On the plane, he thought that if just over two months had put that much emotional distance between them, what would it be like in five months, in a year? He decided that he would come again, if she agreed, in winter. At that point it would be probably be a decision point for them, a decision he wanted to put off indefinitely.

There was a message from George on his phone, asking about his schedule for the coming year. George respected him enough to give him first choice before building the teaching schedule. He went into school the following morning.

"Rob, good to see you. You look refreshed. Had a good summer?"

"I was in the east. It was OK."

"Oh, yeah, your girlfriend." Then Robert's face must have betrayed him, because George added, "I'm getting the impression that absence didn't make the heart grow fonder."

"Well, new life, busy life. We'll see. I'm going back during winter break."

"Good, hang in there, make it work. But between now and then, I've got English classes to schedule. Seems, Rob, that you like alternating between grades nine and eleven one year, ten and twelve the next. Lots of fresh prep work that way. If you want the same schedule next year, it's yours."

Robert thought for just a moment, and in that moment Kelly flashed through his mind. "No, change is good. I'd be happy with ten and twelve next year. Had some great kids, and maybe I can get some of them again next year."

"Love your dedication and enthusiasm man. Hope you never burn out like some of the old timers here. Oh, and one more thing. My wife has gone back to Philly. Her sister's about to have a kid. Well, every August we spend a week at the cabin near Tahoe. Look's like this year, I'm going alone, unless you'd like to join me. There's some good bike trails up there."

This was perfect, it would take him through the rest of the summer, and he wouldn't have to dwell on Sandy. Then school would start, along with the grad classes, and he'd be busy, too busy to brood. He jumped at it.

Kelly, as predicted, signed up for his class, and on the first day, as she walked in and sat down, Robert felt happy just knowing she was there. She had become so ingrained in his life, she was something akin to family. She stopped by after class, during the morning break, asking how his summer had been. He almost blurted out how things went with Sandy, but he caught himself. What was he thinking? You certainly don't talk about your personal relationships with a teenaged student. Instead, he merely said he'd visited her in New York, taken in the town and then toured the DC area, tossing in some details about the museums and the Shenandoah hiking.

She read between the lines almost as quickly as he told his story. "Something happen between you and Sandy?"

"No, not really. New job. She was really busy getting up to speed. We figure it'll be more relaxed when I go back in the winter."

Kelly didn't say a thing. She just looked into his eyes, betraying nothing. And finally, "I guess a new job is like a new school; lots of stress."

111

He asked her about her summer, and she said she'd made another trip to visit her aunt and was gone much of the summer. Did some writing while there, but nothing to get excited over. She was still fishing around for a novel. She asked if it was still OK for her to bring her work in after school, and he told her that was a given, any time, any place. She smiled and told him she'd see him in the morning. Stand there, talking to her, he realized that she'd probably finished growing and that she was now only a couple inches shorter. They stood there eye to eye, perhaps, he mused, a metaphor for their evolving relationship, with her establishing herself as a serious writer.

As usual, Kelly was the star student, often coaching others during writing assignments. There was one bright sign. Another girl, quiet, studious, thick glasses, very bright showed an interest in being friends with Kelly. Robert watched the interaction progressing, with Kelly seeming aloof at first, but slowly warming up to the girl with a name that didn't fit her at all, Peggy Sue.

Looking over the records, Robert found that Peggy had skipped a grade some time back, and that she was just fourteen in the tenth grade, with a very high IQ and a 4.0 GPA. The two girls got into long conversations about who knows what esoteric subjects. Kelly needed intellectual stimulation, and Peggy seemed to be giving it to her.

Kelly seemed to be making another connection. One of the eleventh grade boys in his class was a real bookworm who would rather read than listen to a lecture or do an assignment. He was also a chess nut who was passionate about liberal politics. The long hair and round glasses made him seem like one of those college activists from the sixties. He was a very serious boy; Robert could not remember seeing him smile or hearing him laugh. However, within weeks he was walking with Kelly between classes and at lunch, always engaged in a quiet, intense-seeming conversation. In Robert's view, this boy, Marty, was becoming Kelly's boyfriend. That thought made him apprehensive, wondering if he was the right kind of boy for her to be hanging around with.

On an occasion when Laurie was visiting Pat and Robert showed up, he managed to casually bring up the boy, and Laurie said that it looked like something was developing, but he seemed a bit too serious about everything. She'd been hoping Kelly would find someone more fun loving.

So, there it was, Kelly had a boyfriend, and if her conversation of last spring were any indication, they were either having a sexual relationship or soon would be, and he couldn't or wouldn't let himself understand why that concerned him. He finally scolded himself for being overprotective. She's not my kid, he told himself, and if it doesn't bother her mother, which since Lauri hadn't mentioned it, seemed probable, it shouldn't bother me.

For his part, it was suddenly late September and the holiday visit with Sandy was becoming a looming reality. The letters they exchanged were hopeful. Then both missed each other and were looking forward to getting together. He called her a few times, but she was often working and wasn't too conversational. Also, they both were intoxicated with the written word, so their letters, in both directions, were little literary gems. His were more like highly descriptive essays, while hers were almost prose poems. They both agreed that the letters were the highlight of the week, and it was mostly letters, actually typed, printed out and mailed. There was something sensual about a physical letter, and there was more thought in them than a hasty email, which they also exchanged from time to time.

The visit to George's cabin had turned the two men into friends, rather than friendly coworkers, and they would often stop off for a cold been after work, which tended to be late because George's position required it and because Robert, on the afternoons he didn't have to make the long drive to the university, had lots to do in his room, which was more conducive to work than his apartment.

One afternoon George had a funny look on his face as Robert approached his table in the bar. When he asked, George told him that at a neighboring high school, where he knew the principal, a teacher had been fired after someone found out about an affair he was having with a student. It had made headlines in the nearby town, but rated only a short blurb in the local paper. Turns out the girl was a senior, and the affair had been going on since early in her junior year. Apparently, he did something to upset her, and she told her mother, who called the district, and then all hell broke out. "Interestingly," George said. "This guy was a well liked and respected teacher. No one had a clue."

"So, what's going to happen to the guy?"

"The girl's seventeen, so it's not likely they'll push to prosecute him, but he's been fired, and his credential is history. He'll never teach again, and with this hanging over him, it's doubtful he'll get any professional job. He's going to be competing with high school grads for bottom of the barrel work." George shook his head and added, "A moment of weakness."

"Knowing the consequences, I can't understand why anyone would take that chance." Robert was really trying to understand it.

"Rob, you're thinking with your head. This is at another level. Guys like that get obsessed about some girl, and let's face it, some are very seductive. She might have gone after him. Saw a picture of her. Dress her up and put her in a night club, and you'd swear she was over twenty-one."

"Different context, but in the school setting, every warning alarm should go off at the first sign of temptation."

"I guess some guys have fewer warning lights. Hell, a good looking, baby-faced young guy like you, I'm sure some of these girls have flirted with you."

"Sure, it happens, and like you said, see them dressed up in a night club, but in school, they're just kids, students, and there's a really high wall."

"Right. You know, my first year teaching, I was maybe twenty-two. Seventeen year old in my class, really flirting with me, and I was really attracted."

Now Robert was on the edge of his chair. "What happened?"

"Nothing until she graduated. Then we dated. Now, she's my wife of nineteen years, and our youngest will enter high school next year. Funny how life works out."

That whole conversation unhinged Robert, and it kept him tossing and turning half the night. The fact was, as hard as he'd tried to suppress it, he'd dreamed several times about Kelly since things started to cool with Sandy, in each one she had been the sexual aggressor and he had struggled to resist. He also felt he was too concerned about her dating life. Was he just a thin line of control away from self-destructing like the teacher George was talking about? Robert was a moral man, at least that's what he'd always told himself. Was there a lustful predator lurking just under the surface? He doubted it, but he found himself questioning himself and the true nature of his feelings. To test this, he closed his eyes and imagined himself in a romantic situation with Kelly. As soon as he pictured himself kissing and caressing her, he recoiled from the image. He had to open his eyes and shake it off. Unthinkable! It actually made him feel creepy and immoral.

As he woke, tried from lack of sleep, he vowed to ignore Kelly's dating life. Whatever was going on or not going on between her and this Marty kid was none of his damn business and nothing he would think about. Although he was able to let it go, it wasn't destined to let him go. Less than two weeks later, Kelly came by after school, something she hadn't done in some time.

"Got some writing to show me?"

"Yeah. What's you think?" She handed it to him and settled into a chair, obviously expecting him to drop everything and read it on the spot, which, since she'd long since conditioned him to it, he automatically did.

It was a short story, and he read it quickly. It was obviously based on her and this Marty kid. Girl and boy start a relationship, it turns sexual, and he ends up criticizing her work as being shallow and not political. He looked up at her. "This isn't fiction."

"Is it good?"

"Yes, but it's obviously about you and your boyfriend."

"Former boyfriend. The nerve of him telling me that my writing was just escapist pap, and that I should write political stuff, stuff to, as he put it, 'make a difference.' Then he went on about the rise of the workers. By the time I was able to get a word in, I was so pissed. I told him, no I shouted at him, 'If you like that kind of dreary shit, why don't you write it yourself?' Then I added, 'Oh, that's right, you've got no fucking talent.' Then I walked out."

"Well, that sounds like a break up. You might want to make a few changes so he doesn't see himself in it before you send it off. Like everything else you write, it's good."

As much as he tried not to be, he was somehow please that they had broken up.

It had been weeks since Robert had gotten together with his old pals. Now that they were all married, the gatherings were less frequent, so he was pleased to get a call from Flynn. "Hey, Bobbie, baby. Been awhile."

After a couple minutes of catch up, during which Flynn asked about Sandy, and Robert said something about the difficulties of a long distance relationship, Flynn got to the reason for the call. "As you know Chip got his masters, and his wife already had hers. Well, they've found jobs down in LA and are packing it in pretty soon. We're having a going away party for them."

Robert was naturally in, but disappointed. Ted was already practicing law in San Francisco, not nearly as far away, but just far enough to make meeting for a drink after work impossible. The old gang was falling apart, and Robert hated changes in the social order. Flynn had been talking for some time about moving to Sacramento and working for a company that does business with the state government. That would scatter them all over the state, leaving a summer trip and the odd holiday as the only opportunities to get together.

Robert actually had tears in his eyes when he hugged Chip and wished him well in his new job, promising to get down to see him in the near future. Robert then thought about southern California, realizing that the last time he'd been there was a trip to Disneyland, before he started teaching.

One morning in first period, Kelly came in a few minutes late, something she never did. She was yawning, obviously struggling to stay awake. When she stopped by after school, he asked her about it.

"Last night Peggy Sue took me to hear her cousin's band. He graduated last year, goes to community college. He plays bass. They were at the college music center. After the performance, we all went out. Her cousin seems to like me and wanted to keep hanging out. Before I knew it, it was way late."

Trying to sound nonchalant, Robert asked if she was interested in him.

"He's a fun guy, not like that jerk Marty. And, he's older, a bit more mature. He wants me to go out with him, so I'm thinking why not, like check it out, see how it goes."

16

Mid fall, with the holiday season rapidly approaching, Robert losing one of his best friends, his girlfriend three thousand miles away and making a new life for herself, Kelly, the one person who was always there, dating, possibly starting a relationship and Robert felt he was on the outside looking in.

As November rolled around, Kelly definitely had a relationship. He heard Peggy talking with her about the band and this bass player, who from what they were saying, was sexually involved with Kelly. Robert was having a hard time adjusting to little Kelly being a sexually active young woman. He fought off the urge to use the word "promiscuous," knowing that was an old school sexist notion.

The semester was ending, and Robert had his ticket to New York, assured by Sandy that he was still welcome and they were still a couple. On the last day of school, Kelly seemed a bit upset, and he would normally ask her about it, sit down with her, discuss it, but he had to pack and fly, so he thought it was probably nothing much and would wait until he got back.

He had to admit to himself that this visit was way better than the last. She was far less frantic about the job, and her life had settled into a routine, a busy one, but routine just the same. She had more time for him, particularly since the company gave them the whole week between Christmas and New Year off. They did the town, talked writing and literature, just like the old days, made love passionately and often and were generally pretty comfortable with each other. There was, however, a "but" attached, and it came up one evening in bed.

"You know I still care about you, love you and all. But, you're in California and I'm here, and that makes whatever we have really hard."

He admitted it was for him too, and that he was adjusting as best he could.

"Well," she continued, "Seeing each other for a week or so every six months isn't really enough. It gets lonely, and..." She trailed off.

"And you've found someone else," he finished for her.

"No, not really, but I've done a bit of dating, casual stuff. I guess the point is that I could meet someone I'd hit it off with, and then what?"

"Yeah, it would be unfair of me to keep you to myself, given the situation."

"You understand. I mean, you've probably been dating also."

"Not really," He hated to admit. Then he added, "You're a damn hard act to follow."

She grabbed him and kissed him and smiled. "If you could move here, we could save this, but given the distance, I feel sometimes like it's starting to slip away, and I really hate that feeling."

"I wish I could, but I'm almost done. In a few months I'll only have my dissertation left to do. I'm already set to teach one class at San Jose State, and maybe I'll be able to get my foot in the door. Even if all goes well, I'll be damn near thirty before my career really gets off the ground."

"Don't sell yourself short. You already have a great career as a top teacher. Sure, teaching at the university level would be better, pay better too, but hell, you don't have to feel like anything but a success."

It was great to hear that. He really needed it. Another thing he needed and that they discussed well into the night was their future. They both agreed that come what may, they would remain good friends, and as long as neither got into a new serious relationship, they would be lovers when they were together and still plan for their joint future. It wasn't the perfect situation he'd once imagined, but it was good, it was ongoing and dependable, things he really needed.

It was a new year and a new semester, and Robert went in early to prepare. About fifteen minutes before the bell, Kelly walked in wearing tight jeans and a tank top.

"Did you have a nice trip to New York?"

"Actually, it was quite nice."

"So, you and Sandy still an item?"

His instinct was to not answer personal questions, but he heard himself answer, as if on automatic. "It's not the same any more, living apart like this, but we're still close and vowed to stay friends no matter what happens."

"Still having sex though? Sorry, no need to answer."

Then he remembered. "You looked out of sorts last day of school. Anything wrong?"

"That musician. Guys can be such dumb jerks. Even if they're not jerks, they're usually clueless." The last seemed directed at him.

Ignoring the implication, he pointed to a chair and asked, "Want to talk about it?"

"Well, we were having a good time, music, parties, and you know, sex. Well, one night at a band party, he was drinking, and I was concerned, but he said he was fine. So, he's like driving me home and I realize he's weaving, damn near hitting another car. I yelled at him for putting me in danger, and he called me an uptight little goody goody and said that this is what the big kids do in the real world. I don't like being talked down to, and I don't like someone putting me in danger. I told him to stop the damn car, and he said no. Then I said to stop the fucking car or I'd jump out, so he pulled over, and I called my mom to pick me up. He's telling me either get back in the car or he's kissing me off. I was really pissed, so I told him it was no great loss and that he was boring in bed, which wasn't true."

"So, another big romance ended. Too bad."

"Peggy says I'm too judgmental, too much my way or the high-way. Do you think that's true?"

"Probably, but that's a good thing. You're a strong person. You're not going to be a doormat for some guy. You were right. The guy's got no right risking your life. You wait until you find someone with the good sense and maturity to treat you right."

"You mean, someone like you?"

"Maybe you give me too much credit. You need someone worthy of you, some knight in shining armor. But, the bell's about to ring." Thus he ended the conversation before she could push the subject.

That night he dreamed she was at some wild party. Guys were fighting, drunk, starting fires, and he came to the door, pushed past everyone and scooped her up. Then in the car she put her arms around him, called him her knight and kissed him. He woke with a start and couldn't get back to sleep. This was worrying him. He was looking at her differently lately, and he had to stop himself and realize she was only a fifteen year old kid.

"I'm sorry you're not doing the after school writing club any

119

more." She announced one afternoon as he was reading her latest story.

"Would love to, but way too busy. AP classes mean grading lots of work, and I'm finishing up the last classes in my program."

"So, I'll be calling you Doctor Spagnola this summer."

"Not yet. After the classes, I sign up for dissertation. It's not actual classes, but I do research and writing, and I have a faculty adviser, and it can take who knows how long, maybe a year; some take two or more, a few crank it out in a semester."

"You'll do it before I finish my junior year. Then you'll get settled in a good job at a university, maybe Berkeley and start planning our, I mean your future."

"Kelly, if I believed everything you told me, I'd try walking across the surface of the school pool." He laughed at that, and it set her laughing too. She batted her eyes and said in an exaggerated voice, "What can I say, you're my hee-row."

Then she mentioned some really good poetry one of the kids in the writing club wrote. "The kid's a freshman, but he writes some really heavy stuff, deep and almost musical."

He told her he wanted to see it, and the next day she brought a few poems in. She'd been right. This wasn't what anyone would expect from a freshman boy. It was the work of someone who thought deeply about life. He said he like to meet this kid.

Within a few days, Kelly showed up with the kid in tow. He was a slender blond boy, maybe an inch or so shorter than Kelly, with deep blue eyes. He had that haunted look that reminded Robert of the young Peter O'Toole. "This is Kenny. Kenny, Mr. S, a really great teacher. You should be in his class next year."

The boy stuck out his hand, but looked down, shyly. Then he said, "I've heard about you. Kelly says you're the best writing teacher in the world and you helped her get to... to being the most talented writer. Incredible. Maybe you could help me with my poetry."

"Well, Kenny, I'm not a poet, but I have lots of books by quite an assortment of poets." He pointed to the book shelf in the back of the room. "Feel free to borrow any that look interesting, and after you've looked them over, we can talk about them."

"Thank you, Mr. S. Tell, me, has Kelly always been such a

gifted writer. She says she's known you for like five years."

"She was outstanding at ten, and she's only gotten better every year."

Kenny turned and looked at her like some boys would look at a professional basketball player, basking in her radiant glory. Then he walked to the back of the room and started browsing the poetry.

"Looks like you've got a genuine fan there." He couldn't hide the amusement in his voice.

"Yeah, he kind of follows me around like a puppy. It's kind of cool, especially because he's really an awesome poet. He should have fans."

"Here's a deal for you. You can each be the president of the other's fan club. Unfortunately, most kids your age are fans of movie stars, pop singers and athletes."

Kenny ended up tagging along when Kelly came in after school to discuss her work, and soon Robert was also coaching Kenny, even though he felt his wasn't on solid ground in the world of poetry.

Robert had simply forgotten his mother's birthday, but then Lauri called to tell him she was going to have a birthday dinner party for Pat. She wanted Robert to invite anyone his mother might know. Flynn was the only one of Robert's friends still in town, so he'd already been invited. Was there anyone else?

Robert thought for a minute and then suggested his principal, George, who had met Pat several time.

When Robert showed up at Lauri's place, Pat was already there, and Kelly had Kenny tagging along, which Robert thought was a bit odd.

Flynn and his wife came by and said that they would indeed be moving to Sacramento, and the place they were getting had a guest room, so Robert could visit any time.

Kelly and Flynn hadn't seen each other in a year or more, and while changes in him were imperceptible, Kelly had gone from an awkward-looking teen to a poised young woman, and Flynn's comment was that if it wasn't for the red hair he might not have recognized her. He also asked if Kenny was her boyfriend, and she simply said he was a friend.

George and his wife were the last to show up, and he introduced

121

his wife to Kelly, saying, "This is the writing star Rob is grooming to be a best seller."

"More than that." Kelly insisted, and Robert was afraid of what she might say next. Then, after a dramatic pause to get everyone's attention, she continued. "Mr. S has taught me everything I know about writing and literature. I was a lost little kid, and he taught me how to write and encouraged me. He helped me win a writing contest when I was like only ten. He's stayed after school so many times, postponing his plans, just to help me become a professional writer. He's the greatest teacher in the world, and if I ever write a novel, I'm going to dedicate it to him."

With Kelly, Robert never really knew what to expect, but he certainly never would have expected this, this little drama, the flagrant hero worship, not from a girl who was relating to him more and more as a peer, rather than a student. Perhaps, he thought, this was her way of letting George know that their relationship was strictly mentor and student.

It was interesting how such a diverse group could come together and be so relaxed and at home with each other. George had taken a few educational management classes in his masters program, so he had some common ground with Flynn. Everyone was an avid reader, giving them all a common topic, and Robert observed that Kelly could hold her own, effortlessly making stylistic comparisons between well-known authors and making points that stimulated the conversation.

Little Kenny was the quiet one, only getting talkative for a few moments when poetry was brought up. The rest of the time he sat quietly, mostly looking at Kelly. And at one point, and Robert didn't think anyone else noticed it, Kenny leaned over as if to kiss Kelly, and she gave him a startled and off-putting look. Then realizing what he'd done, he withdrew sheepishly. Why, Robert wondered, would the boy absently try to kiss her if that wasn't a usual part of their relationship. Could there be something going on there? Even though he was only a year younger than Kelly, he seemed so young. He had yet to have the growth spurt that would transform him from a boy to a man.

Kelly had an envelope for Robert, a story. "I wrote this for you, about you. It's kind of science fiction and sort of funny, but I hope you like it."

Robert started to open it to read it, and she told him to wait until after the party.

As George and his wife got up to leave, he shook hands with Kelly and said, "Guess the next time I see you, you'll be insisting I get you into his next year's class."

"Well, maybe the second semester. I've applied to one of those foreign exchange programs, and it looks like it's a go."

Robert did a double take. "You never mentioned this."

"Gee, Mr. S. I don't tell you everything." She drew out the "Everything." Then she added, "After all you're my teacher, not my dad."

It was obvious that Robert wasn't the only one caught off guard by this. Kenny's jaw dropped, and he looked like he might cry. "You're going out of the country. How long?"

"I'll be leaving after school ends and probably get back after the holidays, so maybe seven months."

Pat asked the obvious question. "Where will you be going?"

"Florence. They've got all this great art and history. The pictures look great. There these old bridges over the river, stores and restaurants and stuff on them, and the old churches, the galleries. The statue David is there, the original."

Robert, a bit more composed, asked, "So, what made you want to do this?"

"What do they call it? Broaden my world, get experiences, maybe round out my education. Could be my novel is waiting for me there."

"Won't you have a problem with the language?" Flynn inquired.

"I've been studying one of those programs, Rosetta Stone, plus taking a night class at the community college. Can't write it well, but I'm getting so I can follow a conversation. Besides, I've heard that most of the kids there speak some English."

Robert was surprised that he hadn't heard about the classes, particularly since Kelly loved to share the details of her life. Perhaps it was that teen thing about not communicating with adults.

"What about me," Kenny whined.

"Maybe we should talk in private." Then she gave him a look that said the conversation was over.

Late that night, slightly buzzed, Robert put his book down and turned out the light. Rather than close his eyes, he stared at the ceiling and the shadows of the moonlight through the curtains. Why, he wondered, did he react so strongly to Kelly's plan? This was a good experience for her, perhaps just what she needed to become a more mature writer. Yet, his first reaction was that he didn't want her to go. Two of his best friends have moved, Flynn would be going away in a couple weeks, Sandy was in New York and his social life was null and void. Could it be that he'd come to depend so much on this student for his social connection to the greater world. Was he clinging to her for fear of being alone? There was also that fatherly thing, born of years of watching her grow up. She'd be an innocent in a sophisticated European city. No, she's young and perhaps a bit provincial, but she wasn't innocent. She'd interacted with all kinds of people, young and adult, and she'd had relationships, mostly on her terms. Truth be known, she handled her relationships at least as well as he did.

As he drifted off to sleep, he realized that for whatever reasons, she was an important part of his life, perhaps now that people seem to be going this way and that, she might just be what she claimed to be in the fifth grade, his best friend.

That night he dreamed about her. She was saying goodbye at the airport, and she gave him a passionate kiss that lasted seemingly forever. Then the dream morphed into another airport scene, her returning. She had a handsome young man with her who she introduced as her fiancé. She asked if he would give her away. He asked her about all the talk of her marrying him, and she responded casually that she simply got tired of waiting and decided to get on with her life.

These were the kinds of dreams that made him doubt himself. Whatever his feelings for her in his waking life, they didn't include marriage or even sex. Well, he was a man, and men always have sex on the mind, if not consciously, than subconsciously.

17

"I have a problem and need your help." His sixth period class had no more than cleared the door when Kelly barged in, getting, as usual, straight to the point.

"Problem, huh? Writing or personal?"

"Personal. It's Kenny and me going to Italy."

"OK, I'm guessing there a relationship, and he doesn't want you to leave."

She sat on the edge of a desk, directly in front of him. "Well, yeah, we had, have something going." And then as if in answer to his unasked question, she added, "He's kind of young, but he was so into me. Made me feel so special. Also, I got to kind of teach him about stuff. But it wasn't anything but casual for me. Then one day he says he's in love with me and wants to marry me, and I'm like hold it, wait a minute. I've been trying to put some space there, let him down kind of slow and easy, but he's kind of clingy. He's sweet, and I don't want to hurt him."

He almost laughed. Asking him for advice about relationships was like asking a blind man about Van Gogh's use of color. Still one thing was obvious. "Kelly, no matter what you say or do, you're going to break his heart, first love and all that. That's the bad part, but the good part is that he's young and he'll fall in love with some other girl before you get back."

"You sure?"

"I wouldn't bet money on it, but sure, probably. You've just got to tell him that you really like him but not in that way. I've heard that one more than once." He could hardly believe he'd just admitted that.

"You? No way any girl would reject you, not unless she's totally nuts. So, I should just sit him down and tell him just like that?"

"What choice do you have? You could lead him on, make vague promises about how things will be when you get back, leave him moping and love sick for months. The sooner he knows it's over, the sooner he can go on with his life."

She jumped to her feet and started pacing. "I hate this. Why can't people just have their thing together and then shake hands, part friends?"

"Their thing? If it lasts long enough, then someone gets more involved than the other. So far, that one hasn't been you. You could end up with the broken heart one day."

"Never happen. I always have a plan. I keep my heart safe and sound." She tapped the desk to emphasize "Safe and sound."

"Well, I salute you then. Kelly the unbreakable. So now do what you have to do, and the longer you put it off, the harder it will be."

Then she did the strangest thing. She reached over and ruffled his hair with her hand. She winked, said, "Thanks, you're the best. You always make things simple." and turned and started to strut out the door.

"Wait a minute." He remembered the story she'd given him on Pat's birthday. "That was cute, teacher as superhero, flying through the city to save students from bad prose. Probably couldn't sell it, but it might make a cute animated short. Thank you for the story and the thought. It's the first time I've seen myself as a caped crusader."

"Well," she said with a lopsided grin, "That's exactly how I've always seen you. Bye now."

There was a goodbye party for Flynn, and Robert realized he only knew about half the people there. The others were likely from his job, or rather his late job. He didn't think anyone from his new firm would make a three hour drive from Sacramento.

Robert also was busy with his grad classes. There were orals and other exams, all coming to a head in May, leaving only his dissertation between him and that long awaited doctorate. He was going to focus on that, have it done by this time next year, be ready to start a new life, hopefully at some university. So, as was his style, when without a woman in his life and with friends scattered, he put his head down and started to crank out the work.

Suddenly finals were coming up, and his AP students all had compositions as part of that, meaning hours of reading, correcting and commenting. At times he envied the math teachers: fill in the Scantrons and they can be graded in minutes.

Kelly wasn't coming in after school as much, once a week or so, being also busy with classes, trying to get that 4.0 GPA to get into a good university. Once upon a time, Robert mused, students didn't feel that pressure until their junior year, but now it had become so competitive, that freshmen were sweating, occasionally junior high kids also.

Like Robert, Kelly could focus when needed, pushing everything else aside and just grinding out the work or study. The two of them were alike in that way. Still, when she did come in, these days with no stories to share, they'd have a pleasant chat about each one's studies, the upcoming trip for her and his dissertation. It felt like two young professionals chatting over wine, except one wasn't near old enough to drink and they were in a drab, green classroom, rather than a fancy wine bar.

One day in early May there was a letter from Sandy in the mail. Now, she usually sent emails these days, unless she had something to wax eloquently about, and he hadn't heard anything from her in weeks. He nervously tore it open. It was a "dear Robert" letter, nicely written and sensitive, but one just the same. She had started seeing someone since his last visit, and now it was getting to be a steady thing. She didn't know where it would lead, whether it was serious or not, but she didn't feel comfortable juggling the two of them right now. The upshot was to say it wouldn't be a good idea to come to New York this summer. Something she wrote stuck with him: "Even though you won't be in my arms, you'll always be in my heart." This, however, was small consolation. His once full life was now empty, and he put his head in his hands and dripped tears on the opened letter.

Now, with even more conviction and fervor he dedicated himself to work of all kinds, even turning out several book reviews for the newspaper and publishing an essay in a literary journal. Keeping busy from the time he woke until he fell exhausted into bed, empty wine glass on the table, was his emotional survival. The days had become a blur, a trudge, a death march to some vague new life.

While he often ignored the wad of papers in his box in the office, the large letters on the invitation caught his eye. It was time for the annual faculty end of the year party. That's just what he felt he needed: Be social, drink a lot, flirt with the old maid teachers and forget everything for a few hours.

When he arrived at the party, at George's house, he looked around and realized he really didn't socialize with his fellow teachers that much, and he started to realize how he'd isolated himself. Perhaps, he thought, my loneliness is more of my making than I've allowed myself to admit. The people around him were familiar, and he'd exchanged a few words with most of them. Some he'd talked with extensively in the teacher's lounge, but for the most part, he knew their first names and vaguely what they taught. Sure it was a large high school, but not that large.

He poured a large glass of wine, Said hi to a few people, refilled the glass and started talking to George, mostly small talk that kept him from having the difficult party conversations with people he didn't know as well as he should. There was a bottle of wine on the table next to George, so Robert filled the glass again and took a long deep drink. Soon, other people started tugging at George, and he excused himself. Robert, alone in the middle of the room, refilled his glass and stood there, looking like the act of drinking was keeping him busy.

An attractive little woman, Asian looking, smiled at him, so he thought he'd walk over and chat with her. He quickly took inventory. Helen something, social studies, he believed. Close enough. "Hi, Helen. How's the school year treating you?"

"Wonderful Robert. Good bunch of kids. Got the AP students, always a delight. One of them is a big fan of yours, outgoing young woman named Kelly."

"Oh, yes, I've been mentoring her with her writing for quite some time. She's become an excellent writer, putting away money for college from it too."

"Indeed, your reputation as a writing teacher is well established."

Fishing for more information, he asked. "So which class is she taking from you?"

"History, of course. Tenth grade means world history. She's curious about everything. Asks great questions."

Feeling he couldn't avoid it forever, and figuring it was best to get it out of the way, he admitted he didn't remember her last name.

"Well, you probably wouldn't know it. I've recently gone back to my maiden name, Akimoto. I'm recently divorced."

"Oh, I'm sorry to hear." Sounded lame, but it was the best he could do.

"Don't be. It was mutual. The fire had gone out and we no longer had common interests. We've remained friends."

"Any kids?"

"Daughter, Julie. She'll be a freshman here in the fall."

That caught him off guard. "A teenager? You don't seem old enough. I mean, I figured you were my age or younger."

"Thirty-seven. Blessed with a good complexion. My mother's gray but still has this complexion." She pointed to her cheek.

"So, you were married for a while."

"Almost sixteen years. And, you know, I like not being responsible for another adult, making mutual plans, accommodating another person's needs. I may not remarry, but if I do, it'll be some years down the road. How about you, married, divorced, single?"

"Single. My last serious girlfriend got a great job in New York, and you know how long distance relationships go."

They were hitting it off, and she was cute, getting cuter with each glass of wine. Perhaps, he thought, something might come of this. She didn't seem to be in any hurry to get away from him, and it seems she was giving him positive signs. He asked her for her number, and she quickly gave him her card.

Suddenly, he realized how much the wine had hit him, and he felt he needed to get out of there. "I think I need to go home. I'll call you, OK?"

"No, no, you're in no shape to drive. Leave your car here, and I'll take you home."

In his condition, it sounded very much like an excuse for intimacy, so he consented, believing that he was probably just fine to make the three mile drive.

He had trouble keeping his eyes open in the car, and when they got to his place, he asked if she'd like to come in for a drink or coffee or something, but she said that he needed to get into bed, but he could call her tomorrow.

Robert woke up with a hangover, something he hadn't experienced in a very long time. Always a moderate drinker, he berated himself for letting self-pity drive him to make an ass of himself. He thought about Helen and how nice she'd been about the whole thing,

129

his absurd behavior and all, plus having to drive him home. He wondered if he'd have the courage to call her now, but thinking it over during a breakfast of coffee and toast, he figured that at least he had to call to thank her, and if the vibes were right, maybe he could ask her out.

He put it off as long as he could and then just grabbed the phone and punched in her number. "Good morning, afternoon I guess. It's Robert."

"Feeling better this morning?" Not waiting for an answer, she continued. "I had a delightful time talking with you at the party. Sorry I couldn't come in, but I figured you were not up to entertaining."

He felt relieved; she was making him feel better, a good sign. "You're right. I'm not used to drinking that much, and it just caught up to me. I was better off sleeping it off. But I would like to make it up to you, perhaps with dinner, tonight or Sunday perhaps.?

"Well, my daughter and I have our Saturday night date, but Sunday is free."

Robert was elated. She'd made him feel at ease, and the whole wine thing seemed no big deal. She sounded anxious for them to get together. It was probably good that she had ten years on him. She was mature and had her life pretty much structured, so wherever he fit in would likely be a pretty stable place, and he would be happy to fit in anywhere that he could depend on. Unknowns were uncomfortable, and by definition, unpredictable.

Whatever this thing with Helen was, it took off immediately. Over dinner she laid out what she was after, a comfortable situation, affection, intimacy, friendship, but nothing heavy or permanent. As she'd said at the party, almost sixteen years of being locked into a relationship was enough for now. She seemed to recall a term popular with the twenty somethings, friends with benefits. Would Robert be comfortable as a friend with benefits?

He would be happy with that, much as he would be happy winning a month in Hawaii. Good company, beautiful woman, no worrying about how far to take it or how quickly, just enjoy the time together. He used his denial skills to push to the far reaches of his mind the fact that he was only happy in the long term with a relationship that was progressing toward something more permanent.

One more catch, her daughter. She really didn't want Julie to see men coming and going, so until they establish a fairly steady thing, they'd have to go to his place, which is where they ended up after dinner.

Helen was very direct and very clear about what she enjoyed. She was also a skillful lover, driving him wild to the point where he almost lost control, but then calming him enough to keep him just on the edge. Another plus was her very firm, fit body.

After making love, she snuggled against him, and they talked lazily and into the evening, mostly about how they enjoyed teaching and why they taught what they did. Then she checked her watch and said she had to get home. She dressed quickly, while he slipped on some sweats and slippers. She gave him a quick kiss and told him to call her, and then she was gone.

Robert was kind of disappointed that she didn't stay the night, but he told himself that if he played his cards right and this became steady, he'd be spending the night at her place. The down side of that would be walking out of the bedroom and running into her kid. He knew that something like that would make him highly uncomfortable. Underneath it all, he had to admit to himself, he was pretty conservative and traditional. Orgies and free love were far out of his comfort zone, along with having a teen see him come out of her mom's bedroom.

18

Kelly's plane left the day after her sixteenth birthday. Robert took Kelly, her mother and his mother out to dinner down at the harbor, getting a window seat and watching the sun set over the water, sailboat masts silhouetted against an orange sky. If Helen had been along, it would have been romantic, but for some reason he didn't want these two parts of his life to intersect, at least not now.

He told Kelly how much he'd miss her, and as he said it, he understood how big a hole her departure would leave in his life. The four of them, they were, for want of a better word, family. She listened to his confession and replied simply with, "I know."

With his buddies gone off and busy with new families and with George going on a long vacation with his wife, Robert decided to do a solitary camping trip. He mentioned it to Helen, but she didn't suggest joining him, so he took ten days in July and drove up to the Sierra, turned off highway 108 on a dirt road and drove to the campground at the end, near the Pacific Crest Trail, and close to three small lakes. He brought a stack of books, his camera and a new mountain bike, an expensive treat to help compensate for the loss of so many close friends.

By the end of the trip he was more relaxed and balanced than he'd been in a very long time. His body was exercised, his mind at peace, a comfortable routine of meals, sleeping, hiking and biking having fallen into place. He had hardly spoken to a soul the whole time, and he didn't miss the chatter of his fellow human. In fact, he felt he could easily spend the rest of the summer there, but he'd made plans with Helen for the day after his return, and being one who takes his plans seriously, he packed up and drove down the mountain, stopping at a little roadside diner for breakfast. There he got into a long conversation with several locals, which he found so delightful, he stayed well over an hour.

Upon arriving home and checking his mail, he got on his computer and wrote a piece about getting away and experiencing other people and places. He knew exactly where he could send it, and only giving it a cursory glance for spelling errors, he sent the first draft, which was the finished draft, off. Then he called Helen, told her what a great time he'd had and how anxious he was to see her.

Helen wasn't a biker but she was a hiker, so they spent the warm August days hiking in state parks, from Big Basin to Henry Coe, to Point Lobos to Muir woods, many of which he hadn't visited in some time. It was a beautiful summer, and he hated to see it end.

He did have a couple of emails from Kelly waiting for him on his return. She was living with a delightful host family, a short bus ride from the old part of town and walking distance from the high school. The family had a daughter, just a year older, in her last year of high school. The girl, Francine, had a great group of friends, about seven or eight boys and girls, and they made her feel at home. She was going out almost every day or night, to parks, to clubs, on rides in the country. She was having a ball.

Routine was mother's milk to Robert, and his new routine with Helen was more than pleasant. They got together every Friday night for a date, dinner, a play or club or a movie, with sex at his place. On Sunday they'd go for a hike, taking a picnic lunch. She had not suggested taking her daughter, which was fine by Robert, as he was not comfortable with what he expected to be critical looks and harsh evaluations from a teen.

However, routines tend to make time speed up, and then it was late August and the school year was about to start. Suddenly, the carefree mood of summer changed to getting geared up, which for teachers was like going from a dead stop to freeway speed.

During that time, Kelly was anxious for school to start in Florence. The group of kids she'd been hanging out with were mostly older, some starting their final year of high school, others starting college, a few going out into the work force, assuming there were any jobs to be found. The kids had been mostly pairing up, and there was one boy she described as "cute and funny" who had shown an interest in her. Though intimacy wasn't specifically mentioned, Robert could read between the lines. But again, Kelly was non-committal. It was just a boy. Maybe she really was immune to the romantic crushes that seemed to infect kids her age. She added that she'd encouraged the kids to not baby her by speaking English, and as a result, her Italian was improving daily.

Helen had hinted that they'd been an item long enough that she may soon invite him to sleep over at her place, something he had mixed feelings about, not having met the daughter, but knowing how much attitude the typical thirteen or fourteen year old girl has.

In the old Road Runner cartoons, Wily Coyote is running along a lonely desert road when a speeding truck, out of nowhere, runs him over. That's pretty much how Robert saw the first day of school. No matter how he'd prepared, that first day always blindsided him.

First period without Kelly just didn't seem the same, but there were familiar faces, students that followed him from year to year because he kept switching from ninth and eleventh grade to tenth and twelfth. He was sure some of his better, more talented writers would stay with him their whole four years.

Second period was a train wreck from the beginning. He was taking roll, calling out names. "Ingerson?"

A tall, rangy girl with wavy brown hair responded. "Don't you know who I am yet?"

He looked up, and saw a total stranger sitting in the second row. He shook his head and admitted she wasn't at all familiar.

"You're having an affair with my mom." She blurted out in what sounded to him like a shout that could be heard clear out to the gym. For a moment the class was totally silent, and he was completely at a loss for words. He was so caught off guard, it didn't occur to him that she might by Helen's daughter. She didn't look anything like Helen, who was petite with straight black hair.

When he finally found his voice, he was already starting to get angry. "I don't know who you are and I'm not sure who your mother is, but that was a totally inappropriate comment."

"My mother's Helen Akimoto, and you certainly do know her." She emphasized the word "know."

"You and I will talk later. For now, that will be enough." When it looked like she was about to say something else, he warned. "Enough or suspension. You don't want to start the year off that way." She stared at him, but he stared her down, and she relaxed into her seat.

As soon as the bell rang, he called Helen's room and told her what happened. Helen said to wait there after school for her and Julie. The problem would be solved.

As good as her word, Helen showed up within minutes of the final bell, a sheepish Julie following behind. Helen handed Robert a smart phone. "This is Julie's. You can decide when she gets it back, her penalty for her behavior today. Also, she has something to say to you." She turned to her daughter, who stepped forward.

"I'm sorry sir. That was rude and inappropriate of me. It won't happen again."

A mother who actually was in control of her kid, how refreshing, Robert thought. Looking in the girl's eyes, he could see that she really meant it, that her mother had made her realize what she'd done. Robert couldn't stay angry with the girl. "It's OK, Julie, we all speak without thinking now and then. Anyway, I want us to get a fresh start. You're an AP student and I hope to make this class interesting for you, and I think we can be friends." He put out his hand, and she shook it, a smile starting to come over her previously sad face.

"Thank you Mr. Spagnolo. You have a rep as a great writing teacher. I'm going to study biology, and maybe someday write science books, kind of like Richard Dawkins. Maybe you can help me be a better writer."

"You have my promise on that."

A week later Helen invited him home with her after their date. Julie was already in bed when they got home from a play in San Jose, but she was already up in the morning, when Robert, already fully dressed and put together, sheepishly emerged from Helen's bedroom. This time he was the one on the defensive.

There was a look, rather "the look," but it only lasted a moment, just enough to let him know that the roles were reversed since that afternoon in his classroom. Then she calmly said, "Good morning Mr. S. Coffee's made. Would you like some breakfast?"

He thanked her, poured a cup and sat down in the kitchen. Not knowing what else to say to a teen, he asked her about her first week in high school, and she said it was busy but fun. Then she said she knew about one of his students who was kind of famous.

When Robert looked puzzled, she said. "Girl named Kelly O'Mara. I subscribe to the magazines she writes for. She's great; I am so a fan. She always dedicates her stories to you, the teacher who taught her all she knows. Is that true?"

Robert was actually embarrassed. "Well, she had so much natural talent and she wanted to work with me, learn everything she could, have me criticize and edit her work. She did all the work. I just supported and coached her."

"And she still goes to school here?" Julie sounded anxious, like she might meet her favorite TV star.

"She does, but not this semester. She's a foreign exchange student in Italy. She'll be back next semester."

"That's cool. I want to meet her."

"Maybe she'll help you with your writing. I'll ask her."

That was it. He'd won Julie over, or rather Kelly had won her over and he was profiting by his association with the star. Another reason for Julie to be nice was her phone, which Robert had forgotten he had and as he was far less strict than her mother, he found in his car and handed over.

He could learn from Helen. She was a good mother, loving and respected by Julie, but she also had firm rules that she enforced. Julie, rather than resenting it, respected her mother's code of behavior. Helen had the same reputation in her classroom, strict, fair and caring, and her students responded in kind. Robert had to admit to himself that, while his room was intellectually and creatively active, it was also active in other ways that always bordered on chaotic. He had to constantly refocus the class, and he had to remind himself to pull back when discussions went off on a tangent. He realized that much time was wasted when activities and conversations got out of hand. One night in bed he broached the subject, and she gave him some really good tips that he hoped he could use. The bottom line was personality types. She was orderly and by the numbers, and he was more of a play it by ear teacher.

People, Robert understood, were complex beings, moved by a mix of needs, desires and requirement, often not understanding fully the reasons why they behaved the way they did. If a person were to analyze one simple response to a situation, analyze it fully, chop it into all the primary components, the response would take a hundred times as long, and no one would do much of anything. Rather, all the factors bubble just below the surface, and when an occasion arises, they manifest in immeasurable, often bizarre, combinations.

136

For whatever reasons, Robert had a good working relationship with Helen and Julie, one that could continue indefinitely or go sour on a moment's notice. He was getting comfortable and as such was wishing to have strings attached, even though he knew there were no strings. Should he push for more? He'd tried that in the past and had scuttled those tenuous romances. Best, he thought, regardless of how he felt, to just go along with the routine, and if she indicated a desire to take it to another level, he'd be all for it.

Now that he was spending nights there and the proverbial cat was out of the bag, Julie became included in their Sunday afternoon outings, while still excluded from Friday nights. Since Helen was a hiker, Julie had grown up with it and enjoyed it. She was a very athletic girl, on the tennis team, with aspirations of getting a tennis scholarship. She was determined to be in top shape, lifting weights in the school gym three afternoons a week. She demonstrated to Robert one day that she could knock out thirty pushups and ten pull ups. She even hinted that she could probably beat Robert arm wrestling, and he wasn't sure enough of himself to put it to the test.

Robert was schooled somewhat in history, but was never a history buff or a historian, so when Helen talked about her subject, which was also her passion, he was fascinated. She could talk about events that happened hundreds of years ago as if she'd been there, knew the characters and was caught up in the events of the day. Apparently it was mutual, for when he talked about writing and writers, she was caught up. She even took to reading some of the books he recommended. It was turning into a wonderful intellectual as well as sexual pairing. He was, if not happy, at least content, something he hadn't been in some time. Happy would require a deeper level of commitment, both of time and emotion. But, since things were going so well, it was probably only a matter of time.

Kelly actually wrote a letter, not one she mailed, but one she put as a Word attachment on an email. She described her school, the subjects, students, surroundings the dance of two languages. She wrote with her typical rich style, but now with a bit more maturity. She was widening her vistas, and these were turning her into an adult. She casually mentioned that she wasn't seeing the boy in question any longer, school work taking up too much time, and the boy not being serious enough about work. Playing, she mused, was for either the chronically idle or for highly structured down time. Keeping ones nose to the grindstone may be painful but it makes for a very sharp nose.

There was a mention of some new guy, someone she met while admiring the statue of David. As he was the closest to her while she was falling under the spell of that piece of art, he was the one she'd spoken to when she exclaimed, "Incredible!"

"American, I see," had been his response. He picked up on it right away. He introduced himself as Aldo, a student at the university. He was studying physics and math, planned to become a scientist and work at the new Large Hadron Collider. They had gone for coffee and gelato, talked for over an hour and exchanged phone numbers.

Robert had mixed feelings about this letter. On the surface he was happy she'd met someone who sounded like a decent sort of young man, but beneath the surface was a cauldron of conflicting feelings. In some ways he still considered her a kid, and he was afraid she'd blunder into a relationship that would cause her pain or lead her down some dead end path. There was also her role in his life, still undefined, but important, in a world of people coming and going, Kelly was the one constant, and he'd learned to depend on that consistency.

When he wrote her back, he was guardedly pleased, telling her he was happy for her, but cautioning her to proceed slowly, not to rush into anything with her eyes closed. He also mentioned his relationship with Helen, mentioned it actually in a cowardly way by simply saying he'd been going out with her.

Kelly's one response to that a few days later was her impression of Helen as a nice lady and a good teacher.

Robert was busy working on his dissertation at this point, but it was busy activity he could schedule, as opposed to the set hours his classes had been. It allowed him to work on a schedule that fit his personality, which was putting in long and late hours one day and relaxing the next. This also fit in with the new wrinkle in his romance. Helen had opened the door to a midweek tryst, dinner at her house, which naturally culminated in sex. This was good, he thought, just enough to make him feel like there was something steady there, but not so much that his work suffered.

They got along comfortably. They could talk for hours, and

she, like Robert, was very well read. The more they talked, the more common interests they discovered. Julie was, for the most part, friendly and cooperative, punctuated by occasional outbreaks of teen attitude and moodiness. Helen could usually diffuse her moods, mostly by not buying into her drama, but rather giving her a subtle reality check.

Then Robert got another letter from Kelly. "Incredible things are happening here. I've dated before, but this is something way different, much better, perhaps my first grown up thing. I'm watching this time in my life unfold, and it's taking the shape of a novel, one whose ending is still as much a mystery to me as it is to my protagonist. I'm including the first chapter." Then he started to read the opening pages.

"You can call me Jean. Oh, that's not my real name, but there are people at home I care about, and I have no idea how this adventure will play out. My plane has landed in Florence, my first time out of the United States, and I'm about to become an exchange student, or as the sophisticates say, I'm studying abroad.

"I'm a junior in high school, from a small central California town, not far from the famed Silicon Valley." He continued reading.

This was fascinating. She was writing it in the first person and in the present tense, a tricky style for any writer, a bold move for one so young who is starting her first novel. He read the five pages she'd sent, and he determined that it was working. Robert was anxious to see the subsequent installments.

He thought about sending these pages to Sandy, but decided to wait to see the next chapter, and then a couple weeks later, he received an attachment, a few dozen more pages, covering her settling in and getting together with local kids, a group who were on the surface more adult and sophisticated than her American friends, but once she got to know them, it became clear that they were rootless, hedonistic, and sad because they lacked purpose in their lives. She ended where she decided to give up this crowd, fun as they were, and to explore the fabled city. She ended where a young man spoke to her in front of the statue of David.

Damn, he thought, nothing about this mysterious young man and the incredible things happening to her.

This was enough, he thought, so he combined the two selections and pasted it to an email to Sandy, saying he thought this might be a novel in progress.

Within twenty-four hours Sandy had gotten back to him. "I'm already drawn in, and this is just the part building to something, the real plot of the story, and it sounds like a romance. If she keeps this up, she'll have a hit first novel. Keep them coming." Then she added, almost shyly, "It looks like this little affair has become something more. It's a steady thing now, an understanding. It's looking more and more long term."

Well, Sandy has a new "thing," and Robert also has his new "thing," and that's what the intricate mating dance has been reduced to in the twenty-fist century, some kind of thing. So, everyone is doing his or her thing, but no one falls in love, makes a commitment, whatever. He read the note, shook his head and hit delete, thinking how the delete key is a metaphor for today's human interactions.

He sent an email to Kelly, saying that Sandy agrees with him and that she is in the process of writing an outstanding novel. He warned her not to think about publishing success or anything like that, just concentrate on continuing to tell her story.

Julie had become one of his best students, taking to writing, but while other students wrote personal essays or short fiction, Julie wrote essays connected with her science class. They were quite good, and they explained concepts in a way that someone unfamiliar with the subject would understand, a good foundation for a future science writer or scientist who wishes to popularize the subject.

More than anything else, she seemed to respect him and like him. From what he could tell, and teenagers were always somewhat inscrutable to him, she seemed to approve of him as her mother's boyfriend. He figured he was ahead of the game, since if the kid wasn't on board, these things seldom lasted. Naturally, that brought up a question he was afraid to ask himself and reluctant to even consider. Was there something deeper in this affair, something possibly lasting? Helen had set the boundaries from the start, but that was before they had become closer. As much as he wondered where she stood on this, he questioned himself. Was he just lonely and desperate for something secure? He really hadn't fully gotten over Sandy, and there was something else. When he thought of Helen, there wasn't that hunger to be with her constantly, to be with her for life, to build all the complexity of a long term family. He really cared for her, but what did that mean?

Somewhere deep inside his subconscious there was a feeling he identified as love, he knew it, knew what it felt like, but when he tried to put a face or a name on it, it became like a reflection in a pool after a pebble was tossed in. Something was eating at him, and he was too out of touch with his inner feelings to own it.

Robert was also surprised that Kelly didn't respond immediately to his news about Sandy's reaction. He realized he was living the feeling of a successful first novelist vicariously, like the Olympic coach who beams when his protégé wins a gold medal. While he could understand, if not approve, of his reaction, he couldn't believe that she wouldn't be gushing about it, but he didn't want to press the issue, so he waited for her response.

19

It took a week and a half before he got an email from Kelly. It started out sounding rather bland. "I'm so pleased that Sandy likes my book. I think it is getting better as my situation changes. I've attached another chapter. Things are happening here that I didn't plan or anticipate. It's all kinds of overwhelming and pretty damn exciting. I really don't have any labels for it yet. Anyway, read what I've written, and if you like it forward it to Sandy."

Talk about setting up anticipation. Robert could hardly wait to start reading, and he neglected his grading of papers until he'd read it over twice. My god! He thought. She's in the middle of a full blown love affair, and it sounds serious. The girl who had always prided herself on being in control seemed to be caught up, dazzled, almost giddy, even though "giddy" could never seriously be applied to Kelly. She didn't say she was in love. In fact she seemed to go out of the way to duck the issue, but love seemed to permeate the story.

The writing was exciting, besides being really compelling, so why was he bothered by it? He kept thinking that she was so young and that this was a sojourn from her real life, a bubble that would burst in a few months. Was he afraid that her heart would be broken, or was he afraid that she'd discard everything they'd, no she'd worked for and marry this guy and stay in Italy? What if she never came back? What if the writing ended with a wedding announcement?

Sandy raved about it. It was, in her words, "hot." Every romantic young single woman and girl would be drooling over the pages of this, dreaming of a handsome, suave Italian who would come along and sweep her off her feet. In fact, Sandy added, "If I met this guy, I'd jump his bones in a heartbeat."

She also said something else that Robert hadn't even thought of. "I think the guy's a fiction. I think she may have met some guy, but she's using a lot of literary license to make him prince charming. He can't be this good."

Somehow that made Robert feel better. Also, he knew she was capable of something like that, working her character like a skilled artist works colors on a canvas. He's probably just a charming college boy she'd made into a hero for all those starry-eyed girls who will line up to buy the book.

But he surprisingly didn't have much time to think about Kelly and her future literary success, including his important contribution. His daily dance card was full, what with a full time teaching job, a dissertation in progress, his own writing and reviews and an active romance. He'd actually bought a smart phone to help him keep track of all he had to do each week. Wrapped up in his own life, he hadn't noticed that his mother was spending more and more time with the man she'd been casually dating, that is until he got a call one evening.

"Hi honey. Hope I'm not disturbing anything."

He assured her that he was just grading papers and that he always had time for dear old mom.

"I got some pretty big news."

"From the tone of your voice, it sounds like good news."

"Marty proposed." She paused a moment to let that sink in before continuing. "He's selling his business and retiring with enough money to really retire. He's got his eye on a lovely romantic cottage in Carmel."

Robert felt himself slipping into a combination of shock and sensory overload. "Marriage! Out of the blue. Carmel! Why there?"

"Calm down, honey. It's not out of the blue. We've been dating for over a year, seriously for months. You just haven't noticed, or asked for that matter. And, Carmel isn't exactly the end of the world. It's what, maybe less than an hour's drive. Would that be too far to visit your mother?"

"Of course not. It's not that. I mean, marriage. You're not some girl, you're a mother."

"Good observation, and I'm pushing fifty, not quite ready for the shawl and rocking chair. Been single too long. I'm at the point where I want a nice, secure relationship."

"Well, he seems like an OK guy, but..."

"But nothing. He's more than an OK guy. He's loving, considerate and dependable. He really listens to a woman, cares about what she thinks. Not to be mean, but a bit more of that might make your romances last a little longer."

That hurt, mostly because there was some truth in it. Now that

143

he was in the home stretch for his doctorate, he was starting to realize just how self-absorbed he'd become. For a minute he flashed on Helen and how being more like this Marty might be the key to taking things up a notch. He ended up responding to his mother with approval and encouragement, even though he still had reservations. When he got off the phone, he resolved to get to know this guy a bit better. Let's see, his business was, ah, a car dealership. Must have gotten a good sum. Late fifties, thinning hair, thickening waist, big car salesman's smile.

He'd get a chance to know him better at dinner the following week at his mom's place. We'll see, he thought.

He took his mother's advice and started paying more attention to the signals Helen was sending. Rather than commenting on whatever he said, he forced himself to just listen, soon realizing that most often she wasn't looking for advice, just a good listener.

He mentioned that to his mother at dinner, and she laughed. "You can teach an old dog new tricks." When she shared the joke with Marty, he laughed also, adding, "When you're young and good looking, these things don't matter as much as when you get old and paunchy, like me." Then they both got another good laugh at his expense.

Considering everything, Robert thought, this guy wasn't bad. Naturally, no one was quite good enough for his mother, not even his father, well, in retrospect, especially his father. Still, if the guy makes her happy, and it would be hard not to be happy in Carmel, they had his blessings.

Over the next couple of weeks Robert thought that maybe his new more sensitive approach was working. Helen was giving him more of her time, almost more than his schedule could handle. He was feeling proud of himself for being a more enlightened man.

But, one evening, curled up on the couch with him, glass of red wine in her hand, soft music on the stereo, she confessed something. "I like how you and Julie are getting along." That got his attention. She continued. "You're giving her your time and attention, taking an interest in her interests and including her on our outings. You've become sort of a father figure to her, more so than her father, who was always either at work or on the golf course. Anyway, you've probably noticed that her attitude, well, she has less attitude lately."

He had noticed, and it hadn't occurred to him that he had anything to do with it. In truth, at first he disliked her, but he'd grown to like the kid. She was smart and really excited about going out in nature. If things continued to progress with Helen, having the kid around wouldn't be bad.

There was another lull between missives from Kelly. In the next, her message to him was short. School was interesting, and there were several kids she'd become friendly with. Her Italian was improving and she wasn't really homesick. She'd done every museum and old cathedral in Florence, plus taking weekend jaunts to Sienna and other places. She said that these next two chapters, while fiction, kind of reflected her experiences. There was the attachment: two chapters, thirty some pages. Damn, this kid was prolific.

He sat down to read it and was amazed. She was recounting a relationship that teetered on the edge between a teen romance and a mature love affair. She unpacked each event, each experience as if it were one of those Russian dolls, seemingly endless layers of meaning. This from a sixteen year old kid. In a way it made him jealous. He'd never experienced anything as deep as that, not even with Sandy. If this is more truth than fiction, she was lost to him and to California. She'd never return from something like that.

Still, he reminded himself that she'd specified that this was a fictional account. No matter how he tried to rationalize it, what he was reading bothered him. She had become such a big part of his life for almost six years, more than a student, more than a friend, something like family. She was also one of the main studies in his dissertation. Because of her, he'd taken on that newspaper after school project among other assignments that caused him to become such a valuable teacher. Because of her nagging, he'd enrolled in grad school, so whatever university position awaited him would be in part thanks to Kelly. A huge part of his life would be cut away should she decide not to return.

But then he remembered that she was a minor as well as being bound by exchange student rules and visa restrictions. Yet, this guy was a college student, early twenties, an adult. Robert didn't know the Italian laws governing age of consent to marriage.

The people in his life were a big part of his security. His close friends had scattered, Sandy had moved away, his mother will marry and start a new life and Kelly was a big question mark. He had Helen, or at least a tenuous hold on Helen, but what would happen when he got his doctorate? Would he be offered a job far away, and if so, would he be willing to give up what he had and start over. It was crazy. He was still a young man, not yet thirty; he should be at a stage where change and adventure were tantalizing, not intimidating. What made him nervous and insecure? Was it his father leaving them, his revolving door history with women? At one point the irony of a possible university position in the New York area occurred to him, now that he had a relationship here at home and not in the east. That sort of offer would just be his luck.

He resolved, rather weakly actually, to take what life offers him. His career is the most important thing at the moment. He'd spent his entire adult life preparing for and working toward some professional goals. If he had the chance to work at a university, he'd be foolish to stay at a high school, particularly after Kelly graduates. Still, he did make a difference in a few students' lives, motivating them to seek higher education, helping them to frame their thoughts clearly and to communicate them effectively. Of course, doing this at the university level meant that all, rather than a few, would be motivated. Paying the price to attend college made that a given.

Robert knew he had a tendency to over-think things, to look at every angle, every facet of a problem or decision. Yet, he had the nagging feeling that a big piece of the puzzle, the decisions he would face, was missing. There were things he hadn't considered, but he couldn't put his finger on them. He had some kind of mental block that was driving him nuts.

He danced around his dilemma one night with Helen. "When I get my doctorate, it would make sense to find a university position."

She agreed that it would make sense. Why, after all, waste all that education.

"But, what if the only job takes me far from here, far from you?"

She had been cuddled up to him, but now she pulled away and sat up straight. She pulled her knees up on the couch, put her arms around them and faced him. "I've considered this. I like you, perhaps more than I originally planned. Yet, as I told you, I'm not ready to settle down again, perhaps one day. When I do, you could well be the one, but that's all up in the air. You have yourself, your career to consider. That should come first. I'd hate to have you give us something just for me, and then perhaps things wouldn't work out and we'd go our separate ways."

"So, you're saying that we're temporary, so I shouldn't consider our relationship?"

She shook her head. "No, that's not what I meant. We could be the real thing, but that's a big maybe and also down the road a bit. Right now we're dating, having a romantic affair. That's a good thing, but it's not a total commitment. I don't want to promise anything I might not be able to deliver."

That wasn't a really big help. He was no closer to a resolution than before.

They might be permanent; they might not. He might be better off chasing a dream or staying put in something secure, satisfying and familiar.

The next morning, he didn't hang around her place. He remembered a huge state park not too far away, Henry Coe, and he needed to be alone in nature, so he drove up and started walking. Miles of trails stretched out before him, and he really didn't care which he took. By the time he'd gotten back to his car, hours later, the immediate answer was clear. It was too damn soon to worry about it. He was committed to his job until the end of the school year, about the same time he'd finish his program. Then he'd apply for jobs, starting with the closest universities. He could land one at San Jose State and actually commute from where he was living. He had already taught an extension class for them, and they seemed to like him. He could also find one somewhere on the central coast and be close to family, friends and Helen. Kelly would likely come back, and she might opt to attend whatever college he was teaching at. She did have a long history of being his student. Worst case, he get a great job at some distance and start a new life, find a new love, live happily with a wife, kids and a great job. But all of that was months away. Don't obsess, he told himself over and over and over again.

By the time he got home, he'd given himself the message and he felt better. He had too much on his plate to waste time with a menu of what ifs.

147

20

His graduate adviser was impressed with his work, but she seemed uncomfortable about something. Robert asked her if there was a problem, and the professor said that his major case study was, and she obviously struggled to find better words for it, too good to be true. She wondered if this was a real student or a composite. Robert laughed and pulled out his file of Kelly's clippings. The professor, the mother of a teenaged girl, recognized Kelly's name right away. Then she put the obvious together. "You're the great teacher she dedicates her work to. My god, what a find she must have been."

While most people would assume that Kelly had been his Dr. Frankenstein's monster, his creation, the professor realized that talent like that was natural and that Robert had found a gem and had simply done a great job of polishing it.

"The work you've done with this kid alone is enough to get this accepted. And, I'm thinking that if you rewrite this, it would make an excellent text book, one you'd publish for your classes at whatever university is lucky enough to grab you."

He was elated. When he got home, he wanted to tell someone. He called Helen before he remembered that this was the night she took Julie to karate practice, followed by dinner. His mother was obviously out with Marty, as she often was these days. Then he thought of Laurie, realizing he hadn't spoken to her since they'd seen Kelly off at the airport.

After asking how she'd been, he told her simply that he'd gotten good news about his dissertation. She suggested he come by for dinner so they could catch up. Good. He needed someone to talk with, to share the events in his life.

Laurie was pleased at his news and pleased that Kelly's successes were such a big part of it. Naturally that directed the conversation toward her daughter. "You've heard from her, I know. What do you think?"

He wasn't sure how to respond, as he had a mix of thoughts. "The book she's writing is wonderful. She's shared that with you?"

"Some of it. What about the boyfriend?"

"I guessing it bothers you. I know it does me."

"I'm just wondering if she'd ready for a relationship this, well, this mature. The guy is in his early twenties. I don't want her to get hurt."

"Or," he added, "Rush off and do something foolish."

"You mean, like marry the guy?"

He nodded. And then, needed to say something, "She's on the verge of a brilliant career. I'd hate to see her mess that up."

"And," Laurie added with a trace of a sly smile. "You've got a big emotional investment in her." His discomfort at that must have showed, as she added, "Being the subject of your dissertation and all."

He tried to be philosophical about it. "Well, it's fall, and she'll be home after the holidays. It's not that far away."

Then, after an awkward silence, she asked about his personal life. "I seem to recall you're dating a fellow teacher. Tell me about her."

Robert gave her a quick synopsis, mentioning the subject Helen taught, their common interests, her daughter Julie and the fact that they were just dating, nothing more serious.

When Laurie heard about Julie, she asked how old Helen was, and when Robert answered, she smiled. "You're girlfriend's my age. You get along well with the kid. That's a plus for most mothers. You sure this isn't serious?"

He assured her it wasn't, not specifying that it was Helen's call on that front.

"What does Kelly say about this Helen?"

Odd question, he thought. "She hasn't said much. Mostly that she knows who she is and that she seems OK. "

"No romantic advice?"

"None, thank goodness." They both got a laugh, considering how out of character is was for Kelly not to have a strong opinion and the need to voice it.

Strangely, Robert hadn't thought about how these two women were just about the same age. He looked at Laurie with fresh eyes, not just at Kelly's mother. She was an attractive woman, and she looked a lot like her daughter. Both were tall and rather big boned, but while Kelly still had the slim body of a teen, Laurie was more filled out, not fat by any means but a bit fuller of figure. Robert realized that had Laurie been a stranger he'd met at some party, he'd likely have asked for her number.

That was the wrong thing for him to contemplate late in the evening, the similarities between mother and daughter. He dreamed that he was awakened when the light switched on. There in his bedroom stood Laurie and Kelly, dressed in skimpy nightgowns, grinning at him. As he pulled the covers up over himself, he heard Laurie say, "Don't be coy, Robert. You know you want this."

He woke with a start, feeling rattled and dirty. He didn't even try to go back to sleep, but rather went to his computer and spent the rest of the night working on the dissertation.

On their next evening together Helen was quite effusive about Robert's work, saying how proud of him she was and that she'd soon have to call him Doctor Cutie. When he mentioned he'd called the other night, forgetting their weekly obligation, he turned to Julie, who was somehow watching TV, listening to her mp3 player and doing homework at the same time, motioned that he wanted to talk, and waited until she unplugged one ear."

"What?" She asked.

"Nothing special. Just wondering about that karate class. Black belt?"

"No way, not even close. But," and she got this twinkle in her eyes, "Treat my mom right or I'll karate kick you where it hurts." Then she laughed, plugged in her ear bud and went back to weird multitasking.

She was bright and funny, and he had no problem including her in their dates. However, he never expected to spend a day alone with her. One nice weekend, when Robert and Helen had planned to take a hike to a local waterfall, she complained of a bad case of allergies. She was sneezing and blowing her nose, and her eyes were red. Robert was about to excuse himself and go about the day alone when Helen suggested that since Julie was looking forward to getting out, he might take her.

While he liked the girl, spending the day with her without the mom sounded uncomfortable. He could talk to her, but he didn't think they'd have anything to talk about for an entire afternoon, and could already feel the uncomfortable silence.

However, Julie made a suggestion. "I know you're big on biking, and I'd rather bike than hike. How about we do that long trail that runs along Highway 101, you know, Morgan Hill to San Jose?"

Now, that sounded like a plan. He loved that trail, the long rides without traffic, and he knew that while they were moving, conversation would be at a minimum. They could just get lost in the sensation of pedaling, wind in their hair. He agreed.

He wasn't sure what she could handle, so he started with a vigorous pace, but well below competitive. She was staying right with him, having breath enough to comment on the scenery, the day and random observations. He pushed it up to aerobic, and she hung in there.

After a couple hours they were crossing a street, and he saw a burger place down the block. "Would you like lunch?"

"Great. I'm freakin' starving."

They pulled off. The place had outside seating, so they sat under an umbrella and had their sandwiches. Then, from out of the blue, "So, what's with you and mom?"

His defenses went up, but he calmly answered, "I'm not sure what you mean."

"Well, like are you going to marry her?"

It took him some time to compose his words. "We're not at that place right now. I mean, what does your mother say?"

"She doesn't. She thinks that grown up stuff is none of a kid's business."

"Well, I guess we should respect that, both of us." That, he hoped, would end the subject.

"Come on. Just between you and me. I won't say a word to her. Wouldn't dare. Do you want to marry her?"

He had always talked straight to her, as he did to most students, so he was stuck, unable to put off her kid questions. However, he had to walk a fine line. "Ok, I can't let myself go there. You probably know he doesn't want to get married again. So, anyway, I know that's off the table, so I don't think about it."

"But if you could?"

"I can't think about hypothetical questions. You know what

151

that means?"

She nodded, so he went on. "It's like what if you won the lottery. Unlikely to happen, so you really don't know what you'd do."

"it's not the same." She wasn't going to let it go.

He scrambled to eat the last of the fries in order to buy a bit of time. "Has there ever been a boy you really liked, but who wasn't interested?" She nodded, so he pushed the metaphor. So, what would you do if he suddenly came up and asked you to marry him, you being in ninth grade and hardly knowing him?"

"Wow, I don't know. I'd have to think, I mean if it really happened."

"See, it gets complicated when you add up a bunch of what ifs and try to decide how you'd react."

A different look came over her face. "So, it's about her, about what she wants or doesn't want, not what you want."

"Well, she set the ground rules. She let me know how she felt, and I said I was alright with that, so..."

"So what you want doesn't matter."

"Julie, people have to want the same thing. If I demanded something she wasn't ready for, we'd end up breaking up."

"She's the same way with you as with me. You know, like here is how it is and that's that."

He wasn't going to wiggle out of this, so he might as well own it, and while he was at it, there was a lesson to be taught. "Julie, in every relationship each person has more on less power. The person who is the least committed has the most power, because they have the least to lose if they break up. Are you following me?"

"Yeah. You care about her more than she cares about you, so you do it her way. There's this boy. He's like really lame, but he's all about me, follows me around with those big lovey eyes. If I'm nice to him, he gets all happy, and then I'm mean and he acts like a kicked puppy."

Ouch, Robert thought. "Well, it not quite like that. Your situation is totally unbalanced. Ours is almost balanced."

She was enjoying this, and he was thinking that a career as a prosecuting attorney wouldn't be unreasonable. She leaned her chair back and crossed her legs. "But there's one thing you haven't said, and it has nothing to do with what she wants. Do you love my mom?"

He could feel the nails going into his palms as he hung from the cross Julie had been constructing. "I think we've taken this conversation too far. This is between your mom and me, and I don't think she'd like you poking into it."

"Come on. You said you'd always be honest with me, and I promise that what happens here, stays here. By not answering, it sounds like you are saying yes you do love her."

"Ok, Julie, and this has to be the end of it. It's another hypothetical. I know that kind of relationship isn't in the cards, so I don't let myself go there."

"That's a cop out. Whether you go there or not, you have feelings. Do you love her?"

It was a simple enough question, but he couldn't answer it. He searched his feelings and he honestly didn't know the answer. She was staring impatiently at him, waiting. Finally, he put his hands up. "I really don't know. I'm not being evasive. I really don't know. I like her a lot, but, well..."

"You don't know how you feel." She seemed incredulous. You've been with her for months, and you don't know? You used to have this other girlfriend, the one who moved away. Do you still love her?"

He opened his mouth to answer, but there was no answer. He shook his head, defeated. "I'm not sure."

"Not sure. You were in love with her, right?"

He was facing something he had somehow avoided. "I, I think so."

"Think so. Wow, you don't even know how you feel. I mean, like you love somebody or you don't."

"It's complicated."

"That's what adults always say when they don't have an answer. You know, you're a really nice guy, but you're so messed up. Don't you even think about stuff like that?"

She got up and tossed her trash in the can and grabbed her bike, indicating that the last had been a rhetorical question. As they got on the bikes, and as a concession to her, he said, "You've given me a lot to think about, things I've put off thinking about."

153

21

She had indeed giving him much to think about. That night, he couldn't keep his mind on anything else. What did he feel for Helen? It was affection, caring, need perhaps, but was it love. Could he picture himself living with her night and day, sharing all the little details of married life for years and years. In some ways it appealed to him, but there wasn't that emotion that grabs the heart, that urge to get down on one knee and swear he couldn't live without her. There was also children. He always thought he'd have them someday, but Helen had been there and wasn't interested in doing it again.

And when he thought about Sandy, it wasn't much clearer. He really cared about her and was devastated when she left, but was it really love? If it had been, wouldn't he has chucked it all and taken his chances in New York? But then if it had been real on her part, wouldn't she have done the same, turned down the job and looked for something close to home?

Julie's comment had implied another unspoken question. Had he ever really been in love. He asked himself in the darkness of his room, in the middle of the night, and his answer was a vast silence. He was stunned at his level of denial. Was he some kind of emotional zombie? In desperation he thought that perhaps the real thing had yet to come along. Yes that had to be it, but if so, what of Helen? He drifted off into a troubled sleep.

All one needs to do to avoid deep introspection is to keep busy, fill every hour of every day. A hamster in a wheel doesn't have a contemplative look on its face. Robert met with his adviser, taught his five classes a day, classes that generated lots of writing that had to be corrected individually, saw Helen two nights a week and one afternoon, biked one day with the local club, worked on his dissertation and wrote articles and reviews. That allowed him a few quiet dinners each week, plus an hour late at night for a glass of wine and some TV entertainment. It was only on those troubled, sleepless nights that issues surrounding his emotional, personal life surfaced, and since he was usually exhausted by day's end, these were few. Robert was the twenty-first century man, living on a schedule, externally focused.

He did occasionally have dinner and drinks with George, who had an arrangement with his wife allowing them both a couple nights to themselves. George mentioned a chain restaurant in the mall, one that also had a bar and suggested they meet. Robert needed to come up for air, and he figured a couple hours of relaxation wouldn't throw him off too much.

He arrived a bit early, sat down at the bar and ordered an ale. Then his cell phone rang. "My son twisted his ankle at that damn skateboard park, and I've got to run him over to the ER to have it checked out. Sorry man."

He said he was cool with that, and since already here, he'd eat and drink for a bit.

A woman sitting two stools away spoke up. "Girlfriend stand you up?"

"What? Ah, no. That was my principal. We're friends, meet for dinner now and then. Family emergency."

"Principal? Ah, got it. I know you. You're Mr. Spagnolo, the English teacher."

"Yes, but how did you... do I know you."

She stuck out her hand. "Christine, Christine Baker, English four." She cocked her head and watched him, and as he wasn't responding, she added, "Sixth period, senior English, what, four years ago."

Like sprinkles of leaves on a windy fall day, the pieces started to drift down and form a pattern. "Yes, yes. I didn't recognize you. You were this skinny kid, long straight hair."

She laughed. "Cross country. Greyhound thin. Don't run much these days. Guess I've gotten fat, huh?"

He looked at her again. She was very curvaceous, but anything but fat. "No, you look great, grown up and all that, but what are you doing here, I mean in a bar, drinking?"

"I'm twenty-one now. That seventeen year old has grown up, gone to community college and am an accountant for the Ford dealer, and I'm going to buy you a drink."

Before he could object, she'd called the bartender and ordered another round, margarita for her, ale for him. She held up her glass for a toast, smiled and said, "The word man."

"The what?"

"Didn't you know. That's what all the kids called you. You were always about using the best word. I'm guessing they still call you that. You didn't know. Cool."

The word man. He didn't know whether to consider it a compliment or not. However, this Christine was very outgoing and friendly and had grown into a lovely young woman, sexy actually.

After they finished their drinks, he said the next round was his, and then he remembered he hadn't eaten, so he asked her if she'd like to join him in the dining room. They grabbed their drinks without breaking the stride of their conversation. It was interesting, he thought, how they were talking of nothing special but managing to hold each other's interest.

A meal and another drink later, he reluctantly told her he needed to get home while he could still drive. She shook her head. "Too late. Can't let you drive. I live in the apartment complex behind the mall, walk over here for a drink often. We'll walk to my place for coffee or whatever happens." She followed that with a wide grin.

That was most certainly a proposition, exciting but uncomfortable. "I'm sort of seeing someone," he said, a bit too weakly.

"Well, I'm sort of seeing someone too. Serious? Big commitment? She's not with you."

"No commitment. We're just dating steadily." Then thinking about it, added, "Part time, actually."

"Same with me. Who knows who your girlfriend is with, or my boyfriend for that matter. Come on, I won't take advantage of you, unless you let me."

The cool fall night air woke him up a bit, and he was both nervous and quite excited. There was something about her, this animal attraction. He realized they had nothing in common, but he could no more break the spell than instantly transport himself to his bed.

It was a modest one bedroom apartment, inexpensive furniture, big screen TV, nice stereo, framed prints on the wall, a young single person's apartment. She went to the refrigerator and poured them both glasses of Chardonnay. "You know, this is kind of like an old fantasy."

When he asked what she meant, she said that she'd had a bit of a crush on him in high school, several of the girls did. He was cute, really young looking for a teacher. She'd wondered what it would be like to do him. Then she added, with that wicked grin, "Maybe tonight I'll finally find out."

She was so exciting. He could feel the heat and was turned on. For a brief minute he felt guilty for cheating on Helen, but then he rationalized it by reminding himself that she'd insisted on no commitment. While he very much doubted it, he consoled himself by saying that she could well have another affair going on the nights she didn't see him.   Rationalizations when one is highly aroused don't have to good ones, just remotely plausible. He let her lead him to her bed.

He'd had lots of romantic sex with girlfriends, but this was different, pure sex, no romance, no pretending a relationship, just wild, uninhibited sex, and it felt better than he could ever have imagined.

Afterward, as he lay panting beside her, he looked over and for a moment saw the girl in his class. That made him shiver. "Oh my god."

"What?"

"Ex-student. What am I thinking?"

"Maybe you're thinking you wish you'd done this four years ago. Hell, that was a long time ago. We're just two adults having a good time. Relax. Man you are really old school."

Over breakfast they had to deal with the awkward moment. He brought it up, mainly because she hadn't. "What now? Do we see each other again, or is this a one night stand?"

"Hum. It was a one night stand, but we could do it again. My so-called boyfriend hangs around here a lot, and he sometimes picks up the phone, so why don't we exchange emails, and we'll see what happens. No promises; open ended. Deal?"

It was almost too good to be true. He wasn't obligated to see her again, but if he wanted to, she was open for it, and it was the best sex he'd had in he couldn't remember how long.

Then she added something she thought was terribly funny, but freaked him out. "Maybe I should get in touch with some of my old classmates, bring them over for an orgy. Some of them thought you were pretty hot."

"That's not funny, and I hope you don't broadcast it. Nothing against you, but as a teacher in a pretty small town, my reputation. You understand."

"Chill. I'm just playing with you. But, if you want to really turn the babes on, you've gotta lose the geek look, particularly that hair. Beautiful dark hair like that, all short and neat with a damn part." She reached around his head and ran her hand down the back of his hair to his neck. "Let it grow down to here. Then the sides, over the ears, no part. You'd look like a rock star. Trust me."

Geek, he thought. Not flattering. Old school, too. Uptight was another term that came to mind. He saw himself as a conservative geek, a very uncool man. Hell, he might as well have horn rim glasses and a pocket calculator. The hair, well, why not. It would be a start.

The next time he saw Helen he asked her what she thought of his hair: should he change the style, did it make him look boring. She looked at him as if she hadn't really seen him before and shook her head. "You have a nice, neat, professional look. Don't worry about it. You're at least a decade from a mid-life crisis."

She said those simply words, but in his mind he heard "boring." She liked him to look boring, perhaps so she didn't have to worry about him.

Then he asked her. "Do you ever get restless. You know, look at other guys, want to play the field?"

"Good god, Rob. I scarcely have time for you. Hell, you're busy too, so you know. Between the job, taking care of the house, running Julie to practice, karate plus time at the gym." She stopped and just shook her head again.

Well, that was what they had, clear, simple and naked. They were two busy professionals with a part time relationship they squeezed in between the important chores of life. Perhaps, he thought, the era of great romances is long gone. It's now just pragmatic, work until five, gym until six, dinner at seven, chores until ten and sex from ten to eleven. What happened to the twenty-one year old, filled with passion for teaching and passion for passion? Still in his twenties, he was feeling middle aged. He knew he was buried in work until summer. Then he'd have his doctorate and he would sit down and actually plan the rest of his life, and it wouldn't just be trudging through the days. In less than eight months he would start opening new doors, and if Helen wasn't willing to walk through them with him, he'd find someone who would.

Naturally, he thought about getting in touch with Christine, but with so much on his plate, did he want the additional complications. For some reason, he believed that the boyfriend was merely a place holder, and that he could move into that spot easily. But, if so, what would that mean? It had been great sex, but they had nothing else in common. Also, he realized that every women he'd been with had been his age or older. She was barely twenty-one, working at just a job, no long range career plans. He thought of James Joyce. That kind of relationship had worked for him.

For Robert, being busy was easy, making decisions wasn't. He put it off for a day when his calendar was less full. In the mean time he got a long awaited email from Kelly. "There is something about Europe and Europeans. Maybe it's all the history over here. I don't know, but I feel my life expanding. I had been, as they say, provincial, a small town American girl. I feel like I'm becoming a bit more sophisticated, but maybe I'm just being affected. I do know that whatever is going on, it's making my writing better, at least to me. I'll let you judge, and don't pull any punches. If this sucks, tell me so."

Attached to the email was a few dozen more pages, single spaced. "*The hours and days tick away with a hallow sound, like the measured footsteps of death. There is a day circled on my calendar, a day this ends and I go back to my old life, a life now too small and too empty. He looks in my eyes and we talk, but never about that day. What is he thinking? What will he say, and what will I say when we face each other for the last time in a busy, impersonal airport?*"

Robert couldn't put it down. So much emotion, passion, the type of passion missing in his life. Did she really mean it, he thought, or was this just literary. If this was really her feelings, she'd founds something rare, and as much as he detested the idea, he couldn't blame her if she never returned.

These feelings were only in her manuscript. Her letters gave no hint, other than how travel had broadened her, opened her eyes and improved her artistic vision. What was the truth here? He'd have to wait to find out.

Somewhere between what Kelly described in her writing and what he had with Helen was that one night stand with Christine.

159

Maybe if he gave it a chance, there would be something deeper he could mine. After sitting on the fence for much too long, he decided to contact Christine, throw caution to all the winds and find out if there was something beyond a night of great sex. He emailed his phone number to her, asking her to call.

"Is that Robert, the word guy. I thought you'd died, or worse, got married."

He apologized for the long delay and asked if they could get together for a date, dinner perhaps.

There was a long silence on her end, but finally, "I'd like that, really, but right now things have heated up a bit with my guy, and I want to see if that's going anywhere before I start a marathon fuck fest with you. Look, I've got your number, so if it cools again, and it's done that before, you'll be my first call. By the way, how's the hair looking?"

He laughed weakly, disappointed. "Growing, a bit longer now. Car hardly wait for your opinion."

"Don't forget about me word guy. This romantic shit tends to come and go, so who knows what next week will bring."

While he was listening, he'd scribbled on his note pad, "A day late and a dollar short, like always." After he'd hung up, he pulled off the note and taped it up above his computer, a reminder. Under it he wrote "Carpe diem."

The next time he met George for dinner and drinks he had to tell about about a sexy gal he'd met and spent the night with. He was still uncomfortable enough about her being an ex-student that he left that part out. He didn't want George to think that maybe he'd had something going with her as a student or had even wanted to.

A voice in his head said that this was stupid. The woman was an adult, and after all every woman had been an underage girl at some time. Still, that was a murky area he had no desire to visit.

George, long married, seemed to be getting a vicarious rush out of the story. As an afterthought, Robert mentioned the latest from Kelly. "This kid has matured as a writer. She could have a blockbuster novel on her hands."

George wanted to know what it was about, and Robert told him that it seemed to be loosely based on her experiences in Italy, a

160

romance, a coming of age story, really exceptional writing.

"Apparently the girl's got herself a boyfriend over there."

"That's what she says, but it's not clear how much of the story is fiction and how much is her affair, romance I mean."

22

The holiday season was upon them, leaves turning color, a chill in the air, and soon there would be most of a week off for Thanksgiving, a preview of the three week break for Christmas and New Year. This was the loneliest time of the year, Robert thought, for someone who isn't surrounded by loved ones. He had Helen, but more and more he was realizing that their arrangement was a dead end and emotionally bland. They were little more than friends with benefits, and while the three of them spent days that felt like family activities, they were not and probably never would be a family, not in the traditional sense he envisioned.

He did have family, just his mother, who was getting married in early December. She and her husband to be had invited him to come down to Carmel, which is likely what he'd do, maybe spending Christmas eve with Helen before heading down early Christmas day. He thought of Laurie, considering her almost family, but she was seeing someone and would likely be spending time with him.

Robert's plans for the holidays were adequate, but not great, not something to look enthusiastically forward to. It was at this time each year that he thought that by nature he was the kind of man who needed his own family, a loving wife, some kids, perhaps the cottage with the white picket fence. It was a corny throwback to an imagined ideal time, but deep inside that's who he was.

He was sorry Kelly wasn't going to be back before winter break. She could have left when the Italian school went on holiday, but she opted to stay until the day before the second semester started back home, the second week in January, obviously grabbing every precious moment with her boyfriend. It was odd, he thought, that she never sent a photo of him or even anything personal, other than in the book chapters. If she cared that much about him, it would make sense for her to show him off a bit. Women, even young ones, are always a bit difficult to understand, which, he supposed, was part of their charm.

The students were getting restless, like a tribe of hungry headhunters, their minds already on vacation, and Robert needed something to catch their interest. He assigned an essay, but instead of making detailed notes on each one, he circled a few words on each, scribbling an alternative for one of them. Then he handed them back, and the kids looked around at each other and then him, obviously in confusion.

He gave them a few moments to build the suspense, and then he called for their attention. "The difference between writing that grabs the reader and is remembered and writing that bores is often just the choice of a word. I've circled words that fall flat, and in one case I substituted an alternative. That's just a suggestion. There are other words that would work just as well. You're assignment, due before Thanksgiving, is to go over your work and search for just exactly the right words to fill those places. Each word you use is important, and I know, because I'm the word guy."

That startled them, and they looked around at each other and snickered. Yep, he thought, they still call me that, and they still think I don't know it.

The students came through just as he thought they would. Not having the huge chore of rewriting, just having to focus on fixing a few words, for the most part they dug deep, obviously trying many words before deciding on just the right one. Naturally, the slackers simply slacked, but the majority, the students who were already thinking about the writing entrance test at their chosen university, really pulled out just the right word. Moreover, they seemed damned proud of their accomplishments, some offering to read their passages, a success, and something he would now incorporate into all of his classes, perhaps even add to his dissertation.

He spent Thanksgiving in Carmel with his mother and her intended, in a large cottage on a hillside, surrounded by trees. By the end of the evening, he had to admit to himself that the guy was totally acceptable. He obviously loved Pat, and they had all sorts of great plans. She would be working far less, and they would use the time to travel. They were already planning a honeymoon in France, followed shortly thereafter by a trip to Peru. He'd sold the business he'd worked hard to build, and he sold it for enough to live comfortably. Pat could probably quit working altogether, but she enjoyed work and liked the independence having her own money brought her. What the hell, they even squeezed each other's hands under the table.

He returned the next morning, driving leisurely up the coast before turning inland, and since it was a long weekend for the schools, he had plans with Helen for a good share of the weekend. They were both tired from work and waiting to exhale and relax a bit. There was the typical dinner and a film, and on Saturday they drove to a park high in the Oakland hills for a few hours in the deep redwood forest.

Without the stress of school for a few days, their love making was less hurried and more satisfying. Yes, he thought, it's too early to give up on this. There may well be a future with her.

The period between Thanksgiving and Christmas when everyone's mind is in holiday mode, particularly students, is a difficult time to get serious work done. But, Robert, after his success with the right word, was on a roll. He assigned a writing exercise and stipulated how it was to be done on a couple dozen slips of paper. One said, write it in second person, present tense. Another said to do it third person limited and so on. He even had instructions to do it in blank verse, as a news story, something set in the future or in some historical period. He passed the basket around, and each student reached in and got the luck of the draw. Most were amused, some perplexed. He told them they could conference with him if they were in doubt about how to proceed. Several took him up on it. Final drafts, he announced, would be due before winter break.

Just as he thought, most of them considered this fun, like a puzzle to be solved.

In fact, within a few days, he'd received calls from a few parents complimenting him on getting their kids motivated. Apparently, they were actually telling their folks about how much fun his class was. He shared this with George on their next dine out, and the principal said, "Here you are, becoming a superstar teacher just before leaving us."

Robert was taken back. "Leaving. I'm not leaving, at least I hope not."

"Bob, be realistic. You'll have your doctorate. After all that, I doubt you'll be content to teach high school for the next thirty years. Some university will grab you up for considerably more money than you're making now, plus the prestige. It might be next year or the year after, but I'm afraid you will be leaving us."

Oddly, Robert hadn't really thought that far ahead. Of course, he planned to teach at a university eventually, but his eyes were on the near future, that final push to finish the dissertation and take the orals. Plans to him, beyond the hoops he must first jump through, were tentative. Yes, he would probably be leaving, but then there were high school teachers with doctorates. When he thought deeply about it, he wasn't good at making firm, long range plans, unlike Kelly, who seemed to have had her whole future planned out in junior high. In fact, thinking back, he realized that he might still be putting grad school off had it not been for Kelly's nagging him. She'd not only planned her life, but was intent on planning his, even to the university he'd teach at and where he'd live. He wished he could be that certain about everything in life, and he was certain that she would soon come face to face with the reality that the world doesn't always fit one's plans.

The student work came in and some was delightful to read. One started like this: "So, what have you done? We thought we could trust you. No, problem, you claimed. You knew your way around a lab. We could go home and not worry because you'd finish the experiment. How could anyone doubt your chemistry abilities. And now, the new million dollar lab, gone, up in smoke."

He read through the whole stack after the last day, when most teachers were out on the town, celebrating almost three free weeks. They were, for the most part, fun reading and most were marked with an "A."

Having a few days before the holiday obligations, he decided to take a bike ride. He followed a long series of bike paths to Fremont, where he caught a BART train to Berkeley. He toured the campus, thinking about what it would feel like to work there. He checked into a motel, and the next day he took BART to San Francisco. He visited a friend connected with a museum dedicated to the Beat Generation, a group of writers he'd written essays about over the years. Then he saw an old college friend for dinner and checked into a motel. Then he rode along Skyline Blvd, the ridge between the South Bay and the coast. He got to San Jose in time to get a place to stay and pick up a ticket for live theater. The following day, he rode home, feeling good and proud of himself for all the miles he'd racked up.

Then it was time to see Helen for Christmas Eve. The three of them went out to dinner and caught a local band. It was a romantic night, despite having Julie along with them. However, when they got back, they dropped Julie off at a girlfriends place for some kind of slumber party. They had the house to themselves, so they made love on the plush carpet in the living room that night and first thing in the morning.

After a shower, he jumped in his car and headed down to Carmel to visit his mother for a nice dinner. He stayed in the guest room, walked the beach the next day, ate at a nice Italian place on San Carlos Street and headed home. It had been a great week.

He had some writing to do, both on the dissertation and on a couple articles he'd contracted to write. He was feeling relaxed, well exercised, sexually satisfied and intellectually stimulated. He felt better emotionally than he had in many weeks. And then the phone rang.

"Hey, word guy. What's up?"

"Christine. Didn't think I hear from you again."

"Things change. Boyfriend's gone. It's over for both of us. So, wanna go out and play?"

It was refreshing how she was so to the point, no explanation about the failed romance, no hints to get together, just "It's over, let's play." What could he say to that, other than "Hell, yes."

With only two days left in December, he could be assured that this was the best sex he'd had all year. Her abandon was even more abandoned. There came a point, some time in the wee small hours of the morning when he actually said he couldn't handle any more. Then he fell asleep, passed out actually.

In the morning, over breakfast, the obvious question hung in the air between them, a question he knew she wouldn't ask, so he felt compelled to. "So where are we?"

"Kitchen. Breakfast. My place."

"Come on, Christine. You know what I mean. You and I?"

She shook her head, got up and got the coffee pot. "Man, I don't want to hang a label on this. We're having fun. I just got rid of a boyfriend. Tell me you don't want to be my steady boyfriend, date every Saturday night, holidays with your family or mine. How about this. We see each other when we both feel like it, have great sex and some laughs and no schedules. I fuckin' hate schedules."

166

Robert didn't know what he was expecting or what he was actually hoping for, considering he already had a steady relationship, but whatever it was, it wasn't quite this. Still, on second thought, it might be the best of all worlds, so he just said he was totally cool with it. And he was, or sort of was. Even though he was already involved, and even though he and Christine had little in common other than sex, he still had that old fashioned idea that a woman would want more from him, some level of commitment, other than "Woopie, let's play." It was his male ego, he figured, that made him feel he should be more important than he actually was.

At least he now got her number with the assumption that he could call, and if she were available, they'd play.

Robert went to a faculty New Year's Eve party with Helen, and naturally, he was comparing the two woman. While he was much more compatible with Helen, Christine was far more exciting, the sexual equivalent of an upside down roller coaster. Would that, he wondered, be enough for an extended affair. Christine came with even less strings than Helen, so that should he find someone he could get serious with, it would be an easy thing to sever. But, while Helen was steady, two days and one afternoon each week, Christine was here today and who knows where tomorrow. The obvious choice was no choice. See Helen on a regular basis, Christine whenever the opportunity presented itself.

There would be the lies of omission, something he was uncomfortable with, but then they'd never really discussed it, never agreed explicitly that they were not to see other people. This was true, but there was sort of an unspoken understanding, or at least it seemed that way to him. He soon lost count of his levels of rationalization.

Damn you, he told himself. It's New Year Eve, and you should be having fun, not obsessing. He pushed it back to the cluttered attic of his mind, along with all the other unresolved issues he'd promised himself to revisit at some unnamed future date, and he vowed to concentrate on having a pleasant evening.

Robert waited over a week before he called Christine again, not wanting to appear anxious. She was happy to hear from him but was busy on the night he suggested. Rather than seem desperate and suggest the following night, he said he'd try her again another day. That must have been the best strategy, as a few days later, she called, asking to see him on one of Helen's night. When he said he was busy, she suggested the following night, and he agreed. Score one point for me, he thought.

He ended up seeing her twice more before it was time to slip back into the real world of teaching, as well as the time to meet a plane.

Laurie had suggested that Robert join her to meet Kelly's plane, which came in on Sunday, the day before school started. She was cutting it close. Getting ready to meet Laurie, Robert felt nervous. He hadn't realized how anxious he was to see her, how much he'd missed her, their discussions about writing and books, their easy friendship crafted over six years. He did a final check of himself, changing from a boring white dress shirt to something more casual.

"You look different." Laurie checked him over. "It's the hair. I think I like it, but don't let it grow too long. Remember, casual, not sloppy."

It's a long walk from the parking lot to where the planes unload at the San Jose airport. On the way, Robert told Laurie about the new assignments he was giving the students and how they seemed to be responding. She said she thought Kelly would get a kick out of that, which reminded him that she would be in his class again starting in the morning.

He almost didn't recognize the young woman walking down the ramp. Kelly's red hair was wavy and flowing down to her shoulder. She had on a pair of some kind of jeans that tapered way down to the ankle, in a sort of bright olive color. Her striped, long sleeved shirt was tight at the waste and tucked in, and it bloused out around her breasts and shoulders. She had a wide dusty orange belt and shoes that looked like high heeled sneakers. A necklace of clunky stones finished the picture. She smiled when she saw them.

At first Kelly ran to her mom and hugged her, then she turned to Robert, hesitated for a moment and then grabbed and hugged him. "Robert, I've missed you so."

Then she took another look at him, staring at the hair. She smiled, and her only comment was, "Sexy."

All he could think to say was, "Wow, you look incredible, sophisticated."

"All grown up?"

"Well, yeah, sure."

"Good, because that's how I feel."

Robert grabbed her two huge pieces of luggage and followed behind the two women while they caught up on the interminably long walk to the parking garage, stumbling along while trying in vain to hear the conversation.

They stopped at a chain restaurant on the way home, and Laurie insisted on buying. Kelly was talking nonstop about Italy, the places, the people she stayed with, the school. It was maddening to Robert that she didn't mention this guy who permeated her book, but he didn't want to be the one who brought it up, so he just listened, asking appropriate questions when she stopped to catch her breath.

By the time they got home, Kelly was almost asleep from the exhausting flight. She excused herself and went to bed, and Laurie politely chatted with Robert for a few minutes before he took his leave.

Kelly seemed ready to go, if not fully awake, the next day in school. Even though most of the kids knew her, Robert felt it necessary to say that she'd been an exchange student in Italy and had just returned. Naturally, everyone wanted to know all about it, so Robert took it as a teachable moment and had her get up and talk about Florence, which was mainly about the old buildings, art and Italian culture, nothing personal.

She did stop by after school, mostly to find out what she might have to catch up on. Robert assured her that with the new semester, she needn't worry about past assignments. Then she told him that she was going to be really busy finishing up her book, having only a few months before she turned seventeen. For a moment, Robert was puzzled about the age comment, and then he remembered their conversation about S.E. Hinton and how she'd written her first book at sixteen and how Kelly set that as a goal. He wanted to tell her to concentrate on the writing, not a time table, but by now he knew her well enough to realize how obsessed she could get with her goals.

"So," She said. "I'm not going to be able to hang out with you after school as much for a few weeks."

"No longer needing my editorial advice?"

"Oh, sure." And she laughed weakly. "I know I'm gonna get

stuck and come running for help."

"And you plan to finish this?"

"End of Spring break. I figure I'll use that week to clean it up and get it ready for you and Sandy."

"Well, when you're done, we'll celebrate."

"I was hoping you'd say that, but not at any fancy place. Promise you'll take me to that cute seafood place you like so much."

After class a few days later, Julie asked about Kelly. "I hear she's back from Italy, and there's a rumor that she's working on a book."

When Robert confirmed this, she went on. "I'd love to meet her. You know I've read all her cool stories in magazines. Introduce us?"

"Sure. I think she's going to stop by after school on Friday."

Friday, after the last bell, Julie, who was in his sixth period class stayed in her seat while the others made a mad rush for freedom. Within a few minutes Kelly came in, still dressed in what he called her European chic style. "Robert, I..." And then she stopped, seeing Julie sitting there. "I mean, Mr. S. I have a question about how a transition from one scene to the next."

Robert nodded toward Julie and said he wanted to introduce them. On cue, Julie jumped to her feet and bounded to the front of the class. Without any background information, Robert introduced the two.

Julie spoke first. "I love your writing. It's like you know what's going on in my head." Then she added, for reasons beyond Robert's comprehension, "Mr. S. is dating my mother."

Kelly, in a flat, almost bored tone, responded. "The history teacher. Yeah, I've heard."

Then came the gratuitous few moments of chat about school, the boring classes and the stupid school rules. It was the little social dance before getting to the point.

Then Julie had to stake out her position, her claim to prestige by saying that she was going to study biology and that she was on the tennis and cross country teams. Kelly's comment was that all those things must keep her busy.

Then, almost casually, Julie added. "Maybe we could be

170

friends."

Now Robert was riveted to this verbal chess game, wondering what Kelly's move would be. It was like a seemingly innocent moving of her knight. "I guess so, but I'm so busy finishing this damn book, I'm not going to have a bunch of time to hang out."

Julie, recovering and grabbing a quick save, shot back. "Oh, yes, me too. With school and sports, very little time. Just, you know, when we both have some time, maybe grab a coffee, talk writing."

Kelly bit. "Oh, you write too?"

"Not like you. I'm going into science, and I think I might want to be a science writer. Mr. S. says I'm pretty good at it, that I make science stuff pretty clear to people."

Kelly looked at Robert kind of blankly, and he responded with an affirmative nod.
She turned back to Julie and said. "Cool. Maybe I can read your stuff one day, you know, over a coffee."

Julie smiled and came back with, "Maybe I could see what you're writing."

"Not till I'm finished. I've got a thing about that. He's the only one who can see the work in progress. How about a signed first edition?"

"I'd love it. OK, good meeting you. Gotta go."

Kelly watched her leave and then turned to Robert. "Quite the jock, isn't she?"

Then, leaving the issue of Julie behind, she opened her pages and started to ask Robert some technical questions about her writing, and Robert instinctively knew that no further mention of Julie was needed or wanted.

If was after Kelly left that Robert reflected on the exchange, thinking that women, even young ones, relate to each other in complicated code. This particular exchange, he thought, was pretty easy to decode. They are both very competitive girls: Julie, highly focused physically, and Kelly the same mentally. The two were about the same size and build, and they were both attractive girls, but not what one would call cute or even classically pretty. Neither had the delicate features usually considered feminine. Both radiated a strong self-confidence. Robert then realized that a true friendship probably wouldn't work. Although Julie was slightly awed because Kelly was older, already professionally accomplished and traveled, she was not the kind to be content in another person's shadow. Julie was already a leader, and next year she was going to be team captain, unusual for a sophomore. It would be fun, Robert thought, watching the interaction between the two.

His own interactions were becoming a problem. He was realizing that with the dissertation deadline almost upon him, work pressures and two women in his life, things were getting stressful. Occasionally, both Helen and Christine wanted to see him on the same nights, and, as he was more and more aware, these kinds of decisions were hard for him. He wasn't one of the lucky guys who went with gut reactions. And, frankly, there were times when he didn't want to see either of them, times he rather work, read a good book or just unwind. When romance and sex started to become work, it was time to step back.

Not that Christine was demanding. She still was a very occasional girl, a girl more for the moment than for the day or even hour. She was spontaneous, sometimes calling late at night, saying she was lonely and a bit horny. When she offered to come to his place, he could hardly refuse.

As always, Robert vowed that he'd have to make some decisions. Finishing up his doctorate gave him the excuse he needed to put those decisions off. June, he thought, was going to be a very stressful month.

He got in his car one day and started to back up. When he looked in the side mirror, he noticed the words, "Objects in the mirror are closer than they appear." Although it wouldn't officially be spring for almost two weeks, the central coast was in bloom, blossoms on the fruit trees, fields of bright yellow poppies and deep blue lupine. The days were warm and growing longer. In about two months he'd, he assumed, be able to call himself doctor Spagnolo. It would be a great hurtle, but on the other side lurked a morass of sticky decisions, among them his next career step, along with relationship issues. Why, he wondered, must he put thing off until they land on his head like a gob of bird shit.

172

23

He wondered how he'd approach Helen. "This is what I need in a relationship. Take it or leave it." No, that wasn't really him. The coward's way out would be to just keep things as they are until someone else came along, but that would be a crappy way to do it. At least it wasn't complicated with Christine. For a moment though he pictured her saying that she wanted something serious with him. What would he do with that?

He even, and this was no more than an idle daydream, considered he'd get an offer from some university in New York, and Sandy, hearing the news, would drop her new boyfriend and... and pigs might fly too.

When he got to school, Kelly asked if she could stop by after school for some advice. He said sure, and then he added one more daydream, he'd have a big career as her literary agent, getting fifteen percent of an endless string of best sellers. He could live with that.

When she bounded in after the last bell, she, as usual, launched right into it. "I thought I was being so damn clever with this present tense stuff. Transitioning from one scene to the next is murder." She handed him a flash drive, which he put in his school computer.

"Even very experienced writers tend to stay away from this," he mumbled as he read. After a few minutes' thought he came up with a several ways to handle her problem. The diary entry solution didn't appeal to her, but some of the others perked her up. And as he read, the affair with the Italian boy was heating up while the ending date was looming, and she's written it almost like it was someone getting news from a doctor that they only had a couple months to live. It was very emotional, very compelling.

While he'd vowed to wait for her to bring it up, he couldn't put it off. "You've talked about the school, your host family and the places you've visited, but this," And he pointed to the screen, "Obviously something big was going on here, but you never talk about it."

A sad look rolled across her face. "It's that there's the stuff I did, things that happened, and then there's the story, and I don't want to mix them up while I'm still writing it. It's hard to keep things separate in my head."

Robert looked up from the screen again. "So, this is purely fiction?"

"Oh, no, but, you know, the story is more, what can I say, a story. I really do want to talk just as soon as I finish. I hope I can talk it out with you."

"Kelly. You know I always have and always will be there for you."

"I was hoping you'd say that." She beamed at him and started to reach, as if to hug him, and then seemed to think better of it. "There's a lot on my mind," She finally added.

After she left, her cryptic remarks played on his imagination. Perhaps she was thinking of returning to Florence, trying to make a big life decision. He certainly hoped she wouldn't put that kind of thing on him to wrestle with, to advise her about.

The thick folder was on the desk between Robert and his adviser. She smiled, breaking the tension he felt. "I think you can call this pretty much a done deal. While you've changed your focus since starting this, I like where you've gone with it. Again, you have a potential text book to use on your next position."

"Thank you. Next position, and who knows what or where that will be."

"Look, Robert, assuming you get over all these last hurtles, I have something you might want to look into. I know you already have a job, so this might be a foot in the door, part time only at first, no promises."

Robert was on the edge of his seat, nodding and saying "yes, yes, yes."

Then when she realized she was rambling, she got to the point. "I know some people in the department over at San Jose State. Looks like they'll have a single section unfilled, one night a week. Again, no promise of a full time job, tenure or anything. However, if they hire you and if they like you, who knows."

He was grinning and nodding. "You know, I've already done an extension class for them. So what are the chances?"

"With my recommendation, pretty damn good. Department head was a student of mine some years back."

174

Robert was walking on air. It was the best of all worlds, a decision without making a decision. He had his high school job, solid and secure, while he explored teaching at a university. The commute to San Jose wouldn't be bad, considering it was only once a week. He could leave right after school, grab a sandwich somewhere and make it, seeing that he'd be going opposite to commuter traffic. She promised to talk to the guy and get back to him, encouraging him to get everything wrapped up in the next few weeks.

After school a few days later, Kelly came in with a minor stylistic question, and he had to mention this potential good fortune. She frowned when she heard about a job at a university.

"So, you won't be here for my senior year. I was hoping you'd teach college, but after I graduate."

"No, no, Kelly. You don't get it. This would be a part time position which might lead to something permanent. It would be one night a week, so I'd keep my day job here."

With that she beamed. "Does that mean I'll have to call you professor Robert next year?"

He realized that since she'd returned from Italy, she'd dropped the formal Mr. S, except in class around other students. He thought of making a big deal out of it, but that seemed petty, and he didn't think it was important enough to press, considering that she'd insist on knowing why it mattered. It was, he realized, part of a wider change. Now that she was finishing the book and had experienced some kind of adult relationship, the old roles of teacher and student were replaced with, well, with her regarding him more as a peer. Indeed, they talked like two adults, old friends with common interests. When she came to him, it wasn't for instruction, but to seek his opinion on some writing issue. Would they end up lifelong friends, literary chums who get together over a glass of wine and discuss the finer points of someone's writing?

For his part, he honestly thought of her differently, not so much a student, more a friend, and he realized how much he valued her friendship.

Spring break was suddenly just a couple of days away, and Robert and Helen planned to slip away the first weekend. Julie swore she could be trusted to stay home alone and not have a wild party or get into any trouble. "After all," She said. "I am fourteen."

They drive down to Big Sur and stayed at the River Inn, and it was warm enough to use the pool in midday. They relaxed, hiked, ate, and made love. As always, after spending some quality time with her, Robert again started to feel that they may have something with staying power.

When they got back, Julie gave them that smile that said, "You both look well laid."

He had wanted to stop and see his mother, but he didn't want to impose on Helen, so after relaxing a day, he drove back down to Carmel, spent the day with his mother, wandered through some art galleries and started to think where he'd have dinner. Then his cell phone rang. It was Christine. She was in Monterey, at Cannery Row, and wondered if he were up to driving down. When he said he was already in the area, she told him to meet her at a restaurant on the water. They had dinner, several glasses of wine, and then she said, "Why should two have drunk people drive two cars home? Let's split a motel room."

"Better yet," Robert announced. "I'll pick up the room. Good things are happening, and I want to celebrate." They picked up a bottle of wine and got a place with an ocean view, a bit more expensive than he was comfortable with, but what the hell, he thought. He told her about the potential part time university job. They toasted good times and launched into a night of wild sex.

When he got home, he thought what a great week it had been, and that he still had half a week left. There was some vague talk of having Easter dinner with his mother and tentative plans for the usual Friday night with Helen, but nothing was set in stone. He grabbed the book he was reading and vowed to just relax.

Thursday was a picture perfect Spring day, so he decided to do a sixty mile bike ride, through the hills. When he got home, pleasantly tired, he ordered Chinese food delivered, rented a video, bought some fairly expensive wine and settled in to spoil himself.

The movie over and the wine half gone, he was about to go to bed when the phone rang. It was almost midnight; who in hell would be calling. It was Kelly. "Robert, hope I didn't wake you." Without waiting for an answer, she kept going. "It's done, finished, and I just stuck the last two chapters on an email to you. Please read it and let me know what you think in the morning. I've been writing since six this morning, and I'm going to bed now. Oh, and I think it's pretty good."

He was suddenly wide awake. Finished. He could hardly wait for his computer to warm up again. He opened the file and started reading. Everything was building to the climax, the moment when the protagonist would get on a plane and go back to her old life, and Kelly had built layers of emotion. The writing was designed to carry the reader away, to keep her from putting the book down until the last word.

Then he read the final scene at the airport: *"Like a guillotine hanging over our heads, this moment, always just ahead of us, always pushed back, rarely mentioned, was now a reality, one as cold as these airport seats. He's holding both my hands, looking into my eyes while the noise of the crowded airport swirls around us. I want to speak, but as I'm searching for the right words, he's beating me to it. 'Dear one, I love you.' There are tears in my eyes and I hear myself almost shouting, 'No, no, you know I have to go. Please don't put this on me. I can't handle it.' He's shaking his head. 'You don't understand. It's easier to say in Italian. I love you doesn't mean the same as I'm in love with you. I'm not saying I want you to stay forever, to marry me, for us to live happily ever after. I love you means I treasure you and the time we've had and that you'll always be in my heart. It means I hope we visit each other in the future, that you invite me to your wedding, as I'll invite you to mine, that someday we'll take family vacations together, sitting on a beach while our children play, that some day when we're very old, we'll sit together in a sidewalk cafe, sipping wine and sharing a lifetime of fond memories.' And now I can't stop the tears. 'Yes,' I hear myself say. 'I love you too in the same way, and I'll always cherish you.' And his words somehow moved me over an invisible line. I'd suddenly grown from being a high school girl with childish romantic notions to an adult, an adult who understood the more complex levels of human relationships. And, with the loudspeaker announcing last call for boarding, I'm thanking him for everything he's been to me, as I release his hands and run for the plane."*

The words were blurring on the page, as Robert wiped away the tears and kept reading. If he was crying, he could only imagine the thousands of young women who would soon weep while reading these words. Without even thinking about what might need editing, he attached the chapters to an email to Sandy, with "The book is finished, and it's wonderful," in the subject line.

Then he went to bed, unable to sleep for a very long time, staring up at the ceiling in the dark and thinking about the meaning of "I love you" and I'm in love with you."

It was nine in the morning when Robert woke up. There was already a message on his phone, Kelly wanting to know what he thought. Before calling her, he noticed the computer was left on, the email program still running, and there was a reply from Sandy. It was noon in New York. The email was short: "Wow, the stuff of a best seller. Shared it at the morning editorial meeting. Thumbs up all around. Tell Kelly we want to talk book contract with her, offer her an advance. Does she have an agent?" Kelly was copied on the email.

He called Kelly and asked if she'd seen it. She was ecstatic, bubbling over about the news. "I answered her," she said. "Told her I wanted you to be my agent."

He told her to slow down, that he wasn't really qualified to be her agent, but she cut him off, reminding him of their pending celebration. "Tonight, OK? And I have stuff I've been needing to talk to you about."

24

Of course they'd celebrate. He'd pick her up at five, and they'd drive to the beach for seafood and a long conversation. After he hung up, he remembered the tentative Friday night date with Helen, but this was more important, so he called and told Helen something came up, and he couldn't see her.

When he got to her door, Laurie answered, all excited about her daughter's success, saying Kelly was not quite ready, that she was taking time to look just right. She beamed at Robert and said, "You two have a wonderful time tonight. I couldn't be happier."

When Kelly came out, Robert gasped. Her usual jeans and loose shirt were gone in favor of an actually dress, very unusual for her. There was even a slight nod to the idea of high heels, plus fancy earrings, pearl necklace, her hair done beautifully, flowing over her shoulders. She was even wearing makeup, also unusual for her. The teen had been replaced with a beautiful, sophisticated young woman, a stylish, best-selling author. She simply smiled and asked, "How do I look?"

He blithered some lame answer back at her, gushing about how great she looked. Then she took his arm and they walked to the car.

Driving down the highway in the dead zone between small talk and real conversation, Robert had to ask. "That ending. Powerful stuff. Is that really what happened?"

"I dressed it up a bit, but basically Also, he did say he loved me but that wasn't exactly the same as being in love with me. He also said he wanted to remain friends, perhaps visit each other from time to time. He did wish me luck with a relationship back home, and I'm still not sure whether to put that in the book or not. Anyway, the rest I added to make it more dramatic."

Robert wanted to ask what she meant about a relationship back home, but he thought it better that he hold off on that. Then she added, "It made me think about love, what you can give and what you can expect." Then since she didn't elaborate, he let the silence engulf them again until they pulled into the parking lot by the docks.

Since they were there early, there were many tables to choose from, and Kelly pointed to one back in a corner by itself. Once seated, she added a bit to her car conversation. "Anyway, that whole thing about love and being in love, that's something I want to talk to you about tonight."

Robert swallowed hard but responded cheerfully, reassuring her that he was open for any conversation. But, then the waitress came up for drink orders.

She jumped right in, pointing to the wine list. "Robert, isn't that the chardonnay we had our first date here? Yes, of course it is. I know you like the merlot, but let's have the chard, OK." And without giving him a chance to answer or protest, she continued. "Great, yes, we'll both have a glass of that. Thank you."

Robert thought for sure she'd be carded, but the waitress just took the order and left. "Kelly, you're under age. I'm surprised they didn't card you. I didn't know you drank."

"It's perception. I dressed older and talked about having it before, so she assumed I was over twenty-one. And, I've had a glass or two, though I'm not really a wine drinker. They're a bit less fussy in Italy about age, and we often had a glass with dinner. Also, this is a special occasion."

"Of course, your book, very special."

"Oh yes, but more than that." She had a serious look on her face, and he nodded for her to continue, half fearing the unknown lurking in her look.

"This is hard," She said. "Anyway I've been thinking about love and in love, and I realize that just because one person wants something, that doesn't mean the other person has to be on board with it. I know you love me, like a friend, a student, whatever, but I'm having to face the fact that you're not in love with me and my plans for marrying you aren't going to happen." Her face was dead serious as she leaned in toward him. This was a prelude to her closing the book on over six years, and suddenly he didn't want that to happen.

"Well, Kelly, I never said I didn't love you. I mean I do, but I never said I wasn't in love with you."

"You never said you were, and your omission was said it in a very loud voice."

"That's not a subject I could have gotten into, you being

sixteen, a student."

"That's an excuse. The truth is those feelings aren't there, and I've got to accept that." He could feel her pulling off years of strings, and a feeling of panic came over him.

"No, Kelly, I do love you. I mean I am in love with you." And now it came pouring out, the pressure of long hidden feelings bursting through his wall of denial. "I don't know how long. I mean I've loved you in a different way from the start, but it grew into something else, gradually. I don't know, but it's been years, maybe even when I thought I was in love with Sandy, but you were so young, and those kinds of thoughts were so wrong, and me, a teacher, but yes I'm so in love with you it hurts just to think about it." He was having trouble holding his voice down so as not to be heard by others, and he found tears coming to his eyes. He took her hands and said, "I'm so sorry. I've been crazy, in denial. I'm in love with you and I want to marry you, what a year and a couple months, if you still want me."

"I've never stopped. Even Aldo understood that, and that's why he probably held a bit back emotionally. Our life together starts tonight."

"Yes it does, and we can be engaged secretly for now. Obviously we can't tell anyone."

"I don't care about that. It's us I care about." She smiled the most radiant smile, and he was so filled with love, he couldn't understand how he'd kept his feelings hidden, even from himself. He was holding both her hands, and he should have felt self-conscious about it, but he didn't.

They talked about their future plans, his moving from high school to a university, her publishing her book, writing the next and also going to college. "Could you handle a wife who's also a full time writer and full time university student?"

"Why not. I'll iron and do the dishes."

"After a hard day teaching at Berkeley."

There was that again. "Christ, Kelly, I'm not even in the door part time at San Jose yet, and that's a long way from Berkeley."

She reached over and stroked his face. "Trust me; you'll get there. And there'll be the house in the Berkeley hills."

As they were leaving, he sighed and said, "I'm sorry the

evening is ending."

"Oh, no," She corrected. "It's just getting started. We're going back to your place."

"I can't do that. Remember you're still my student, and you're only sixteen. You're talking about my career, my credential, maybe being dragged into court."

"Hold it, my love. First, do I seem to you 'only' sixteen? I doubt it. I'm not some innocent kid you're taking advantage of. Remember I celebrated Aldo's twenty-second birthday. I've done adult love affairs. Second, no one is going to know. Do you think I'm going to blab to my best girlfriend? Oh, that right, I don't have one of those, something you've reminded me of often. I'm sure as hell not going to risk our future after all we've been through."

Robert was near panic, but he wasn't sure why. "What about your mother? She expects you home."

"No she doesn't. I told her that if I came home tonight it was because you rejected me and it was all over."

He was uncomfortable picturing Laurie knowing about them spending the night together. "And she's fine with that?"

"Well, you know, she said she wished I'd wait, but since I was already sexually active, it was better I was with the man I'm going to marry than with a string of high school boys."

Even though he realized that this was just what he wanted, he still felt trapped. She was making these decisions about them having sex, and frankly he was a bit nervous.
His only response was, "I hope you don't mind a little case of anxiety."

"You're not the only nervous one here. I'm thinking about a fantasy that goes back to puberty."

On the freeway, as he stole occasional glances at Kelly, Robert saw the images switch between the sweet but precocious little girl he'd mentored for years and the lovely woman he was in love with. He was afraid that, if these images didn't resolve themselves by the time they got home, an intimate disaster awaited him.

Robert was glad he was a neat person and had made up his bed and picked up his clothes and dishes. The place was suitable for company, and Kelly walked around his apartment like a mother bird sizing up a nesting sight.

Standing there, feeling awkward, Robert offered her a glass of wine, which she refused. Instead, she came up to him, wrapped her arms around his neck and kissed him passionately, while kicking off her shoes.

After a few moments, she reached up and unbuttoned his shirt. He took a deep breath between kisses and undid her dress, which dropped rather quickly to the floor, leaving her standing there in her bra and panties. She pressed against him once again and then unbuttoned his pants, giving them a pull down. Now they were both standing in a spreading pool of clothing. She pushed him back, and they both stepped free and kissed again.

She gently pushed him in the direction of his bedroom, and he, getting the hint, led her to his bed. The light was off, but a waxing moon filled the room with a soft glow. He pulled back the bedding, and when he turned back to her, the bra had disappeared. She was, he noted, quite well endowed.

Kelly dropped her panties, leaving Robert the only one with anything on, so he quickly dropped his shorts. Then she leaned into him, pushing them both down on the bed in a tight embrace.

As much as he struggled against it, that damn image of the young girl kept getting in the way, and he felt his erection slipping away. This was really awkward, as he really wanted the woman at the same time as the girl intimidated him. "Darling Kelly, I'm having a problem tonight. There's a lot of old images and taboos messing with my mind."

In a soft, husky voice, she responded. "My love, we have a lifetime. Let's just curl up together and enjoy the feeling of being close."

With the pressure off, Robert calmed down, and as she nuzzled his neck with her lips and stroked his chest, the nervousness gradually subsided and was replaced by the stirring of an erection. He realized how desperately he wanted her, and then he was kissing her lips, neck, breasts, her smooth belly and her upper thighs. She was wet and groaning, and his face was buried deep between her legs.

Soon she was writhing and saying, "Now, darling, now."

She came almost immediately, and he didn't last much longer. As he rolled over he realized that this was a notch above anything he'd had before. She was physically as exciting as Christine, and emotionally

183

an order of magnitude better than any of his affairs. So this, he thought, was what really being in love felt like.

They cuddled, kissed and talked well into the night, and they made love again just before dawn. Right or wrong, they had started something lasting, and they would have to deal with all the unintended consequences.

Over breakfast, they talked about some of the restrictions imposed on them by a society that would look at them through rigid rules. They couldn't go out in public in town or within fifteen miles, just to be safe. They would have to be very careful to be strictly teacher and student at school, and they would have to take care not to be obvious about her coming over. She even suggested that they take a motel at the beach or in San Jose from time to time. Her car, when she visited him, would have to be parked some distance away, where he would meet her and bring her home. With only one night behind them, the paranoia was already seeping in.

Then she added the obvious. "You need to end it with your teacher girlfriend and any others. After all this, I'm not going to share you."

He knew he had to do that, but breaking off any relationship was painfully uncomfortable for him. "Yes, I've got to do that."

"Today." She said flatly but firmly. But then she changed the subject. "I'm going to use some of my advance money to buy a really nice bike, so we can ride together."

"Really, Kelly. I didn't think you were that into serious riding."

"I'm not, at least not yet. I like to ride a bike, but you know, part of being together is sharing interests, and I know how you love it. Once I get a good bike and get in better shape, I'll enjoy it much more. Maybe I'll end up being a hard body like that Julie you admire so much."

That took him aback. "I don't admire her. She's just a nice kid, the daughter of a woman I dated."

In a mocking tone, Kelly responded, quoting him,"Oh, I was amazed that she could keep up with me on a twenty-five mile. She's really in good condition."

"That's not funny, and you know I didn't mean it that way. You know I'm not that kind of person."

184

She apologized and said that she was feeling kind of fat and unattractive, since she'd just been writing and not getting exercise. He assured her that she was neither fat nor unattractive. And now, she unfortunately needed go home, and that brought up another uncomfortable situation, facing Laurie in the middle of the day, after a night of sex with her teen daughter.

Laurie was going out of her way to be good with it all, asking them if they'd had a nice evening and all that small talk. Kelly got right to the point with the announcement that they were now secretly engaged. She even knew the exact number of days before her eighteenth birthday and the wedding.

Robert's place seemed empty and alien without Kelly in it. Being an emotional coward, he took the easy situation first, calling Christine. A simple, "I've got a girlfriend now, so I can't see you anymore," was enough. She said that when it went sour, he had her number.

Helen was another matter. He picked up the phone, and as he dialed, he understood that he couldn't do this over the phone, even though it would be the coward's way out. "I have something important to talk to you about, can we meet for lunch."

She had tentative plans, but picking up on the tone of his voice, agreed. He showered and dressed, wishing that the earth would open up and swallow him on the way to the restaurant.

Robert had long known that he lacked a good poker face. Within minutes, Helen was picking up on the purpose of the meeting. "This is something about you and me, isn't it?"

Not being able to tell her the whole truth, he told her a half truth, a lie of omission. "You know I'm looking for more, and I know you've had your marriage and a great kid. I haven't, and the clock is ticking. I need the wife, kids, white picket fence and all that."

"I know, Rob, and I've always said that what we have can only go so far. I take it you've found someone."

Now the lie, he thought. "I'm not the kind of guy who can go looking while with someone, even if I had the time. I can't establish," and he deliberately avoided the outright lie that would be implied if he's said 'find,' " a new relationship while still in one. It wouldn't be fair to anyone."

"And you always care about being fair. I see. So, you're breaking up with me to go search for your true love. It's kind of sudden, but I'm not really in a place to offer you what you want. Yeah, it hurts. I really like you, but sure, I guess I understand."

Lunch was the longest hour of his life. They made pleasant conversation, the emotional issues swept away with the dirty dishes and empty coffee cups. And then he was free, free to follow his heart with Kelly. In his need to deal with this, he hadn't thought about Julie and how she'd react., considering she's put him in the role of substitute father.

Before the following week was out, Julie, who had been rather sullen in class, stormed in the door after school. "Did you break up with mom because of me?"

That was totally out of the blue and his only best reply was "What?"

"You dumped her because she has a kid. You didn't want to deal with a teen, some snot-nosed kid."

Robert had to jump to his feet for this one and to slow her down. "It had absolutely nothing to do with you. In fact, I'm sad about it; you've been the closest thing I've ever had to a kid of my own. But, a wife and kids, that's what I want. Your mom and I are just on different wavelengths, different timing. I'm still looking for the life she had with your dad when you were little. In fact, when I see you, you remind me of something missing in my life."

That caught her off guard, and she softened. "Maybe we could both work on mom, and she'd maybe want to marry you." Then she added something that gave him a chilling jab. "Did that Kelly bad mouth us to you? I don't think she likes me, and I didn't do anything to her."

After profusely assuring her that Kelly never said a word, he continued. "We've talked all that out, and I don't want to work on her. I want her to be happy, and if getting tied down doesn't make her happy, you shouldn't want that for her either."

`   There were tears in Julie's eyes, even though she was trying to hide them. "Well, I'm going to miss you. You're a real cool guy."

Now, sitting alone in his classroom, some elevator music on the computer, he felt like shit. Julie was a great kid, and he'd inadvertently led her to expect something lasting, maybe even a real family, and now she felt betrayed, and there was nothing he could do about it. He couldn't keep being her pal, particularly with Kelly around.

The road to true love, he thought, is strewn with wreckage.

Then Robert's mother called. "Laurie said that you and Kelly are now a couple."

"That's not for publication, mom, and she shouldn't have said anything to you."

"Hell, son, it's not like it wasn't expected."

When he asked her what that meant, she answered that Kelly's intentions were clear from the beginning, and that she'd always appeared a step ahead of Robert, adding that in matters of the heart, he seldom really got it until it was spelled out for him.

"Does that mean you approve or you don't?"

"Actually, you need someone like her. If it was up to you to instigate something, you'd die an old but still single man. The girl's strong in ways that you need. In fact you complement each other. Oh, yeah, I really like her too. She knows what makes you happy, even if you don't." She trailed off from that with a mischievous laugh.

"Damn, mom, you make me sound clueless."

"When it comes to women, you are, but that's part of your charm. You have that bumbling professor air about you. You're sort of the messy house that women love to put in order. You'll be good for each other, and you'll make me a grandma."

25

Robert's world shifted suddenly, going from idle to full speed. By the time he'd spent two more weekends with Kelly, he had earned the right to add Ph.D. to his name and he'd been accepted as a part time instructor at San Jose State for the fall semester. Seeing that he was in honeymoon mode and would be spending Friday through Sunday with Kelly, and knowing that her advance was yet to come, he took money out of his savings and bought her a bike.

The weekends were either spent in his place or when out, they drove someplace away from town, often to the long bike trail that follows Highway 101, the one he'd ridden with Julie. It took Kelly three weekend rides to build up to twenty-five miles, but being young and healthy, she got into shape quickly, dropping almost ten pounds in the process. Sometimes, since it was still spring, they'd find a county park, one with wild flowers, and just go walking hand in hand. Life couldn't get much better, unless it would be not to have to hide their affair.

There was a flurry of phone and email exchanges between the publisher and Kelly, editorial changes and suggestions, discussions about the title and other details leading up to publication. On the dedication, she decided on "To Robert Spagnolo Ph.D., who taught me everything I know about writing." This, she claimed, would be helpful when, not if, he applied to teach at Berkeley.

In the middle of the whirlwind that his life had become, he found himself writing up his final exams, actually, with Kelly's help one Saturday night over dinner. And this effectively marked the end of another school year, his seventh with the district.

Sandy called and said that in the last minute rush to get the book published, it would be helpful if Kelly could come to New York. Kelly, listening, nodded yes and pointed to Robert and then held up two fingers, meaning "you too." And so they booked a flight the day after school ended.

Robert wanted to do it up right, so he booked them into a nice hotel not far from the publisher. He also got tickets for a couple of Broadway plays and made arrangements to take in a few tourist destinations.

When they all sat down together, Sandy immediately understood. "You two are a couple now, aren't you?" Robert, uncomfortable, was trying to be noncommittal, but Kelly jumped right in with, "Yes, we're having a wonderful affair and we plan to get married in just over a year."

Sandy smiled and said she always suspected it would turn out this way. And then she asked Kelly if Robert was acting as her agent, and she responded that he was the only one she trusted to do it.

Then came the last minute corrections and changes, followed by the proof. Sandy and her bosses agreed that this would be a good summer book, something romantic for girls' summer break reading, and they wanted it out before the summer was too far gone. Fortunately, Kelly had done such a skillful job that editing was minimal.

Kelly had a check, and they had the whole summer to enjoy their new found love, so they spent a couple more weeks in and around New York, visiting the museums, beaches, trendy restaurants and all the rest. With no one around who knew them, they were just another young couple on summer vacation. Kelly looked at least a couple years older, and Robert had that eternal boyish look, so they gave the appearance of a college couple on break. However, just to avoid embarrassment, they agreed not to order wine with meals.

They decided to celebrate her seventeenth birthday in Washington DC, catching an early train one morning. They did the museums, visited the Capitol, saw all the monuments and memorials and had her birthday dinner in a restaurant near the White House.

Finally, the image of the other Kelly, the young girl, his precocious student, faded away, leaving only Kelly the passionate and beautiful young woman, so Robert no longer felt any apprehension in bed with her. Making love was incredible each and every time, and there was nothing shy and girlish about her responses, and Robert was secretly thankful she'd had an experienced lover in Florence.

When they finally flew home, a big dinner party was planned at his mother's new place in Carmel. Pat and her husband, Laurie and her steady boyfriend and Robert and Kelly. It was a new twist in the relationship, three adult couples dining, sipping wine, talking, sharing the richness of their lives, and life was indeed rich for all of them. Pat was happy in her new life, Laurie's business was doing great, her relationship long, steady and comfortable. Naturally, Robert and Kelly couldn't be happier.

Laurie did mention one thing. "Kelly, you probably shouldn't be in his class next year. You could say or do something to give it away. You know how kids pick up on subtle hints."

"But I've always made a big deal out of being in his class. Wouldn't it look strange now?"

Robert had the solution. "Every year George asks me if I want the same schedule for the following year, easier than new preps, but each year I welcome the change. This year I'll tell him that with teaching one night in San Jose, I'd rather stick with the familiar, freshmen and juniors, leaving both Kelly and Julie out of my classes."

They all wanted to know why Julie might be a problem, and he told them how she took the breakup kind of hard, blaming first herself and then Kelly. Better not have to deal with her at all, he figured, even though he still felt guilty about not being her substitute dad.

Suddenly it was August and the end of summer vacation was only weeks away, and in what seemed to Robert to be a superhuman effort, Sandy had kept her word and got Kelly's book out in time for hungry young women to still have a literary feast before hitting the dull text books. The book not only came out but was highly publicized and thus highly reviewed. Within two weeks it had made the New York Times list of best sellers, and Kelly was suddenly awash with a good income, enough to afford her upcoming university education.

She took it all in stride, almost as if it was all long expected. In fact, their brightly burning romance also appeared to be long expected. There was never the "pinch me; I'm dreaming" moment with Kelly. She acted always as if she were checking off items on a long list. Sometimes she seemed seventeen, going on forty.

Robert got up on the first morning, finding strands of red hair on his pillow from the weekend, knowing that they'd have less time together now, possibly nothing during the week. This would be his first year in sometime when Kelly wouldn't be sitting in the first row, tapping her foot impatiently, waiting for some educational revelation. It wouldn't be the same. He'd no longer be looking forward to each day.

George stopped by his room after school that first day. "So tomorrow night you teach your first university class. Nervous?"

"Yeah, I'm going over my syllabus again tonight. I want things as smooth and seamless as possible, get off on the right foot."

George settled down on a desk top, but his hands behind his head and leaned back. "You'll be a busy boy. Maybe put a strain on your thing with Helen."

That's right, he didn't know, but how to phrase it, Robert being the word guy.

"Well, George, this new job got me thinking. My life is getting serious, more and more adult, career moves and all. I have to admit, part time and temporary affairs just aren't enough. I'm looking for something permanent, something like what you have, and it's not there with Helen, so I've had to reluctantly end it."

"Ah, and the little hottie you picked up one night?"

"Seriously, yes, her too."

"So you burned your bridges."

"I did, and I'm cool with that. After all, life is going to be busy. Probably no secret that I'm hoping for a full time position at the university, maybe tenure one day."

"Buddy, I, or actually all of us, will miss you, but I don't blame you. You're good; you're dedicated: you deserve it. You already have my recommendation. Since you don't have a girlfriend, we've got to get together."

"Thursday's good." He didn't want to take a night away from Kelly. George nodded, adding that Friday nights were his date nights with the wife, Saturday being family night.

To Kelly's obvious discomfort, she became a sudden celebrity at school. Not only did many of the girls buy her book, but a surprising number of boys did also, possibly picturing themselves in the role of the charming Italian lover. Students were approaching her to have their copies signed, and while enjoying the fact that her book was popular, she was, at least she claimed to be, uncomfortable with her personal fame.

One night, over dinner at Robert's, she said, "If I wanted to be a celebrity, I would have become an actor or singer. I'd rather people just buy and enjoy my books and not make a big fuss over me."

She also complained that besides the girl fans, there were also the boys, who wanted to be more than fans. "Guys are hitting on me all the time, some are really pests. Mostly I tell them I have a boyfriend, a college guy." Then she grinned and added, "Not exactly a lie, is it?"

This celebrity buzz came to a head on Homecoming Day. Naturally there was a big rally, the varsity team and cheerleaders were featured, and the principal and coach spoke. And then George announced that the school has a literary star, and he asked Kelly to come up and say something. Robert looked down at her and saw the pained expression. She got up and said, "The only thing I can say is to follow your dreams and never give up, and you can all be successful at whatever you love doing."

Short and sweet. On paper, she could have turned this into five thousand words, but she got up and said it in twenty-six. She was followed back to her seat with a standing ovation, giving George a menacing look on the way.

There was, she said, one bright spot at school. While she was suddenly popular with many of the various school groups, she wasn't interested in most of them, not the jocks, the socials, the rockers or the party crowd. There was one group, however, that interested her. It was a book club, all girls, a very serious and smart group. They approached her, saying that they'd read and discussed her book and were inviting her to join them. Perhaps these were finally the friends she'd been doing without for so long, and she liked them. Robert had long understood that Kelly bestowed the blessing of liking someone very sparingly. She had long ago built a protective wall around her.

Robert could never fathom how she could be so self-confident about herself as a writer but so insecure when it came to friendships. She seemed to always assume that any friendship would end in disappointment and rejection. He'd known her for almost seven years and loved her deeply, but she was still somewhat of an enigma to him.

There were two girls in particular that she seemed to click with, Mayra Espinosa and Pauline Gross, and Robert got the opportunity to meet them one day when Kelly asked him to address the group's luncheon meeting, his topic "Nonfiction as fiction: Information can be a page turner." The girls were sharp, their questions serious and thoughtful. He paid particular attention to the girls Kelly had talked about. Mayra, thin, braided dark hair, tattoos on her shoulders and arms, a dress style vaguely Goth. It was clear she wanted to send the message that she was a rebel of some sort, and part of her image was a dead pan expression. Pauline, on the other hand, was a somewhat less attractive version of Kelly, a couple inches shorter, but maybe a bit heavier. She wore her dishwater blond hair short and nondescript. Her style, if one could call it that, was like Kelly's, no style at all, Kelly having gradually retreated from stylish Italian. They both dress for comfort and convenience, faded jeans, tee shirts, sweaters, no make up, sneakers. Unlike Mayra, Pauline tended to smile a lot. They talked after his presentation, and he liked them both immediately, and they seemed to feel the same.

Mayra carefully studied how Robert and Kelly interacted, much to Robert's discomfort, and finally, she, while not smiling, seemed to wear a knowing smirk.

Naturally, the students who bought Kelly's book noticed the dedication and obviously knew who Robert was, so there were questions, mostly innocent. However, it was only a matter of time before someone with a suspicious mind put two and two together, and that person was Julie, still smarting from the perceived abandonment.

Julie still came into Robert's room from time to time, ostensibly to get a bit of writing advice, but mostly to keep the remnants of the security of being an almost family.
Whenever she arrived at a time Kelly was there, she noticed that there seemed to be an intense conversation, one that stopped abruptly when she entered. Then there was obvious discomfort, particularly on Mr. Spagnolo's face. Robert realized this from the first and wished he could keep the inscrutable look that Kelly had mastered. It was obvious that Julie was suspicious.

For their part, Robert and Kelly were never behind closed doors. Whenever she stopped by his room, which wasn't too often, the door was wide open, and they never touched. That was enough to curb suspicion, unless someone was looking for something deeper, which Julie obviously was.

One night, Robert mentioned it to Kelly, who dismissed it. "Doesn't matter what she thinks, only what she can prove."

Naturally, while it would be a scandal for Kelly, it would be Robert's credential and career, so he was justifiably more paranoid. He made it a point to chat with Helen in the lunch room fairly often,

193

hoping to hear about Julie's suspicions. Rather than divulge any information, Helen instead asked him seemingly innocent questions. "So, what sort of things did you teach her that turned her into a best seller?" One day Helen said, "Apparently the girl has been published for years, even before she got to high school. Robert reminded her that he'd been the adviser for the junior high newspaper, where Kelly had been editor.

Were Helen's questions innocent, and was Robert being paranoid or perhaps wracked with guilt? Or could it be that Helen and Julie had figured out what was really going on and were setting a trap for him?

When Robert talked to Kelly about it, she admitted that Helen was smart but added that Julie couldn't find her ass with both hands. Kelly refused to let it bother her, saying, rightly, that they had taken every precaution to avoid discovery. "Sometime I think we're acting out some dumb spy movie." It was clear to Robert that as a young woman in love, she was dying to tell the world and was frustrated by all the secrecy.

Robert took to walking outside on weekend mornings, strolling innocently around the block, while carefully looking around. Only when he was convinced that no one was watching, did he leave with Kelly. Again, all their activities were away from the community: Bike rides, hikes, dinning, films.

The tension was hard on the both of them, so when the winter break came, they caught a plane to Hawaii, spending two weeks free to stroll hand in hand, lie on the beach together and express open affection.

When they got home, Laurie told Kelly that Julie had called to talk to her, which in itself was unusual. Laurie had simple told Julie that she was out of town, taking a vacation. When Julie wanted more information, Laurie had suggested that she ask Kelly about it when school started again.

26

As the second semester started, Robert and Kelly had fallen into a routine, mostly weekends, always cautious, usually a bit nervous. Then George asked Robert to stop by his office. There was a look on his face that said he didn't really want to have this meeting. "Robert, I wish I didn't have to do this, but my job requires me to follow up on any complaint I get, particularly from a student or another teacher. Please understand that it isn't me, I'm just going by the book here."

"Come on George, out with it. How bad can it be?" Of course, Robert suspected how bad it could be but didn't want to betray his fears.

"Ok. Helen and her daughter have both claimed that there's something going on between you and Kelly."

"Something, like in... Oh my god. Why?"

"Well, everyone knows by now that you have a history, mentor and friend for years, her dedicating her book to you and all."

Robert interrupted him. "You know about that. Our families are friends. You've been to dinner with all of us."

"I know, and to those gals, it seems suspicious. Then Julie says she's seen really obvious, really guilty looks between you two."

Robert interrupted again. "She's seeing what she wants to see. She's still upset that I broke up with her mother."

"I realize that too. Helen says she's noticed things too, the awkward way you and Kelly act around each other, and then Julie says she was at a drive through one Friday night and saw the two of you driving by late in the evening."

"George, you know I'm not only her friend and mentor, but her agent as well. We probably had been out for a business dinner, and I was taking her home."

George took a deep breath and got a sad look on his face. "That's what I told them, but Julie claims you were on a direct route from the freeway to your place, that Kelly lives in the other direction."

"I don't know how to respond to that. Who knows where we

were going or coming from. Sometimes I stop and buy her an ice cream or a soda, we talk about her book, business. Check with her mother. She'll tell you there's nothing going on."

"Don't think I haven't thought about having to do that. Trust me. I'd rather have a tooth pulled without Novocain. How do you ask a mother if her daughter's having an affair with a teacher?"

"Do you think I'm doing that?"

"You're not that kind of guy, but this isn't the usual situation and I can't let my opinion stop me from going through the steps on this. Jesus, Robert, don't shoot the messenger. All I need from you is to say it isn't true."

"OK, it isn't true."

"Good. You know I do have to talk to Kelly. I don't want to, but." He shrugged as if to say he had no choice.

Robert left with the feeling that George didn't actually believe there was something going on but was still suspicious, and suspicion, once planted, tends to grow like a weed, friend or not.

Robert brooded over it for a couple of days before mentioning it to Kelly, who said, she'd been told the principal wanted to see her on Friday afternoon. She added that her mother would be adamant about there being nothing to this.

On Friday evening, Robert anxiously awaited the news of Kelly's meeting with George. She had a self-satisfied smile on her face as they sat down to dinner at a hotel, miles from home, near the San Jose airport, where he'd booked a room for the weekend. She was obviously enjoying the building drama, while Robert was going crazy waiting for the news.

Finally, settled in a corner booth, he asked, "Well?"

She did something he'd never seen her do before, the fist-pump in the air. "I should have gone into acting instead of writing. I deserve an Oscar." Then she stopped and let the dramatic tension build again before continuing.

"When he asked me about it, and that dumb Julie had more to add – She's been watching me damn near everywhere I go – I totally freaked." Then she got into character. "I got all indignant with, 'How can you accuse me, an innocent girl? Are you trying to ruin my reputation? Do you think I'm some kind of cheap slut? I guess you think I don't deserve my grades, that I'm sleeping my way to an A. God, I'll never get into a university now. You're trying to ruin my life. I'm going to tell my mom to call her lawyer. We're going to sue you, the school district and that history teacher bitch for slander and for defaming my character.' Well, you should have seen his face, white as a ghost, look of total panic."

Just watching her recreate her speech was mesmerizing. She was actually shouting in a voice subdued enough to avoid disturbing other diners. Robert thought that she might have been somewhat over the top and that he'd have to deal with a very angry George. "So what did he say?"

"He was all over himself apologizing to me, saying he was only doing his job, following up on a complaint. He was, he said, primarily interested in protecting his students, and an accusation like this has to be taken seriously because of the teachers who take advantage of innocent girls like me. He promised that he'd done his investigation and the matter was put to rest, no more would be said."

She'd pulled it off, but did George really buy it, or was he just trying to avoid a law suit. He'd have a better idea next week when they talked again. That thought put a slight tarnish on the weekend, one even Kelly couldn't completely erase.

When Robert suggested to George their regular dining out, the principal, usually up front, was evasive. "Damn, Robert, I've been terribly busy, here and at home. Let's take a rain check, OK?" He added a forced smile. It was clear that the bond was broken and he could also feel it with the other teachers, who were cordial enough, but not at all friendly. This bothered him, and he told Kelly about it.

"It's become uncomfortable at school. They all suspect us, but naturally, no one is saying anything. There's talk of a regular non-tenure track teaching position at State next year, and I'm hoping so. I don't think I'd be comfortable staying."

Kelly was matter of fact. "I'm graduating, and we're getting married, and that will confirm the rumors. Besides, you've got that Ph.D, and it's time for you to move up. It's all working out."

Trauma for him was little more than another item to check off for her. She could be so self-possessed, an island unto herself. However, later that evening, cuddled in front of a rented movie on the TV, she surprised him. "I'm starting a new book."

That in itself was startling news, her first one still a best seller, but the next part of it was even more surprising. "I've been Suzie Serious for a long time, obsessed with my goals. Now, I look up and I have the man I love, I'll be getting married in a few months, and I have two good friends. Life is a bit lighter now. And, the girls and I have been talking, laughing really about dating, I mean how it is for high school girls. You have no idea what these boys are like, clueless, weird. Well, we've been telling stories and laughing our asses off, and Mayra suggested I write about it, so I've been jotting down the stories, and it's sort of coming together into a humorous novel."

"Let me guess," Robert ventured, "Hysterical to girls, humiliating to boys."

"I'm guessing. Well, enlightened boys, the few, the almost proud, will appreciate it."

Robert thought for a few moments. "That would be a major change for you, unexpected by your audience. However, if you pull it off, it would show that you're versatile. You gonna to show it to me?"

"In a couple of weeks, both you and Sandy. I'm turning the first bunch of stories into a book, you know, a real story line, continuity. I made up a girl who has had the bad luck of having all those guys in her life, you know, smart but really unlucky."

As the weeks went by, Robert noticed the small changes in her. She laughed and joked more, told funny stories about the conversations and antics of her group of literary girls. But the old Kelly was still there, planning and plotting.

She told him that she was all over the social media about Robert as this great teacher at State. She even had Pauline, who had applied to State in the Fall, ask the counselor if she could get Mr. Spagnolo's class, having heard so many good things about him. Kelly even somehow managed to get a book signing at the university book store, using the occasion to stress how she'd learned everything she knew from this world class teacher. Kelly was on a roll, and all Robert could do is stand back and watch her relentless promotion of him as a teacher.

Sandy didn't send Robert her usual email. She called and was laughing as she talked about Kelly's book. "God, Robert, I remember high school. For a girl who was bright and mature, the boys were almost swinging from the trees by their tails, and she's nailed it."

"Robert was a bit indignant, having been one of those boys himself. But, Sandy clarified. "Sure, it's over the top, and not all teen boys fit her 'Seven deadly hims,' but there's enough truth to it to be outrageously funny. This could go on the shelf next to *Catch 22* and *A Confederacy of Dunces*, and I can tell you, I'll sell the movie rights. Tell her to drop everything and finish the damn thing."

So there it was, she could write serious fiction and humor. Her career was made. And now with the strong possibility of him becoming a full time university instructor, late 20s, with a Ph.D, Kelly, even if she quit school today and never got her high school diploma stood to make more money. Sure, Robert's income would be steady, while hers would fluctuate, but averaged out over any given year, she would be the dominate earner in the family. This went down like bitter medicine, not that he begrudged her success, but he realized that his role as head of household would be ceremonial at best.

Then came the night when everything seemed to come full circle. The girl who had pursued him relentlessly from a precocious preteen, through her adolescent years, through her sexual awakening, and who now had him signed, sealed and delivered as her soon to be husband, was now sitting in his dining room one Friday night, bent over her laptop. "Come on sweetheart. It's late; let's go to bed."

She looked up as if she'd been summoned back from some remote place, looked up at the clock and answered, "Go ahead darling. I'll be along soon. I'm right in the middle of this chapter, and I want to finish getting it down."

By the time she came to bed, he was sound asleep.

27

Preparations for her impending graduation were already starting, the ordering of cap and gown, photos, invitations and all the stuff
designed to make the occasion feel special, to make the kids feel
they've accomplished something and were now prepared to take on the
world, a world each generation felt they could conquer. For some, it
was exciting, but for Kelly it seemed just another thing to check off the
list. She'd already applied and been accepted at San Jose State.

Mayra, who was headed to Stanford in the fall, called her on
this, as she related to Robert over the phone. "With your grades and
accomplishments, why go to State? You could get in anywhere."

"I've got my career, so where I go and what I study doesn't
matter so much. I just want a good, liberal education. I want to be
knowledgeable and informed. I'm not studying to be anything in particular."

"And your boyfriend teaches there." Kelly said she felt cornered. How could Mayra know? Mayra had said it was obvious to anyone who had eyes and knew her. Then she'd sung a few bars of "The
Look of Love."

Pauline, who was also headed to State, also knew. Kelly had
objected, even denied it at first, until her friends told her not to worry,
that her secret was safe with them.

Naturally, this news bothered Robert. If they knew, how many
others did? Still there were only weeks left, and both Kelly and Robert
would be gone, would be married, would be starting a new life.

Then Kelly, always looking to the future, always planning,
made an announcement. "We need to buy a house." Just like that, out
of the blue.

Robert was caught off guard, but Kelly explained her reasoning, which would have been obvious to him, had he been focused on
the future. "No point in staying here and commuting down a busy freeway to school every day. This apartment is too small for both of us,
and we'll no longer have a connection to town. Besides, we need to in-
vest our money. I'm making serious royalties, you've got a good paying job and tons of money in your savings. As my mom says, rent is

throwing money away, buying security for your landlord."

It made perfect sense, Laurie had bought almost as soon as she started her own business and now her house was worth more than she paid for it. Kelly was right about his bank account. He'd never been extravagant and had always been a saver. Now, after eight years teaching, he had ample money for a down, and between the two of them, a house payment would be easy. He agreed to contact a real estate agent.

They found a lovely place in Campbell, just a few minutes from campus, but in a very nice neighborhood. At first there was some issues about the two of them, she being still in high school and only seventeen, but when Kelly showed her income and said they had no intention of closing until her birthday and their marriage, no one saw a problem. A ninety day escrow would put them in their new home when they returned from their honeymoon.

A couple weeks later, Kelly made a suggestion. "Pauline is going to State, and her parents don't have much money. She's looking at living at home and commuting every day." Kelly waited for that to sink in and for Robert to indicate that he was waiting for the suggestion or solution.

We're buying a three bedroom place with a small den. So, we have our bedroom and office space for both of us, and one whole bedroom to spare."

"So, you want to offer it to Pauline?"

"If it's alright with you." She sounded almost apologetic.

Robert liked the girl and was glad that Kelly finally had some really close female friends. "No problem. She doesn't even have to pay rent, just her share of the food."

Kelly actually squealed, that silly girlish sound that he'd never heard from her. "
Thank you, my wonderful loving man. I'll tell her in the morning."

In a very odd, but very wonderful way, Robert finally had the feeling of having his own family. Life was good, better since the dean confirmed a full teaching schedule for the Fall.

Graduation was not a big deal to Kelly, what with the wedding, college and a new home just around the corner. Robert actually took her to a local restaurant after the ceremony. He was also taking leave of the school, and where he was once popular, few people now congratulated him or wished him well. Most were either friends of Helen or George or were just angry that he'd gotten away with an affair with a student. A few people shook his hand, told him what a great teacher he'd been and wished him good luck on his new job.

Then it was the wedding, a small affair. Laurie and her longtime boyfriend, Neal, Pat and her new husband, Pauline and Mayra, each with a date, Flynn, Ted and Chip, who had come back for the occasion, and even Sandy, who had flown out to support her ex-lover and her current best writer. Notably absent were his former colleagues, something that Robert found painful. A door had opened, another one had shut, and there was no either going or looking back.

One guest Robert hadn't expected, Aldo made the trip from Florence, along with his intended, fulfilling the promise he'd made to Kelly at the airport. At least that part of the story wasn't fiction.

Robert thought to himself, after meeting the handsome, charming young man, his warm, brown eyes and ready smile. how fortunate he'd been not to lose Kelly to her Italian lover.

After a honeymoon in England, they moved into their first home, along with Pauline, and settled into university life.

28

"We'll have to do something special for your twenty-first birth-day," Robert said over breakfast one Saturday. Then he added, "You got in pretty late last night. How was that address at Berkeley?" She had somehow managed to convince the English department to let her address the graduating students, saying they needed to hear that with their new degree, anything was possible, with her as an example. After all, at age twenty, she already had three best sellers and was busy writing a forth. It was ironic that she was still an undergrad, addressing students a year older.

She told him all about it, about how she spent the day with the dean and department head, how they'd given her a tour of the campus, which she pronounced as beautiful. She had even taken these guys out to dinner at a nice restaurant. On top of that she said she wanted to transfer to Berkeley and do graduate work there.

"I didn't think they had a grad program in creative writing." He said.

"No, the closest is journalism, but that's OK."

"So, now you want to be a journalist? New York Times, I'll bet."

"Oh, silly. No, I might not even finish the program. It was all about buttering them up for you."

He smiled, took her hand and kissed it. "Sweetheart, are you still hoping I'll get on at Cal?"

"You should know me by now. After the address, dinner, lots of wine and a constant enumeration of your talents as a teacher, I think they're ready to bite. I was told to have you call and make an appointment. They think they'll have an opening in the fall, and they like the idea of getting both of us, a high profile student and her high profile mentor."

"Seriously? I always indulged this fantasy, but never thought it could happen."

Then she got up, walked into the next room and came back with some fliers. "I picked these up yesterday afternoon. Remember the pictures you showed me ten years ago, the view of San Francisco from the Berkeley Hills? Well, I found an agent and told her what view I wanted, and she found this place, perfect for us." She dropped the flyer with the pictures of the inside and the view over the bay from the deck.

Robert looked at the price and whistled. "That's a pretty expensive view."

"I know, but here's what they're paying, here's what we can get for this place, here's what's in the bank, and here's my projected royalties for the next year. We can do this, we really can." she jumped up and threw her arms around his neck, smothering him with kisses. Then she added, "It's everything we ever wanted."

"Well, I wanted it more in the abstract, pie in the sky, but you obviously took wanting it to a new level."

"But, this is what you want?"

"Of course. I just didn't allow myself to dream this big. But then I had you to do that. So, is there anything left of your grand plan for us that I should know?" He smiled and winked at her.

"There's just one more thing my love, the last thing on my list."

Robert nodded and waited through her dramatic pause.

"I'd like to have a baby."

"Would that be a boy or a girl?"

"Don't be silly darling. You can't plan everything." She squeezed his hand and laughed.

Other books by Meade Fischer

With The Sea Beside Me: An intimate guide to California's central and north coast. Part guide, part travel literature, this books takes the reader along on an outdoor-lover's trip from Santa Barbara to the Oregon border, withcamping, hiking, kayaking, surfing, hidden beaches, brewpubs and other interestig attractions along the way.

Messiah Chronicles. The story of Jesus and his friends, preachers and religious reformers, sans the supernatural. Set in the cultural and political climate of the times. A secular novel.

Spinning Real Life. This satire on comtemporary politics, enviromentalism, romantic relationships and human weirdness traces the misadventures of Scott, a young and very clueless writer who hopes to write the great American novel, but doesn't see it unfolding around him.

Cosmic Coastal Chronicles. Adventures along the west coast. A solitary adventurer seeks out the perfect moment whether in a kayak in Canada, surfing some deserted beach, hiking in wild redwood groves or camping in some remote spot.

Shattering the Crystal Face of God. Part environmental exploration, part outdoor adventure, part manifesto, the Tripper explores the meaning of his life and his relationship with the land.

www.baymoon.com/~eclecticpress